"All right," Ryder found himself asking, "what do you intend to do with the ranch?"

Eve's lips curved wryly. "I'm sure you'll be glad to know, cowboy, that I'm leaving most of the land as it is. However, I have some real changes planned for the main house."

Surely she just meant nothing more than some new drapes, a few rugs scattered about, he assured himself. Simple stuff. Then he remembered that *simple* simply didn't apply to this woman.

"Exactly *what* kind of changes do you have in mind?"

As she'd done earlier, Eve met his gaze head-on and didn't so much as blink. "To be exact, I'm turning a portion of this house into a day-care center. A day nursery, actually."

She waited a beat, wanting his full attention for the final blow. "For babies."

Dear Reader,

Harlequin American Romance has rounded up the best romantic reading to help you celebrate Valentine's Day. Start off with the final installment in the MAITLAND MATERNITY: TRIPLETS, QUADS & QUINTS series. *The McCallum Quintuplets* is a special three-in-one volume featuring *New York Times* bestselling author Kasey Michaels, Mindy Neff and Mary Anne Wilson.

BILLION-DOLLAR BRADDOCKS, Karen Toller Whittenburg's new family-connected miniseries, premiers this month with *The C.E.O.'s Unplanned Proposal*. In this Cinderella story, a small-town waitress is swept into the Braddock world of wealth and power and puts eldest brother Adam Braddock's bachelor status to the test. Next, in Bonnie Gardner's *Sgt. Billy's Bride*, an air force controller is in desperate need of a fiancée to appease his beloved, ailing mother, so he asks a beautiful stranger to become his wife. Can love bloom and turn their pretend engagement into wedded bliss? Finally, we welcome another new author to the Harlequin American family. Sharon Swan makes her irresistible debut with *Cowboys and Cradles*.

Enjoy this month's offerings, and be sure to return next month when Harlequin American Romance launches a new cross-line continuity, THE CARRADIGNES: AMERICAN ROYALTY, with *The Improperly Pregnant Princess* by Jacqueline Diamond.

Wishing you happy reading,

Melissa Jeglinski
Associate Senior Editor
Harlequin American Romance

COWBOYS AND CRADLES

Sharon Swan

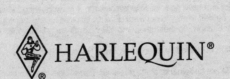

TORONTO • NEW YORK • LONDON
AMSTERDAM • PARIS • SYDNEY • HAMBURG
STOCKHOLM • ATHENS • TOKYO • MILAN • MADRID
PRAGUE • WARSAW • BUDAPEST • AUCKLAND

For Ann, who always loved a cowboy hero

ISBN 0-373-16912-4

COWBOYS AND CRADLES

Copyright © 2002 by Sharon Swearengen.

ABOUT THE AUTHOR

Born and raised in Chicago, Sharon Swan once dreamed of dancing for a living. Instead, she surrendered to life's more practical aspects, settled for an office job, concentrated on typing and being a Chicago Bears fan. Sharon never seriously considered a writing career until she moved to the Phoenix area and met Pierce Brosnan at a local shopping mall. It was a chance meeting that changed her life because she found herself thinking what if? What if two fictional characters had met the same way? That formed the basis for her next novel, and she's now cheerfully addicted to writing contemporary romance and playing what if?

All underlined places are fictitious.

Chapter One

He rode into her life like a god on horseback.

If she hadn't been so busy slamming on the brakes, the startling sight might have actually thrilled her.

Bits of desert dust, red-tinged and light as air, still swirled around them as she discovered he was mortal—and far from thrilled with her. "Give me one good reason why I shouldn't tell you exactly what I think of your driving skills, lady."

Eve Terry squared her shoulders, instinctively reacting both to the words and the clipped tone. He was human, all right, she told herself. And big. Looking up to meet his gaze would be necessary, she knew, even if he climbed down from his saddle and she stood to her full, taller-than-average height. He clearly outweighed her, as well, by more than a few pounds, and she was no lightweight. Still, she refused to let his size, the whole muscled length of him, intimidate her.

Or at least she refused to appear intimidated. Despite a pounding pulse and a racing heartbeat, aftereffects of their near collision, she managed a calm reply. "I can give you a great reason for keeping your opinions to yourself, cowboy. I just happen to be your new boss."

Beyond a dirt-specked windshield, she watched a

sudden frown appear under the wide brim of a battered tan hat. Honing in, she studied well-formed features, unhampered by the thin coat of dusty grime half concealing them. She'd drawn enough faces to recognize good bone structure when she saw it. High cheekbones, a straight nose and a firm jawline. Cleaned up, he would be attractive, she had no doubt. Not that she was interested. Right now she had a list of priorities, and men, even attractive ones, weren't on it.

"The boss? Not hardly," he said, his voice low and a bit gritty, tinged with a Western drawl. "This ranch belongs to an outfit in Dallas by the name of E. T. Holdings."

"I'm Eve Terry, the owner of that company and—as of ten days ago—this ranch."

She relished the abruptly stunned look in his green eyes before it disappeared in a flash as his frown deepened. Obviously, it would take more than a formidable surprise, even one as plainly unwelcome as this, to really shake this man. "Would you mind telling me why you rode straight in front of my Jeep?"

He stiffened. "*You* headed straight toward *me*. Do you always drive down dry gullies like a bat out of hell?"

She'd never driven down a gully before in her life. The Jeep was less than a week old, a last-minute purchase in Dallas, and she'd been testing the four-wheel drive and her ability to handle it. And she *had* handled it. She'd actually been enjoying the bumpy ride, with the canvas top down and a warm breeze ruffling what there was to ruffle of her dark-blond hair. Until he'd shown up out of nowhere, racing down one steep side of the gully. She'd stopped in the nick of time to avoid a crash.

"You scared the bejeezus out of Lucky," he added when she didn't respond to his terse question.

Lucky? He had to be referring to the caramel-colored stallion he'd brought to a swift standstill. It was the biggest horse she'd ever seen. Not that she'd seen all that many from a distance of less than a yard, of course. City life didn't lend much opportunity for close encounters with horses. Nevertheless, she knew it was male. There was no missing a certain portion of its anatomy. And it was a huge animal. If they had collided, the Jeep would probably have come out the loser.

"I think Lucky can take care of himself," she said dryly, tapping a finger tipped with red on the steering wheel. "Now, I suggest you get back to work. That is, if you work for this ranch and aren't just trespassing."

"I work for it, all right," he muttered. He didn't seem any happier about that fact than her earlier claim of ownership.

Great. Just what she needed: another disgruntled employee. The ranch cook she'd met yesterday afternoon upon her arrival could give lessons in how to be a grouch. Yes, she'd shown up unexpectedly, but she hadn't meant to. Signals had gotten crossed somehow, and her lawyer in Dallas hadn't contacted the broker in Tucson who had handled the sale. Letting the people here know she was coming would have been the courteous thing to do. Still, whether they liked it or not, she was the boss, and she had to make it crystal clear that she wouldn't take any guff from anyone.

Especially when they discovered her plans for the Creedence Creek Ranch.

Eve shifted into reverse. "Well, I'll leave you to do…whatever you were doing." With that, she shot back a few feet, then made a swift U-turn and headed back the way she'd come. She thought about looking in the rearview mirror to see if he watched her departure. *Or maybe to get another look at him, Eve,* something inside her said. She didn't look, didn't so much as glance. Bad-tempered cowboys were not on her agenda—no matter how good a sight they made.

The man she'd left in a rush stared after her, squinting into the brilliant sunshine seldom absent for long periods in southern Arizona. A trailing cloud of dust faithfully followed the Jeep until it and the dust disappeared, leaving a view of flat desert and rolling hills, with the jagged-peaked Santa Catalina Mountains looming in the distance. Some would call it a picture-postcard setting. He called it home.

She'd taken him for one of the ranch hands. Which was hardly amazing, he told himself. After all, he'd put on his oldest pair of jeans and an equally beat-up denim shirt when he'd given in to the urge yesterday morning to do something he hadn't done in years. Checking fences, as tiresome as it could be, meant miles of open spaces and some solitary time to decide what he'd do next.

Stay or go?

Even after a wakeful night stretched out on a narrow bedroll under a wide sky crowded with stars, he hadn't come up with a firm answer. Reason told him to get on with his life and leave behind what fate, or maybe sheer bad luck, had placed out of his reach. Yet a stubborn streak in him that had nothing to do with reason said stay, anyway.

The outcome of that inner war remained in doubt. But one thing was dead certain: the ranch's new owner was in for a surprise. Those smoke-gray eyes, as big as they'd seemed, could well get bigger. Those elegantly arched eyebrows, dark in contrast to burnished-gold hair worn in a mannish cut shorter than his own, just might take a hike up a silky smooth forehead. Those full lips, shaded a soft red, might even drop open.

He could only hope. Leaning forward, he gave the stallion a brief pat on the neck. "We'll at least stick around long enough to enjoy the moment, friend."

Snorting, Lucky nodded his agreement.

HANK SWENSON didn't look like one of the most successful real estate brokers in the Southwest, Eve decided, viewing him across a large knotty-pine desk that took up a major portion of the ranch's modest-size office. A small man, he was inches shorter and probably pounds lighter than she was. Yet beneath that deceptively slight frame, she knew, lurked a huge dose of business savvy.

"Sorry about the mix-up, Hank." They had already progressed to first names. "You should have been told I was coming."

He nodded a balding head rimmed with gray and settled back in a scuffed leather chair. Like most of the office furnishings, it had seen better days. Only a personal computer and other business machines set up against one wall could be considered even close to new.

"No problem," Hank replied mildly, "although I have to admit I was a little surprised when you didn't come to look things over before the final papers were signed."

Eve's lips quirked in a faint smile. "I didn't need to. Several years ago I visited this area and saw the ranch from the main road. By the time I learned it was for sale, I was already certain I wanted to buy the place.''

She could still recall her first sight of the house, its large adobe exterior stark white against a backdrop of desert green and sandy beige, its wide terra-cotta tile roof warmed to a glaze of orange by the sun, high overheard. Far from being new and firmly linked with the present, it was old and rooted to the past…and somehow that made it perfect in her eyes.

But the desire to own the ranch was only one of the results of that brief visit. In many ways it had been a life-altering experience.

''You could have made a better deal by bargaining with Amos Cutter's heirs,'' Hank commented.

Her smile widened. ''If that's a diplomatic way of telling me I paid too much, I'm well aware of what the property is actually worth.''

The figure she named sparked a gleam of respect in Hank's shrewd gaze. ''Which is almost exactly what Ryder Quinn offered.''

Eve leaned forward, propped her elbows on the desk. ''But he didn't get it. I did.''

''True, but can you run it without him?''

''No,'' she admitted bluntly. ''Or at least not without someone like him. Do you think he'll leave?''

Hank's expression turned thoughtful. ''Maybe. I've known him on a casual basis for a long time, ever since Amos hired him on as a lanky ranch hand. He filled out over the years, took on the job of foreman when it opened up, then went to college nights and became a surprisingly shrewd business manager when Amos's health started to fail. During all that time, he never made any secret of the fact that he'd be interested in buying if Amos ever chose to sell. More than interested, it always seemed to me. I believe Quinn wanted this property very badly. Why, I couldn't tell you."

"Hmm." Eve absorbed that information. "And Amos Cutter never chose to sell?"

"I think he was seriously considering it toward the end, before that last stroke took him suddenly. Under the terms of a will he'd made out as a young man, his only living relatives—two daughters back East—got everything. Amos hadn't seen them since his wife left him and took the kids with her nearly forty years ago. They had no interest in the ranch and didn't waste any time contacting me to put it up for sale."

"And how did Ryder Quinn feel about it being sold to someone else?"

Hank shrugged a bony shoulder. "He didn't have much to say. Still, he must have been disappointed. Of course, my friend Amos wouldn't have said much, either, if he'd been able to see you walk through the front door yesterday." Hazel eyes took on another gleam, this time of amusement. "He would have been too busy swallowing his tough-as-jerky tongue."

It was Eve's turn to be amused. "I didn't know I was such a dreadful sight."

Thin lips curved in a wry smile. "On the contrary. You're a mighty fine sight, Eve." He paused. "But you *are* a woman."

She lifted a brow. "So?"

"The last female to cross that threshold was Amos's disgruntled wife, and she was on her way out."

After a startled moment Eve said, "Now it's clear to me why Pete Rawlins's mouth worked like a guppy's when I dropped my luggage on the doorstep and introduced myself. Apparently Amos Cutter had no fondness for women, and I wouldn't be at all amazed if the ranch cook feels exactly the same way.''

Nodding, Hank straightened a bola tie looped under the collar of a checked shirt worn with a suede vest and corduroy slacks. ''Pete's got about as much regard for the opposite sex as Amos had.'' A sudden twinkle in his eyes belied the fact that he was probably close to seventy. ''Now, myself, I enjoy every glimpse I can get of a good-looking woman.''

Eve cocked her head. She liked this man. He was certainly the only one who'd made her feel welcome since her arrival. ''Are you by any chance flirting with me, Hank?''

His smile was wily as a fox. ''I'm trying, ma'am.''

''Sorry to interrupt this party,'' a low voice said.

The swivel chair creaked softly as Eve made a half turn to see a tall figure standing in the doorway. Her eyes widened as recognition hit. It was him—the ticked-off male she'd confronted hours earlier. As she'd concluded, his features were attractive minus a layer of dust. But he wasn't, as she'd assumed, a ranch hand. No ranch hand could afford this man's wardrobe.

Eve knew fabrics. Quality told. So did expert tailoring. While the Western cut of the charcoal-brown suit that she quickly ran her gaze over might be more casual than a Manhattan banker's three-piece pinstripe, it was every bit as impressive. The clothes didn't make the man, though. Not this one. He made the outfit.

No, he wasn't a ranch hand. But he *was* a cowboy. And he didn't need a horse under him to prove it. From polished brown boots emphasizing a solid stance, to glossy dark hair worn just long enough in the back to brush the collar of his ivory shirt, he had a distinct air about him. *Rugged.* That was the word, she decided. It had taken rugged men—and women—to tame the West and make it theirs.

Oh, yes. He was a cowboy.

Suddenly aware that her lips had parted of their own accord, Eve snapped them shut and looked straight into his green eyes, firmly refusing to let her gaze falter. Something told her that was the best way to deal with this man. Head-on. And she'd have to deal with him. He was Ryder Quinn. All at once she was as sure of his identity as she was of her own.

Hank's brief introduction confirmed it. "Eve, I'd like you to meet Ryder Quinn. Quinn, this is Eve Terry, the new owner."

Deciding not to mention that they'd already run into each other, almost literally, she rose to her full height and issued a polite greeting. "I'm happy to meet you, Mr. Quinn."

RYDER TOOK A DEEP BREATH, filling his lungs full, and tried not to look as though he'd just been punched in the gut, which was exactly how he felt. Stubborn horses had thrown him, wild-eyed steers had done their best to trample him into the dirt, a surly bull had even gored him on one memorable occasion. Never in all of his thirty-three years, though, had a woman threatened to bowl him over. Until now.

Earlier, he hadn't been able to see much more than her face. Now he had a top-to-toes view. And it was quite a sight. Every bit as shapely as he'd always preferred a woman to be, with plenty of soft flesh to cover strong bones, Eve Terry was a curvy goddess decked out like a cowgirl. An urban cowgirl.

Not for a minute did he believe the fitted jeans hugging well-rounded hips or the stylishly embroidered

denim shirt outlining full breasts had so much as
brushed against a dusty corral fence. And if those
cream-colored boots with the elaborate carving had
ever come within sniffing distance of a mound of cow
dung, he'd eat the fancy leather belt circling a nipped-
in waist—glittering silver buckle and all.

Yet, beneath the sophisticated exterior, there was
something earthy about the woman that stirred his
blood. Quite simply, she made his mouth water.

She's also your boss, Quinn, he reminded himself
grimly. He was her employee—the hired help—at least
temporarily. His boot heels clicked on hard tile as he
stepped into the room.

She'd said she was happy to meet him, but he didn't
say the same. It would be a lie, and he didn't care much
for lies, even social ones. When she extended her right
hand, he took it in his own, found its texture to be just
as he'd expected: soft as satin, with an underlying
strength.

"Ms. Terry." He didn't have to dip his head far to
reestablish eye contact. Since he was over six feet, she
had to be around five-ten.

"Call me Eve, please." Again the tone was soft,
with an edge of quiet self-assurance.

He kept her hand in his a second longer than he'd
meant to before releasing it to cross his arms over his
chest. "All right…Eve. I'm Ryder."

They took each other's measure before she finally
turned to resume her seat. "Hank tells me you've been
with the ranch for a long time."

He considered it a victory that she'd been the one to
look away first. A minor one, true. But winning at anything, however small, felt good right now. He had re-

cently lost a great deal. "I've been here almost fifteen years, in one capacity or another."

Imitating his body language, she leaned back and folded her arms under her breasts. "You wanted to buy it."

He had to admire that blunt statement. Apparently, she didn't care to beat around the bush any more than he did. "Yes."

"And I got it instead."

"Uh-huh."

"Because I paid more for it than it was worth."

Her droll frankness almost surprised a laugh out of him. Another study of her gray eyes found intelligence, and more than a hint of good-natured humor.

He nearly groaned. A smart, curvy goddess with a sense of humor. It was a potent combination, one that appealed on several levels, challenged and seduced at the same time. If she'd been anyone but who she was, his male ego might have been afraid he'd wind up begging. When an all-too-clear image of himself doing exactly that slid into his mind, he swiftly shoved it aside and deliberately made his reply curt.

"I figured you had more money than you knew what to do with."

He didn't add that he would have done his best to match her offer if there'd been time to seek additional financing. But time had been denied him. Amos Cutter's daughters had wanted the sale over and done with as quickly as possible.

Eve's gaze narrowed. "If you think I was born rich and spoiled rotten, you can think again. What I have, I've earned."

"The same goes for me," he shot back.

Her chin went up. "Want to stay and earn more?"

"Maybe."

"Good. Let's talk business."

Hank cleared his throat, reminding Ryder there was another person in the room. "Well," the older man said, "I'll leave you two to…get to it."

SHE WAS READY to get to it, Eve reflected as she sat forward and set her forearms on the desktop. More than ready. But it wouldn't be wise to let her temper rule now. She needed a cool head to deal with this—and him.

Rather than taking the chair Hank had vacated moments earlier, her companion braced one hip against a desk corner and looked down at her, his arms still crossed. The significance of that pose didn't escape Eve. She held the power position behind the desk, but Ryder Quinn had no intention of assuming a visitor's role.

How to begin? she wondered, and decided to just dig in. "What would it take to get you to stay on as business manager?"

"That depends on how much you need me."

Trust him to cut to the quick. And it would be pointless to dodge the issue. If he stayed, he'd discover the truth soon enough. "What I know about horses and cattle could be written on a sticky note, with room left over."

One corner of his firm mouth hiked up. "I figured as much from that fancy outfit you're wearing."

His opinion shouldn't matter, she told herself. But somehow it did. "Do you like it?"

He hesitated, looking as though he might not want to answer. "Yeah, I like it," he said at last.

Because she sensed that was the truth, she allowed herself a smile. "I designed it."

He lifted a dark eyebrow. "A hobby?"

Her smile widened. "A business." She couldn't help it, she just had to go on. "A big business, actually. When I sold it to an even bigger clothing manufacturer, the profit I banked was enough to buy the Creedence Creek, with a considerable amount left over."

Now both brows went up. "You mean you bought this place with money you made from *clothes?*"

Oh, it felt good to finally jar this man. And she still had what she felt would be an even greater surprise in store for him. Eve began to enjoy herself.

"Not just *clothes,*" she told him, echoing his astonishment. "Upscale Western wear for women, sold under the label Sassy Lady. As I said, it's a profitable business, and even though I no longer own it, I still design for the line."

There was pride in her voice, she knew, and she *was* proud of what she'd achieved. It had taken long years filled with hopes, dreams and sheer hard work to put the Sassy Lady line on department store racks across the country. And it was a vindication of sorts that her designs were done with the full-figured female form in mind.

She'd been chubby as a child, chubbier yet as a teen. Those years bridging the gap between childhood and college had been the most difficult of all for her, and she remembered them well.

Yo, hefty hips.

Sometimes she could still hear that mocking chorus of deep voices thrown from a passing convertible, one crowded with a bunch of thoughtless punks out for a joyride on a hot summer night. Not that they'd been punks to her. Back then, they were her peers, boys she went to high school with, which only gave their taunting remark all the more power to hurt her.

And, of course, it hadn't ended there. In a society that valued thinness almost as highly as wealth, she'd felt less than worthy throughout her young adulthood, a feeling she'd since discovered was familiar to others standing on the wrong side of the scale. Although she'd lost weight as she'd grown older, she continued to struggle with more than a few extra pounds she could have done without. Still, she'd won the battle not to let that bother her too much. Not most of the time, at any rate. Trying on swimsuits under a store dressing room's unforgiving light could still make her wince, she had to admit.

Not that those swimsuits had been anywhere near dowdy. Not any longer. Clothing styles for women with bodies not built along Barbie lines had taken a dramatic turn over the past several years. She'd been a part of that transformation and had reaped its rewards—all of which had her proud enough of her achievements to burst the pearl snaps on a shirt that fit well *and* made a fashion statement.

"Sassy Lady," Ryder murmured, breaking into her thoughts. "Somehow it seems to suit."

His sudden grin, flashing a string of strong, white teeth, was so starkly male—and so all-out appealing because of that fact—she felt the impact ripple a path through her and had to steel herself to keep it from showing. The last thing she needed, she told herself, was to let him know he could affect her that way. The very last thing.

He was used to being in charge, that was as plain as the nose on her face. Regardless of what he seemingly had no trouble making her feel—right down to her toes, she couldn't deny—she had to keep her wits about her and maintain as much control as she could over this conversation. Too much depended on the outcome.

"So I suppose we'll agree that where ranching is concerned, I'm over my head," she said, marshaling her forces.

"Seems to sum things up," he said, his tone as dry as dust.

"I need you…badly," she added, seeking to be bluntly businesslike yet regretting those last words the minute they made it past her lips. Far from her intention, they'd come out loaded with innuendo.

For a split second something sizzled in the air. Something that had nothing to do with business. Something far closer to silk sheets than balance sheets. "That is, I need your expertise," she tacked on hastily.

His grin had turned just a bit smug around the edges. "And I take it you can afford to pay for it."

"I'm not opposed to giving you a raise," she replied, glad to be on less dangerous ground. "Name your price, and we'll see if we can make a deal."

Ryder drew in a breath and shifted his gaze to a large, bare window. *Name your price,* he thought as the words rang in his mind. He wondered what it was.

Did he really want more money?

It seemed to have lost its appeal, he had to admit, now that his main use for it had disappeared. What remained was a long-held goal that might never be attained. He could move on and start over somewhere else, of course, maybe even try city life for a while.

But he discarded that last notion in a heartbeat as he watched a hawk streak past in the distance, cutting a swift path through the sky. Whatever he chose to do in the future, he knew down deep that he'd spent too much time in open spaces to live in a cramped city for any length of time. The sprawling desert, rolling hills and low mountains of the Southwest were almost as much a part of him as they were of the bird he'd just viewed. He'd never be able to—

It rose up and hit him squarely between the eyes. Something he should have realized the minute he got a good long look at Eve Terry. From her stylish haircut to her manicured fingernails to her—no doubt—manicured toenails, the whole fancy package said she belonged in the city. A big, thriving, fast-paced city. Like Dallas, where she'd come from. A ranch on the outskirts of Tucson wasn't the end of the world, but it was hardly the world she was used to, not by a long shot.

She wouldn't stick it out. Couldn't, he was certain—certain enough to waste no time in using that newfound knowledge to his advantage.

"I don't want a raise," he said, breaking the silence. He turned his head, locked his gaze to hers. "What I want is the right of first refusal on buying this place if you decide to sell." *When* you decide, he added to himself. "I'll give you exactly what you paid for it, down to the last penny." Given a little time, he could come up with the extra financing, surely. She'd probably last at least a couple of weeks.

As though she'd guessed his thoughts, Eve's jaw tightened. "I'm staying," she said flatly. "I subleased my apartment, sold my furniture, gave away my plants, shipped what I'll need to continue my design work here and sent out 123 change-of-address cards. I'm here for good."

"Then it shouldn't be difficult to give me what I want," he countered.

They stared at each other for ten humming seconds before she nodded. "Okay. You've got the right of first refusal, and I'll be glad to put it in writing."

Ryder heaved an inner sigh. He felt better than he had in weeks. Losing Amos Cutter, as mule-headed as the old man could be on occasion, had been a blow. Amos, along with cantankerous Pete Rawlins, had been the closest thing to family he'd had for many years.

But things were looking up again. For the moment he'd still be part of the ranch. And when his boss got bored with playing cowgirl and went hightailing it back to where she belonged, he'd—

Eve's voice hauled back his attention. "Now, since I've given you what you asked for, I'd like something in return."

He should have known it wouldn't be that simple. *Simple,* it was becoming as clear as daylight, was not a word to be used in connection with this woman.

"And what's that?" he asked warily.

She didn't hesitate a second. "I want your agreement that you'll remain with the Creedence Creek for the next six months, no matter what I decide to do here."

Ryder ran his tongue over his teeth. Agreeing to stay was no problem. Long before those six months were up, he'd probably be the owner. It was the "no matter what" that bothered him.

Somehow he'd assumed the ranch would remain pretty much as it was, going on as it always had. A foolish assumption, he now realized. Yet what could she possibly plan to do with it? he asked himself, frowning in thought.

Suddenly something occurred to him, and it was horrible enough to make him shudder. "Oh, no. Don't tell me you want to turn this place into one of those god-awful dude ranches. *Please,* whatever you do, don't tell me that.''

Looking amused, she shook her head and sent shiny silver hoops swinging from delicately shaped ears. ''I won't tell you that.''

He let out the long gust of air he'd been holding back. ''Thank the Lord…and thank *you.*''

''You're welcome. But I still don't have your agreement,'' she reminded him.

Since, in his opinion, practically nothing could be worse than playing mother hen to a bunch of greenhorns who didn't know a horse's rear from a hole in the ground, Ryder nodded. ''You've got it—and I'll put that in writing.''

Eve slapped her palms on the desktop and stood up. ''Good, that's settled then. It's been a pleasure doing business with you.''

He should have been equally pleased—would have been, if the last turn the conversation had taken wasn't still bothering him. She wanted him to ask, was waiting for it, in fact. A sly glint in her eye told him that. If he had a lick of sense, he wouldn't open his mouth. But he had to know.

''All right. Spill it. What do you intend to do with the place?''

Her lips curved in a slight smile. ''I'm sure you'll be glad to learn that I'm leaving most of it as it is.''

He threw a swift look up at the beamed ceiling. *Thanks again, Lord.*

''I have some real changes planned for this house, though,'' she tacked on with an appraising glance around a room that contained no more than the basics.

And this woman would want more than the basics. Of course, she would. Curtains, drapes, a few rugs scattered about. Some pictures on the white stucco walls. That's what she had in mind, he assured himself. Simple stuff.

Then he remembered that *simple* didn't apply here. She didn't even travel simple. He'd already been told she'd arrived with enough luggage to sink a battleship, and more stuff was likely on the way.

Again, he didn't want to ask. Again, he found himself asking anyway. "Exactly what kind of changes do you have in mind?"

As she'd done earlier, Eve met his gaze head-on and didn't so much as blink. "To be exact, I'm turning a portion of this house into a day care center." The words were soft, the underlying tone firm. "A free day care center."

He frowned. He couldn't have understood her correctly. Surely he couldn't have. "A day care center?"

She nodded slowly. "A day nursery, actually."

"A nursery?" His frown deepened.

"Mmm-hmm. You know...for babies."

Chapter Two

"Babies."

Eve had to bite her lower lip to keep from laughing out loud. Judging by the blankly stunned expression on Ryder Quinn's face, she had surprised him, and surprised him well. "Yes, those little darlings who pop out nine months after mom and dad go to bed and do a lot more than sleep."

He looked at her as if she had just said she'd landed from another planet. "You are flat-out crazy!"

"You're welcome to think so," she calmly informed him. "However, the attorney general of this state, being a perceptive woman, considers it a great idea."

Ryder chewed that over for a second. "And where did you happen to bump into her?" he asked, raising a skeptical eyebrow.

"At a charity fund-raiser during Super Bowl celebrations a few years ago. We've kept in touch for quite a while. She loves the Sassy Lady line, by the way."

"Uh-huh. Sure."

"Believe what you want, but the end result is that she's willing to help me deal with all the bureaucratic regulations involved in this type of thing. If she's as good as her word, which I don't doubt for a minute, the center should be up and running in a couple of weeks.''

Ryder sat down on the edge of the desk, looking so disgusted she almost felt sorry for him. Almost. ''Is the first lady, or maybe the Queen of England, in on this too?''

She had to smile. ''No, they both missed that fund-raiser.''

''What other big shots do you know?''

She searched for someone who would truly impress him. Unfortunately she'd never run into Clint Eastwood. ''Well, I did meet Brad Pitt once.'' *For about thirty seconds.*

After studying her for a long moment, Ryder blew out a resigned breath. ''You're not making any of this up, are you?'' Since it wasn't really a question, she remained silent. ''This isn't a bad dream. You really are going to turn this place into a *Bonanza* for babies—the old TV show with a big twist.''

''Yes,'' she agreed, ''if you want to put it that way. My plan is to give new mothers who can't afford other forms of day care a chance to either work or go back to school. The service will be free of charge, but if it allows even one woman to keep a child she wants to keep, I'll consider myself well paid.''

Something in her voice must have alerted him. His gaze was suddenly probing. ''This is personal, isn't it, Eve?''

She turned to walk toward the window, saw the sun low on the horizon. Sunsets here, she'd already discovered, could be spectacular. ''Yes, it's personal,'' she replied quietly. ''I want to help mothers keep children, because mine didn't keep me.''

Eve lifted a hand and rubbed a dark smudge from

the glass. "The thing was, she wanted to keep me, which I only learned a few years ago. She wasn't married when I was born. She is now. Her husband seems like a good man. They lived in Tucson when we all met for the first time, in probably a nicer area of the city than I suspect she once lived in. Now they've moved to El Paso. I stopped by to see them again on the drive here. They have three children. It appears to be a very happy family. I might have been part of it, if the woman who gave birth to me had had the resources at seventeen to care for a baby."

"What happened after she gave you up?" Ryder asked softly.

Eve switched back to face him. "I was lucky. Two great people adopted me. When I was old enough to understand, they were straightforward about the adoption, and I was comfortable with it because I never doubted they loved me. I grew up in a middle-class area of Dallas, had lots of friends. I was happy. Yet something was always…missing. A link with the past, I suppose you could say. For instance, my adopted parents were small in stature—I was taller than both by the time I was thirteen. Where had my height come from? I often wondered. Then, too, I loved to draw almost from the time I could walk. Crayons were far more treasured than toys. Neither of the people who raised me had any artistic leanings. I learned from my birth mother that she'd always loved to draw. And my biological father, who didn't stay around long enough to see the child he'd created, gave me my height. Apparently, he was a very tall man."

Ryder ran a hand through his hair. "Okay, I guess I can understand this whole thing a little better now. But why here? A nursery setup on a *ranch*?"

"One that's close enough to the city to allow a mother to bring her child here if she has access to a car," Eve pointed out. "If she doesn't, I'm willing to provide transportation. As far as babies are concerned, they don't care if they're being cared for in the biggest skyscraper or the smallest hut on the planet. A full tummy, a dry diaper, someone to hold them—that's their world." She paused. "You may think I'm crazy again, but after meeting my birth mother I took a drive. I needed some time alone before I went to the airport for the flight back to Dallas. Somehow I wound up on Creedence Creek Road. I saw the ranch in the distance and—I'm not sure how to explain it—something just clicked. Right from that moment I wanted to live here."

She smiled faintly. "Perhaps there's a homesteader, or maybe a cattle rustler, in my family tree. Anyway, I asked a local real estate agency to let me know if the property ever went on the market. You know the rest. Long before I signed the purchase papers, though, one of my goals was to establish a free day care facility someday, somewhere. It seemed as though fate was working in my favor when I was able to do it here."

"I'm glad fate's working in someone's favor," he muttered, seemingly more to himself than to her.

She'd been going on and on, she abruptly realized. This man now knew a good part of her life history, and she knew practically nothing about him. Except that he'd wanted the ranch just as much as or maybe more than she had. Perhaps far more.

"Why did it have to be the Creedence Creek, Ryder?"

She'd struck a nerve. The way he stilled completely for an instant told her that. He didn't pretend not to know what she referred to. And he didn't respond immediately. Several silent seconds passed before he spoke.

"It's a long story."

A civil way of saying, *Mind your own business,* she knew. And she would. Yet she couldn't help wondering.

"Well, all my cards are on the table now, and I suppose I should give you a last chance to back out." She stepped forward, held out a hand. "Do we still have a deal, cowboy?"

Ryder studied her for a long moment before he took her hand in his for a firm handshake. "We still have a deal, lady."

JUST OVER A WEEK LATER, Ryder watched a large truck pull up to the back of the ranch house. Although he was more than fifty yards away, standing near a corral, he had no trouble making out what two uniformed deliverymen quickly began to unload. One sparkling white baby crib after another was hauled out and lined up in a long row.

"You got to do something, Ry. The woman's a pure menace."

Ryder clamped a companionable hand around the sturdy shoulder of the person standing beside him. "Hang in there, Pete. I told you she won't be here long."

And he didn't plan on revising that statement, Ryder reflected. No, not for a minute. Eve Terry was sincere about the whole thing, he had to give her that. She'd meant everything she'd said before they'd shaken hands to seal their agreement. But she hadn't changed his mind about anything. She wouldn't be able to stick it out.

Right now he had to hope Pete Rawlins could dredge up enough patience to make it through until the inevitable happened, well aware that to the solidly built man on the far side of sixty only four things in life were truly important: a tender steak, a decent brand of whisky, a big-screen television and no fussy female around to spoil his enjoyment of the other three.

"How long's long?" Pete asked.

Ryder shrugged. "A few weeks. Maybe a couple of months."

"Months."

"Could be," he had to acknowledge. "So far she's had plenty on her plate to keep her busy. She hasn't had time yet to start getting bored."

"She's been busy, all right." Pete snorted his displeasure. "Amos must be turning over in his grave. Jeez, he's probably spinning like a tumbleweed on a gusty day! Frilly curtains and fancy rugs all over the house. One whole side of the place looking like a circus ad with that clown wallpaper everywhere. And the kitchen… Why'd she have to mess with the kitchen?" A hint of anguish underscored that question.

"All she did was buy a new refrigerator and put in a dishwasher," Ryder said in a soothing tone.

"The old fridge was fine, and we don't need a dishwasher."

We will when the baby bottles start piling up. Ryder decided not to voice that thought. Pete obviously had enough to handle at the moment.

"Do you know what was in one of the dozen shopping bags she hauled in this morning? A *tablecloth.*" If Pete had said *horse manure,* it would have come out the same way. "Jeez. How's a man supposed to enjoy his supper when he has to face a tablecloth?"

Ryder's lips twitched. "It's a new experience, I know." He waited a beat. "Of course, you could always eat with the bunch down at the bunkhouse."

As expected, that suggestion was turned down flat. "There's been enough changes around here. For more years than I care to count, I fed the whole crew, and then Amos and I had our supper in the room off the kitchen where we could see the mountains. Along the way, you joined us. Now Amos is gone, but you and I are eating together at that old oak table, even if it does have a fancy-dancy cloth on it."

"I appreciate your sticking by me, Pete. I'd hate to face that trial alone."

He knew he'd laid it on too thick when a sidelong glance found midnight-black eyes narrowing. Once Pete's hair had been as dark as his eyes. Now black hair had given way to silver, although it was still as plentiful as ever.

"This is nothin' to joke about, Ry," the older man said. "It's serious. And you wouldn't be alone at that table. You'd be eating with *her.*"

As if on cue, Eve stepped out of the house, wearing more "upscale Western wear for women," as she'd termed it. She began to instruct the two deliverymen, and the lined-up cribs soon made their way up the short porch steps and through the back door.

Sharing the evening meal was about the only time Ryder had spent with his boss since their initial meeting, a deliberate decision on his part. He was staying out of her way as much as he could, but she probably hadn't even noticed. She'd been busy as a bee giving the house a makeover and driving Pete crazy.

Much of his own days had been spent outdoors. While the good weather held, there was plenty to be done. March, typically a dry month, might turn out to be wetter than normal. A large storm was brewing in the Pacific, and rain was a definite possibility, the forecasters said, hedging their bets, as usual. But rain or not he had to put some time in at the ranch office soon. He had records to update and investments to check on. Ordinarily, he enjoyed working at the computer, but he wasn't looking forward to the next session. It would put him too close to Eve Terry.

"How old do you suppose she is?"

Since Ryder had already given the matter some thought, he had a ready answer. "Around thirty, I'd guess."

"Humph. She looks younger. Of course, that makeup females use can probably change night into day."

Ryder had a hunch Eve would look just as good without a stitch of makeup, and he didn't even want to consider how she'd look in nothing at all. A vivid dream picturing that sight had already rattled his peace of mind. It was one of the reasons he was staying out of her way.

Okay, make that the first and foremost reason, he admitted. Certain parts of him were way too attracted to her, and if he didn't keep a rein on his libido, things could get…complicated.

Ryder's brow knitted under the wide rim of his black Stetson. If he had to come up with a single word to describe his past relationships with women—and there hadn't been all that many after his younger, wilder days—that word would probably be *uncomplicated*. Complications were something he'd never felt he could afford, not as long as the major part of his time and attention was solidly focused on eventually owning the Creedence Creek—a firmly held goal grounded in the past, with roots going back many years.

Thirty-three years, to be exact.

Those roots could be traced back to the day he was born, a fact he'd always kept to himself.

Now, at least for the present, a woman stood between him and his ability to achieve that goal. When she packed up and left, he'd have what he wanted. The last thing he needed was to start wanting her, as well. And if he were foolish enough to act on it, things were bound to get complicated in a hurry.

So it has to be kept simple, Quinn, he told himself. But he hadn't forgotten that simple didn't apply with *this* woman.

"Must be close to time to start supper," Pete said. He took a step forward, then stopped dead as the rev of an engine suddenly made itself known. "This must be the other female who's supposed to show up today. Jeez, it's a regular invasion!"

After negotiating a bend in the gravel road with a flourish, a bright-red coupe zipped neatly into a spot behind the truck. A woman with a trim figure and copper-colored hair got out. She wasn't young, yet there was nothing at all matronly about the yellow, short-skirted suit she wore, her fashionably high heels or the spring in her step. As she approached the back door, it opened and the deliverymen walked out. She turned and gave both men a frankly appraising glance as they departed before continuing on her way.

"Well, will you look at that. She was checkin' out their rears, Ry."

Ryder's chuckle was deep and low. "She's seen quite a few, I imagine. Remember, she's a nurse."

CLORIS MUNROE was like a breath of fresh air, brisk and invigorating. Eve had come to that conclusion minutes after meeting her in Tucson earlier that week. A hint of a Southern drawl, a legacy of her Louisiana childhood, seemed to be the only thing remotely lazy about Cloris. Her credentials were top-notch, her references excellent. During her thirty-year career as a pediatric nurse, Cloris had cared for untold numbers of children. She had also raised two of her own.

Eve felt downright lucky to have won this woman's agreement to act as the sole full-time member of the day care staff. She told her as much as they got better acquainted over coffee in the long dining room off the kitchen, where a wide landscape could be viewed through tall windows now framed in ivory lace.

Cloris aimed a small smile over the rim of a stoneware mug. "Thanks, Eve, I appreciate that. But I think I'm the one who lucked out." She set her mug down on the floral-print tablecloth, leaned back in a rustic oak chair. "When my husband and I split up after our kids were grown and on their own, I have to admit I felt sorry for myself. Too sorry for too long. Finally I got up the spunk to face myself in the mirror and say, 'Cloris, you need to get on with your life, get rid of a house that's too big for one person and get involved in something new.' Caring for children isn't new, of course, but living on a ranch definitely qualifies. I'm looking forward to it."

"Good." Eve took a short swallow of the coffee she'd made. It might not be the best in the West, she conceded, but it was better than the take-no-prisoners brew Pete favored. "The nursery area is already set up, for the most part. I'll show it to you shortly. It used to be the largest bedroom and a smaller connecting room. Your bedroom will be directly across the hall from the nursery. Mine is next to yours. We'll have to share a bath. I hope you don't mind."

After a quick shake of her head, Cloris said, "I made some inquiries about additional help. Anna Montez, a retired nurse who lives in the area, is willing to work on a part-time basis."

"That's terrific." Eve nodded. "Things are moving right along. I've made arrangements with a couple of used-car dealers in town to provide cars to women who want to bring their babies here but don't currently have transportation. Whether they're going back to school or work, they'll probably need them for that, as well, and the dealers will bill me by the month."

Cloris pursed her bright-coral lips. "I hate to say this, but cars can be stolen, and you'd be liable."

"I know. But if someone trusts us with her child, wouldn't it be petty in comparison not to trust her with a hunk of metal?"

"You have a point. And a soft heart, I think." She smiled. "But it's clear that you also have a sharp mind and a lot of determination. This is a wonderful thing you're doing here, Eve."

"No, it's just something I feel I should do, since I have the resources." She had already shared her reasons during their earlier meeting. "What's wonderful is being able to talk to someone who's equally enthusiastic about it."

A teasing twinkle entered Cloris's blue eyes. "Don't the cowboys around here appreciate your efforts?"

"Not exactly," Eve replied dryly.

"I saw two of them standing near a fenced-in area behind the house as I pulled in. I have to admit one caught my eye."

Ryder Quinn, Eve concluded without hesitation, having seen him and Pete over by the corral, watching cribs being unloaded and no doubt wishing her a thousand miles from where she was. Her business manager had probably caught the eye of scores of women, though he was avoiding her as much as possible. She was certain of that, and hadn't made an issue of it because it suited her to keep some distance between them for the time being. The humming awareness that had leaped to life for a sizzling moment on the day they'd met remained fixed in her memory, despite her considerable efforts to forget it.

Unaware of Eve's thoughts, Cloris went on. "He was very distinguished looking, with a splendid head of silver hair."

Eve blinked as realization struck. Then she began to laugh. Then she began to roar. Ryder wasn't the cowboy under discussion. It was Pete!

"How about letting me in on the joke," Cloris suggested when Eve finally got herself under control.

She wiped a tear from the corner of her eye. "I'm sorry, that was probably rude of me, but I couldn't help it. I'd be willing to bet that Pete Rawlins, the silver-haired man and our ranch cook, would rather be boiled in oil than be the object of any woman's attention."

"He doesn't like women?" Cloris ventured.

"That's putting it mildly. Pete firmly believes a woman's place is anywhere other than within a mile of him."

"I see. Obviously, he's one of those poor, unfortunate males who don't have the good sense to appreciate a woman.''

"You got it."

Cloris smiled in a way that boded ill for poor, unfortunate men. "Do you mind if a Southern belle has a little fun?''

Eve grinned. "Not at all—as long as I can watch.''

The back door opened, then closed with a familiar near slam. "There's Mr. Charm now.'' Raising her voice, Eve called, "Pete, would you come here for a minute?''

Boots stomped their way closer. Seconds later Pete poked his head through an arched doorway and viewed the two women with a crystal-clear scowl. "I'm here.''

"I'd like you to meet Cloris Munroe,'' Eve said. "She'll be heading up the day care staff. Cloris, this is Pete Rawlins.''

Cloris draped an arm over the back of her chair and flashed a million-kilowatt smile. "I sure am glad to meet you…sugar.'' Her smooth-as-silk, rich-as-cream tone would have made Scarlett O'Hara proud. The playful wink that followed would have turned an entire generation of younger women who had never mastered that trick green with envy.

Pete's jaw dropped and stayed down.

If possible, Cloris's next smile was even more brilliant. "Eve's been telling me you do the cooking around here. I'm sure you're a marvelous chef.''

Dead silence reigned until Pete got his bearings and shut his mouth with an audible snap. "I'm a plain cook, not some fancy chef,'' he muttered, jamming his hands into the side pockets of well-worn Wranglers.

"Now, there's no need to be modest. I can hardly wait to taste the treat you have in store for us tonight.''

Oh, so slowly Cloris ran her tongue over her lips. "I'm really looking forward to it…sugar."

Pete's throat worked as he swallowed hard. "Yeah, well, ah, I got to go." He spun around on one heel and all but fled.

"I do believe Mr. Charm has met his match," Eve remarked with satisfaction.

"Could be," Cloris said, eyes sparkling. "What's he cooking for dinner tonight?"

Eve's expression turned rueful. "I can almost guarantee beef in some form. It's occurred to me during the past week that the link between cowboys and cattle may be so strong they can't bear to eat anything else."

RYDER DEFTLY CUT another slice of T-bone and listened to a conversation that seemed to be ruining someone's appetite. Raising his gaze, he aimed a look down the length of the table and found Eve's expression to be perfectly innocent. Too perfect. She knew exactly what was going on, he thought, chewing his meat. She might even have put Cloris Munroe up to it.

"No, I didn't say beef was bad for a person," Cloris corrected softly, batting her eyelashes at the man sitting across from her. "And, in case I haven't mentioned it, you do have a way with a steak, sugar. It's just that red meat isn't good for a body all the time. Now a lean piece of chicken—"

"I like my chicken fried," Pete broke in, clenching a knife and fork in opposite hands as though they were weapons and he was a desperate man.

"Oh, fried is scrumptious, sugar. No one south of the Mason-Dixon line would disagree with that. Still, we all have to remember our cholesterol count, as depressing as it can be, and lean chicken, baked fish, or even boiled shrimp—''

''Shrimp! I'd rather eat a bale of hay than a plateful of those slimy things.''

Cloris pursed her lips. ''Come to think of it, hay could be a good source of fiber. But a whole *bale,* sugar?''

A sudden cough didn't quite smother Eve's chuckle. She was in on it, all right, Ryder told himself.

Pete's chair tottered as he shot to his feet. ''Real food for real men is what I cook. It's been good enough for the folks around here since God knows when, and it's good enough now.'' That said, he grabbed his plate with one hand and stomped out.

''Isn't he a darling man?'' Cloris asked of no one in particular. She forked up a helping of mashed potatoes and continued her meal as though nothing at all unusual had occurred.

Ryder's gaze met Eve's. ''You'll be lucky if he doesn't leave.''

''I doubt he'll do that,'' she replied, her tone confident. ''He's probably waiting for me to leave.'' *Like you are,* a glint in her eye added silently. ''But I'm staying.'' She paused for a beat. ''And since I'm staying, I think it's time I took some riding lessons. Can you suggest someone here who could help?''

Not me.

As determined as ever not to spend more time in her company than strictly necessary, he considered the alternatives as he polished off his steak. It didn't take long to come up with one. ''Zeb Hollister will get you started. He's our most experienced horseman.''

And he was bound to be less than thrilled about riding herd on a greenhorn. But the old wrangler would do it and keep her out of trouble at the same time, Ryder decided. He'd make it an order if he had to. When it came to the working part of the ranch, he was still in charge. Zeb and every other man on the place knew that. He'd made certain they knew it.

Eve reached for her water glass. "Fine. Early tomorrow afternoon would be a good time for me."

"I'll set it up for one o'clock." Ryder tossed his napkin beside his empty plate and pushed back from the table as pots and pans clanked loudly in the background. "Pete's probably thrown out dessert, so if you'll excuse me, I'll check in at the bunkhouse. There may be a few stray crumbs of pie left, if I'm lucky."

He was barely gone when Cloris slid a sidelong glance Eve's way. "That man does things to a pair of jeans."

Having just watched a tight male backside depart, she could hardly argue the matter. "Mmm-hmm," was her reply.

"He doesn't look like a business manager," Cloris tacked on.

"He does when he wears a suit, trust me."

Despite the fact that she hadn't seen him in one since the day they'd met, Eve had no trouble recalling the sight. He'd done it to make a point, she was sure. Ryder Quinn, businessman. Impressive? Yes. But then, he'd probably be impressive stripped down to—

No, Eve, don't go there, she warned herself. Fully clothed, he already captured too many of her thoughts. Much too many of them, she had to admit.

Showing flawless table manners as she had throughout the meal, Cloris dabbed her napkin at the corners of her mouth. "Does Ryder stay at the bunkhouse he mentioned?"

Eve went back to her dinner. "No. Although the single hands stay there, as a rule, while the married ones have homes of their own, Ryder lives in the original house that was built when the ranch was first settled. I've been told that it's a short drive from here, up a steep road toward the mountains. I haven't had a chance to see it yet."

Truth was, she'd made no effort to see it, although it was part of her property. And she was in no hurry to change that situation. She knew she'd be better off not being able to picture where a certain man spent his evenings when he left after the late-day meal they regularly shared.

"Pete stays here," she added. "His bedroom and a small bath are on the other side of the kitchen."

"So only the three of us will be living here," Cloris summed up, then winced as metal met metal with a sharp clang.

Eve carefully removed a thin edge of marbled fat and stabbed a last piece of steak. "That's right. It's just you and me and Mr. Charm."

THE FOLLOWING AFTERNOON Eve walked down a gravel road, headed for the corral and adjoining stable located closest to the house. Other ranch buildings, a tall tin-roofed barn, sheds of various shapes and sizes, together with the large stone bunkhouse, marked the landscape. Up above, fluffy white clouds drifted, creating a moving patchwork quilt of sun and shade on hard-packed ground.

Cloris had left after lunch to visit a friend who was actively involved in several local charities; it was time to spread the news about the day care center and what it had to offer. Pete, sulking to beat the band, had stationed himself in front of the large-screen television in the living room.

And Eve had set out for her date with Zeb Hollister. She'd met Zeb, along with many of the hands, on her second day at the ranch. The bearded man might resemble Willie Nelson more than John Wayne, she thought, yet his bowlegged stance said he'd been all but born in a saddle.

As she approached the corral, taking quick strides in her cream-colored boots, a cowboy came into view leading a stocky gray horse out of the stable. He lifted a gloved hand and waved when he saw her. It wasn't Zeb, or anyone she readily recognized. Tall and lanky, he couldn't have been more than in his early twenties.

"Hello, Miz Terry," he called, his voice ripe with an easygoing twang. Turning his head, he aimed a look over his shoulder. "Come on, Buttercup, old girl. Step lively and meet your new owner." In response, Buttercup continued to plod along, clearly unenthusiastic about the news.

"I'm Cody Bodeen," the cowboy said as he and Eve faced each other over a slatted wood fence seconds later. In a courteous gesture that took her by surprise, he lifted his dusty beige hat and tipped it forward, revealing sun-bleached hair before he resettled it on his head. A friendly gaze assessed her in a sweeping glance too quick and casual to give offense.

"I'm glad to meet you, Cody Bodeen," she said, reaching up to touch the pristine rim of her own creamy Western hat. "I don't think you were here the day I met a bunch of the hands."

"No, I was helping stubborn strays fixed on leaving find their way back to the herd." He grinned ruefully.

"They usually save that treat for me." Then his grin widened. "But I lucked out today. I get to help you."

Eve arched an eyebrow. "Did Zeb head for the hills when he found himself elected to give riding lessons?"

"Uh-uh. He had an emergency—nothing real serious," he tacked on before she could ask. "His oldest granddaughter called from Bisbee. Her husband's out of town and her car broke down in the middle of the highway while she was driving one of her kids to a doctor's appointment. Zeb and another hand went to see if they could get it started again, or at least get the kid to the doctor. If the head honcho were around, he might have taken Zeb's place instead of me, but he left for Tucson this morning and he's not back yet."

Puzzled, Eve asked, "The head honcho?"

"Ryder Quinn. To the men who work here, he's the head honcho. You're the owner now, so you're the big boss."

Not only the boss, the *big* boss. Because the title amused her, and because she was sure it would not amuse the "head honcho," Eve smiled. "Why don't we get started?"

Cody nodded his agreement. "Come in through the gate next to the stable and I'll introduce you to Buttercup."

If the long-suffering look in her eyes was any indication, Buttercup wasn't overjoyed to meet her owner, and Eve decided the feeling was mutual after a frustrating hour of coaxing the mare around the corral and achieving no more than a snail's pace.

Finally she'd had it. She halted at the spot where Cody leaned against the fence. "There have to be horses on this place with a little more zip."

He nudged his hat back and gazed up at her. "Buttercup's the one the head honcho picked out for you, Miz Eve.''

That information didn't merit a second thought, not as far as she was concerned. ''Well, I'm ready to pick something else. I've got the basics down, but I'll never get beyond them if the Old Gray Mare won't even break into a trot.''

Cody pushed away from the fence. ''Guess you have a point. But the head—''

''I'll deal with him,'' Eve assured the ranch hand, and went on before he could offer any further objection. ''Let's look at some of the other horses.''

There were three in the stable, she found as they entered through wide double doors with Buttercup trailing behind. The huge stallion she'd almost collided with occupied the first stall they came to. He snorted a greeting.

''This is Lucky,'' Cody said. ''He belongs to Ryder Quinn. No one else rides him,'' he added hastily, as though he were afraid she might decide to do exactly that.

She ran her tongue around her teeth to foil a grin and moved on. The two remaining occupants were less impressive than Lucky, she had to admit. Still, they had to be more lively than Buttercup. She'd parted her lips, ready to ask a question about a cinnamon-colored horse, when a high-pitched whinny drew her attention to the back of the building.

''That's Sable,'' Cody told her as she turned toward the sound. ''She's only been here a few weeks. Could be they'll hitch her up with Lucky when the time's right.''

Sable. A fitting name, Eve decided after walking forward for a closer look. Black as coal and sleek as satin, the mare pranced to the front of the stall, then tilted her head at a playful angle and blew out a soft breath. Obviously far beyond lively, she was a strong, spirited mixture of muscle and grace. And a beautiful, dark-eyed flirt, as well.

Eve was entranced. "Does she belong to Ryder Quinn, too?"

"No, she's yours," Cody replied, moving to stand next to her.

Hers. Up to that moment she'd considered the animals that had come with the ranch as merely part of the property. Now she knew just how wrong she'd been. There was a bond here, she realized, and with it came responsibility. Ultimately the fate of this and every other animal she owned rested with her. And, when it came to this particular one, there was also a thrill of possession she couldn't deny.

She reached up and gently rubbed the mare's ebony forehead, watching as dark eyes viewed her with a saucy gleam. "I want to ride her."

"I don't think that's a good idea, Miz Eve." Cody's easygoing manner abruptly turned serious. "Sable can be a handful when she sets her mind to it."

Eve dropped her arm and turned to face him. "Are you saying she's dangerous?"

"No," he admitted reluctantly. "Just…frisky."

One corner of Eve's mouth quirked up. "Hmm. Maybe even…sassy?"

He lifted a hand to rub the back of his neck. "Yeah, I suppose."

That did it. In a flash, the prospect of riding Sable became irresistible. "Saddle her up, Cody Bodeen."

He let out a resigned sigh. "The head honcho's

probably gonna be teed off when he finds out about this.''

''And I told you I'd deal with him,'' she countered smoothly yet firmly. ''Remember, I'm the big boss.''

Another high whinny seconded that statement.

Chapter Three

Ryder had spent the better part of the day dealing with bankers and was glad to be back at the ranch, out of a suit and dressed in his usual denim. Not that he regretted the lengthy questions he'd answered or the stack of forms he'd filled out. They'd tried his patience, but his spirits were far from dampened. With any luck at all, the extra financing he needed would be at his disposal by the time Eve Terry decided to throw in the towel.

Maybe her riding lesson this afternoon would speed her on her way, he thought as he parked his dark-blue pickup along one side of the ranch house stable and swung to the ground in a single, easy movement. To him the world was made up of two kinds of people: those who genuinely loved horses, and those who were convinced they loved horses until they'd spent a few hours on the back of one. If Eve was part of the last group, her nose would have already wrinkled at a good whiff of horse sweat, not to mention the barnyard smell of horse sh—

A woman's laugh, soft and light, broke into Ryder's reflections. If it was Eve—and who else could it be?—she seemed to be enjoying herself. Well, she just might be, even if she was in that second group, he conceded with a shrug, since he'd handpicked the oldest and slowest mare on the place for her first lesson. Buttercup didn't move fast enough to work up a sweat.

Next time, assuming Eve was game for another lesson, he'd have to pick something a bit more challenging. Not too much, though. He didn't want her to break her neck. He just wanted her gone.

But when Ryder moved past the stable and got a view of the corral, he was ready to break someone's neck, or at least wring it for a satisfying moment. Zeb Hollister's immediately came to mind. The old wrangler was supposed to be riding herd on the ranch's new owner, and here she was, clearly having a grand time smiling down on young Cody Bodeen, who was checking her stirrup and managing to get very close to a shapely leg in the process—a leg clenched around a horse Eve had no business being on.

Three long, rapid strides took him to the edge of the fence. *"What the hell is going on here?"*

The black mare reacted first, surging up on her hind legs to paw the air. Cody's swift tug on her bridle brought her back on all fours, and it took him another moment to bring her to a complete standstill. Then he faced Ryder with a wary look.

"I know I'm supposed to be up on the north range, but Zeb wasn't able to give Miz Eve her riding lesson." He rushed on to explain what had happened. "So with you and Zeb gone," he added, "I offered to help."

And avoided hunting strays at the same time, Ryder thought. His steely gaze didn't waver. "And just how did Miz Eve—" he copied Cody's twang for those last words "—wind up on a horse you know damn well she shouldn't be on?"

"I'm riding Sable because I wanted to," Eve said calmly, interrupting before the younger man could reply. "In fact, I ordered Cody to saddle her up."

Ryder turned his gaze on her, not softening it in the slightest. "*You* ordered him?"

"Yes," she replied in that same calm tone. "The mare *you* picked should be put out to pasture, since she's probably old enough to collect Social Security." One tawny eyebrow rose. "Or did you bring her out of retirement solely for my benefit?"

He had, but he wasn't about to admit it. "Buttercup," he replied with what he felt was admirable restraint, "is the right horse for a beginner."

"And I began with her. Now I'm ready for something else."

"That brief demonstration a minute ago should tell you the something you're ready for isn't Sable," Ryder muttered. He didn't miss the way Cody watched their exchange like a verbal tennis match, eyes shifting back and forth.

"You scared her with your bellowing," Eve protested. "We were getting along fine before you arrived on the scene. I've already taken her around the corral several times, and she's been an angel."

"She can also be a devilishly uncooperative female when the mood strikes." He was no longer talking strictly about the mare, and Eve knew it, if the sudden spark that lit in her gray eyes was anything to go by.

"Maybe it depends who's on her back."

Ignoring that zinger, he blew out an exasperated breath. "I'm not going to argue the point with you.

Why don't you just get down and we'll drop the subject?''

"I don't plan on arguing, either," she promptly informed him. "It would be wasting time better spent taking Sable for a real ride outside this corral."

He counted to five under his breath, then ten. And his temper still got the better of him. "You want to take a *real* ride? Okay." Reaching up, he tugged the rim of his black Stetson low on his forehead in a gesture as challenging as an Old West gunfighter's. "Cody, saddle up Lucky. Miz Eve and I are going to tour the ranch."

And he'd do his best to make sure she came to no harm, he told himself, even though he was now certain whose neck he wanted to wring.

EVE GRIPPED THE SADDLE with tender thighs and issued a quiet sigh. Although an hour and several miles had clipped by since their confrontation in the corral, she had no trouble recalling how she'd watched Ryder mount up for their ride with such effortless grace, or how the soft curse she'd muttered under her breath had been directed as much at herself as at a wide male back. She'd been well aware of the mistake she'd made. Rather than attempt to compromise as she usually tried to do, she'd dug in her boot heels. And look where it had put her.

Not only was she spending time with someone she'd been going out of her way not to spend time with, she was doing it on horseback when parts of her had already been headed toward saddle sore before they'd even started out. Still, she'd never so much as considered backing down at any point, and on that she remained firm. Pride was on the line and she was seeing this through, no matter what.

No Complaints and No Regrets. That was her motto for the moment. Besides, without the physical discomfort, she knew she'd be totally enjoying the ride.

Sable had resumed her angelic ways, responding to the slightest tug on the reins. Not that Ryder was impressed, Eve noted with a sidelong glance. He continued to watch the mare like a hawk, clearly waiting for a devilish side to appear. An occasional word or two was all he'd offered so far, which was fine with Eve. The lack of conversation as they rode side by side allowed her to concentrate on her surroundings, and what she saw all around her made that effort more than worthwhile.

The desert, far from barren as some believed it to be, was a starkly beautiful place. The variety of cactus alone, from short and squat to tall and stately, created a constantly changing landscape. Trees, delicately green paloverdes and darker, gnarled mesquites, also flourished, along with a surprising amount of animal life.

The cattle were expected, of course, and every now and then groups could be glimpsed in the distance, Herefords with white faces and rusty-brown coats. But there were other animals, as well. Big-eared rabbits, tiny lizards, bushy-tailed prairie dogs, chattering birds. They were all here if one looked carefully, before they darted away as the horses got too close.

Something Eve had suspected she might see, and was very grateful not to have seen so far, was anything slithering along the ground. She'd never considered herself a coward, but the mere thought gave her the shivers. She'd rather face a hungry lion than a…

Snake!

Without warning, it was there, coiled near the side of the narrow dirt trail they rode down. Instinctively reacting to the sudden sight, she let out a small shout, jerked back on the reins, and almost instantly found herself airborne as Sable shot up on two legs to paw at the sky.

Ryder's curse, brief and graphic, followed a thump as Eve landed on her rear and rolled—right into the snake! Something pierced her upper thigh before she scrambled up and lunged back toward the trail, only to come up against a solid chest.

Strong arms wrapped around her, held her so close she could feel Ryder's heart pounding and knew her heartbeat matched his. "Good Lord, are you hurt?"

She sucked in a breath and raised her head. "No, I don't think so." Then she remembered the instant of piercing pain she'd experienced and realized the spot still smarted. Her eyes went huge.

"Oh, my God. I may have been bitten by the snake. I almost rolled on top of it."

Dark brows snapped together. "What snake?"

"It was on my side of the trail, just coiled there. Scared the living daylights out of me. That's why I yelled."

He eased her an arm's length away, ran his gaze over her. "Where did it get you?"

She twisted slightly and pointed to a spot high on her outer left thigh, noting a jagged tear in the denim fabric there.

Plainly seeing it, too, Ryder cursed again while he maintained his grasp on one arm and led her to a short, rounded boulder located on the opposite side of the trail from where she'd fallen. "I have to get a better look," he told her, then made quick work of unbuckling her belt and shoving her jeans nearly to her knees. That done, he urged her into a makeshift seat on the boulder and crouched down beside her.

"It's a puncture wound, and it's not bleeding much," he said after a moment, taking a snowy white handkerchief from his back pocket to pat it against her skin. He tipped his hat back and gazed up at her, his expression sober. "I want a good look at that snake."

Her blood went cold. "What if it's poisonous?"

He snagged her left wrist, pressed her palm on the soft cloth to hold it in place before getting to his feet. "It could be totally harmless, but even if it isn't, there's rarely a grave danger when the victim is a healthy adult. I just need to make sure exactly what we're facing here."

She fought for control, took a steadying breath and managed to achieve it. "Okay."

He launched a probing glance. Apparently satisfied that he didn't have a hysterical woman on his hands, he turned away and headed for the place where she'd landed on her rump.

Left alone and prompted by a gentle breeze gliding over bare skin, she became fully aware of her exposure. Granted, the long front and back tails of her ecru cotton shirt covered more than short shorts would have. Still, enough flesh remained on view to make something inside her clench at the unbidden thought of a certain male mouth sucking venom from a wound that was scant inches from other parts of her.

Back to reality, Eve, she told herself briskly, fairly sure modern medicine frowned on that technique. If it turned out she was in any sort of danger, the head honcho would probably put his take-charge attitude to good use by hauling her off to the nearest hospital. And she'd be grateful, despite the fact that no one had taken charge of her since she'd gone off to college.

At the sound of footsteps Eve raised her gaze and watched Ryder approach, swinging something from one large hand—something that had her shuddering before she realized it was too stiff, too rigid as it cut a path through the air, to be what she'd thought it was. At the same time, it was something she recognized all too well.

He stopped directly in front of her and held up the object. "Is this the snake you saw?" he asked mildly. Too mildly.

She knew she was on very shaky ground. "It looks like a snake," was all she could come up with to say.

"It's an old, wind-twisted mesquite branch. A sharp edge must have pierced your skin when you rolled into it."

"It looks like a snake."

"It's a damned hunk of wood."

"It looks like a damned snake," she said stubbornly.

With clear disgust, he flung it backward over a broad shoulder. "Heaven save me from greenhorns and their imagination," he muttered as he turned away. "I'll get the first-aid kit and patch you up."

Ryder whistled for Lucky, and the stallion was immediately at his side. He reached into a saddlebag and pulled out a small plastic box, still grumbling. The fact that he half blamed himself for what had happened only added to his dark frame of mind. He should have just flatly refused to let Eve ride a horse she wasn't ready for, he groused inwardly. And he would have done it…if she wasn't his boss. Cripes, how was a man supposed to deal with that?

And how was any male supposed to hide what a glimpse of smooth-as-cream thighs did to him? At first, with health issues in question, he'd been too concerned to consider anything else. Then he'd found the twisted piece of wood no seasoned outdoors person would have mistaken for anything threatening, relieving his mind and rousing something else when he got another look at his companion, jeans at her knees. If her attention hadn't been fixed on the bogus snake, she'd have probably noticed that his zipper was no longer as flat as it had been minutes earlier.

Ryder pried open the kit and knelt next to Eve. He drew a deep breath and instantly regretted it. God, she didn't even *smell* simple, he thought, taking in a sophisticated blend of exotic flowers and warm woman. He willed his hands to remain fixed on their objective as he slipped the handkerchief from her grasp, letting it fall to the dusty ground, and began to clean the wound.

"The antiseptic may sting," he told her with a trace of huskiness he couldn't hide.

Her leg jerked slightly when he gently touched torn skin, but she didn't make a sound. He continued his task, trying to ignore a scant inch of pink lace that peeked out from between the slit sides of her shirt, and failing. At that moment, ignoring a rattler primed to strike might have been easier. By the time he applied a flesh-colored Band-Aid, he'd started to sweat. "I'm no expert, but I don't think it's serious enough for stitches. It should heal fine on its own. You'll need a tetanus shot, though," he tacked on, dropping his gaze and making a bigger production of repacking the kit than necessary.

"I got a shot before I came here." The soft rustle

of clothing, the low rasp of a zipper, accompanied Eve's reply. "I know it's important when you live around animals."

At least she knew that much, he griped to himself, rising. He ventured a glance, discovered she was fully dressed and, after a moment, also noted a tendency on her part to look everywhere except his way. It suddenly occurred to him that he might not have been the only one affected by their enforced intimacy. Somehow that put him in a better mood. He didn't like what was coming next, yet if it made his boss half as uncomfortable as it was bound to make him, maybe she'd think twice before overriding his judgment.

Ryder checked the time on the plain gold watch Pete had traded hard-earned money for to proudly produce as his college-graduation present, something he wouldn't have traded for the fanciest Rolex. "It's late. I'll take a look around for your hat, then we have to start back."

Eve resisted the urge to wince and told herself not to be a wimp. Despite various aches and pains, most of which centered where she'd be sitting, she had to get back on a horse, and there was no sense whining about it. "Don't bother with the hat. If my memory serves me right, I landed on it when I fell."

Ryder replaced the kit and turned to her. "Okay, let's get going. Fortunately, Lucky can carry both of us."

Eve frowned, puzzled because she knew her horse was uninjured. She'd already been reassured by the sight of the black mare standing several yards away, head dipped to munch on sparse grass. "Sable's fine. I'll ride her."

Crossing his arms over his chest, Ryder propped one

shoulder against the stallion's saddle. "I have a feeling that won't be so easy."

Eve's chin rose right along with her renewed sense of pride. "I am perfectly capable of riding her."

One corner of his mouth tipped up. "First you have to get her over here. Go ahead, call her."

Recognizing the challenge underscoring those words, Eve called. Sable lifted her head, viewed her owner with gleaming dark eyes and stayed put. She called again. And nothing happened. When she took a determined step forward, the mare took a step backward. When she stopped and coaxed in a soothing tone, the mare went back to munching grass.

After several frustrating minutes of more of the same, Eve placed her fists on her hips. "Get your butt over here right this minute, Sable," she ordered, stomping a foot to emphasize that statement.

The mare's only response was to bob her head up and down, snorting all the while.

Eve's spine stiffened in indignation. "I think she's *laughing* at me."

A sudden cough may have masked Ryder's own laugh. Eve couldn't be certain, since a quick spin found nothing to confirm it. "Are you ready to go now?" he asked calmly.

Still bristling, Eve returned to where he stood. "We can't just leave her here. You try something."

"I'd have to chase her down, and there's no time for that if we're going to make it back before the sun is history. Don't worry, she'll follow us. She's smart enough to know there's plenty of food and water waiting for her." He bent over, linked his hands. "Put your foot here, and I'll give you a leg up."

She went up and up, and met the saddle with a small groan she couldn't restrain.

"A bit tender, Miz Eve?" Now he *was* laughing at her. She was sure of it, even though she couldn't see his expression as he mounted behind her.

Two people could indeed share a single saddle, she learned a second later—if the two in question were plastered to each other from shoulders to knees, if an unyielding chest melded to a supple backbone, if hard thighs cradled far softer ones, if some very private male anatomy came flat up against some very sore female anatomy.

It gave, she decided, a whole new meaning to the phrase *up close and personal.*

"Everything okay?" a low voice at her ear asked as Lucky ambled forward.

"Uh-huh." She could hardly tell him that her nerves were stretched as taut as some of her muscles.

A skillful flick of the reins had the horse turning to retrace its steps. "We'll take it slow and easy."

"Uh-huh." She wanted it fast and done with. A foolish wish, she knew. The stallion couldn't handle both their weights and run a race at the same time. And, truth be told, her body wasn't up to being jostled more than necessary.

As though well aware of the shape she was in, Ryder grasped the reins with one hand and slid an arm loosely around her waist. "If you tense up now, you'll suffer for it later. Why don't you lean on me and try to relax?"

The offer caught her off guard. Yet it shouldn't have, she quickly realized. By and large, cowboys seemed to be naturally chivalrous. Fantasy knights in shining armor? No. Gallant in their own way? Absolutely. She recalled how Cody Bodeen had automatically tipped his hat. Ryder's suggestion probably meant nothing more than that. Knowing she was bone tired, he had reacted accordingly.

What he didn't know was that she seldom leaned on anyone, physically or emotionally. Her parents, special souls that they were, had raised her to be independent, encouraged her to never be afraid to try her wings. And she blessed them for it every time she met capable people too bound by what others thought they should be doing with their lives to try theirs. In her own way she had soared. Not to great heights but great enough for her. And she'd done it on her own. Still, that didn't mean she couldn't lean on someone else just a bit right now, just for a little while.

Eve let out a long breath and reclined slightly against the man behind her.

"That's better," he told her. "You won't even have to put anything extra in my paycheck for the service."

It made her smile faintly, eased more of her tension. "I'll stick a gold star on your personnel file instead," she promised, tongue in cheek.

"Thanks. I was afraid I'd have to do something truly amazing, like stand on my head on the back of a horse, to get one of those."

The image had her chuckling. "Have you ever actually tried that?"

"Yeah," he acknowledged, "when I was young and stupid."

Although he'd certainly been young once, she didn't believe for a second that this man had ever been less than intelligent. Reckless, perhaps. Stupid, never. "What happened?"

"I landed on the head I was trying to stand on."

Now she gave in to the wince she'd held back earlier. "That's a mental picture I can do without. Recent
experience has proved it's painful enough landing on
the other end." She let out a breath. "I have to admit
I've been waiting to hear you say I told you so."

"I told you so."

His all-too-ready response had her grumbling.
"Guess I should have kept my mouth shut." But there
was no real heat in that statement. "Is Sable following
us?"

Ryder's chin brushed her temple as he turned his
head. "She's there, all right, keeping her distance and
having a great time, judging by the way she's dancing
around."

Despite her exhaustion, Eve's jaw set with determination. "I'm going to ride her again."

"Eve—"

"But not outside a corral for the time being," she
assured him before he could continue the stern warning
she was sure would have followed. "Not until I feel I
can handle her no matter what we come across."

His tone turned wry in a flash. "Does that include
dead mesquite branches?"

Eve still had her pride, and she was sticking to her
story. "It looked like a damned snake."

RYDER VIEWED the sight of ranch buildings in the distance with sheer relief, grateful to know they were almost there. The return ride had seemed endless, and
time had little to do with it. He assumed Eve was at
least half-asleep, since she hadn't said a word in some
time and now leaned heavily against him, obviously
totally relaxed.

He, on the other hand, was as tense as a steel fence post and quietly going crazy.

Even if Eve had been fully awake, her backside might be too numb to feel what pressed against it with growing enthusiasm, unmistakable evidence of a physical reaction he'd tried to curb. And failed. Thoughts of ranch business, which normally won his full attention, had proved to be no match for the lure of a woman's softness.

And added to that, he supposed, was what he'd learned today about this particular woman.

Eve Terry could take it when the going got tough, and she did it without complaint. With some people, he knew the whining would have long since started. Hell, being thrown from a horse and then coping with a possible snakebite would have left more than a few shaken to the point of tears, not to mention hysterics.

But not his boss.

He had to admire her for it, although that admiration only seemed to heighten an attraction he'd done his best to squelch from the day they'd met. *You're complicating things, Quinn,* he told himself. Too bad certain parts of him didn't appear to appreciate that fact.

Soon the black mare ran ahead as they approached the stable she recognized as home. When Cody rushed out to catch her reins and bring her to a standstill, Ryder didn't stop to answer the questions he saw in the younger man's puzzled look. His priorities were set. Take Eve to the ranch house, drop Lucky back here, then climb into his truck and head for his place and a cold shower. If he was quick, he might get away before anyone suspected his control hung by a thread. It was one piece of news he'd rather not have Cody spreading to the rest of the hands along with the usual stories traded over the bunkhouse's long, rough pine dining table.

And the less the ranch's owner knew about the whole thing, the better.

Riding to the edge of the back porch, he brought the stallion to a halt, loosened the tight grip he'd kept on Eve, and gave her a gentle shake. "We're back," he told her, pitching his voice low in an effort not to jar her.

In spite of that, she sat straight up. "Already? I guess I must have dozed off."

"Probably," he replied shortly, dropping the reins. In a flash, his boots met gravel with a crunch. Then he reached up and caught Eve around the waist to lift her down. He had to grit his teeth to foil a groan as their bodies brushed briefly before he set her on her feet. A scant moment later after waiting only long enough to be sure her stance was steady he grabbed the reins and bounded back into the saddle.

"Cody's taking care of Sable. I have to get Lucky settled. See you later."

That said, he was off and running, and he didn't plan on stopping for long until he hit that shower.

AFTER A RESTORING BATH doused with a large helping of Epsom salts, Eve felt almost human as she dressed for dinner. Well aware that there was no way she could wear jeans without moaning every time she took a step, she chose a loose-fitting jumpsuit of gauzy red cotton. With a dash of makeup and scarlet-enameled hoops swinging from her ears, she decided she looked nearly human, too. At least the sight of her wouldn't send anyone running in the opposite direction without so much as a backward glance. Which was basically what had happened earlier.

Who was that masked man? she'd found herself thinking as she'd watched Ryder take off in a flash, leaving a trail of dust behind him. The rueful question had hit her from out of the blue even as it summed up exactly how she'd felt.

She'd been dropped like a hot potato, Eve was forced to admit. Plainly things hadn't changed. A certain male still had no intention of spending any more time in her company than strictly necessary.

It was foolish to be disappointed by that. After all, it was what she wanted…wasn't it? Eve shook her head. Her brain must be even more worn-out than the rest of her if she was having doubts about the wisdom of maintaining a discreet distance.

Especially after today.

Today had proved to be a revelation, mainly about herself. Like it or not, she had the niggling suspicion that only sheer exhaustion had stopped her from doing something truly dumb, such as letting everything inside her dissolve into a warm puddle at the feel of a strong arm at her waist, the steady brace of a rock-solid body at her back, the rough purr of a deep voice at her ear. And a lot of good that would have done her.

It was crystal clear that her business manager wanted to keep things businesslike, even after the all-too-personal nature of some of the day's events. If she had any sense, Eve told herself, she'd make damned sure Ryder Quinn got what he wanted. Fortunately, she had plenty of sense; she just had to use it.

When a soft voice called from the hallway, interrupting her thoughts, Eve crossed the bedroom to open the door and discovered Cloris holding a brimming wineglass in each hand. "I thought this might come in handy," she said, offering a glass. "When I got back a few minutes ago, Pete unbent enough to tell me that you'd returned from your lesson looking like you'd been, and I quote, 'rode hard and put away wet.'"

"Although it galls me to say so, I have to agree with him," Eve replied. She accepted the glass and stepped back to let the other woman enter. "What's Mr. Charm fixing for dinner?"

"The good news is that it's not beef," Clovis told her. "The bad news is that it's chicken—dipped in egg, floured and fried to a crisp."

Eve grimaced. "It figures. And we're probably having biscuits and gravy to go with it. At least I used up enough calories today to indulge without guilt," she added as she closed the door. "Let's sit down."

Gesturing with her free hand, she indicated two chintz-covered chairs placed in one corner of the room. Newly purchased, they were done in shades of green, as was the quilt stretched over an antique brass bed she'd unearthed from a jumble of old furniture and polished to a high sheen. The modern furnishings so in tune with her Dallas high-rise apartment would have struck a woefully wrong note here, and knowing that, she'd given them up with no real regrets, along with the cell phone and pager that had once tied her to the business she'd sold.

Cloris sank into a seat, looked toward the curtained window that provided a backdrop for a plain chrome drafting table and matching tall stool. "Is that where Sassy Lady clothes are created these days?"

"Mmm-hmm." Eve settled gingerly on her chair. "Not that I've spent much time there lately, with everything else going on. Then again, it seems to come in spurts, no matter where I am or what else is happening. Back in Dallas, some days I'd work for a few hours, others until I couldn't see straight.'' She took a sip of the white wine. ''Those can be the best days, when it grabs you by the throat and won't let you go.'' Turning ideas into genuine designs would always be important, she knew. It was something she would never willingly surrender. Even if no one wanted what she created, she would continue to do it. For her.

Eve leaned back and enjoyed the smooth taste of the wine on her tongue. ''How did your afternoon go?''

''I didn't have nearly as much fun as you obviously did—'' Cloris cocked a wry eyebrow ''—but it was productive.'' She twirled the stem of her glass between her fingers. ''After talking with my friend Barbara Ridgeway, I've learned of a few prospects who may be interested in bringing their babies here. One, in particular, stands out. Her name is Theresa Conroy.'' Cloris paused. ''Or at least that's who she says she is.''

It was Eve's turn to lift a brow. ''There's some doubt?''

''Only in Barbara's mind, I have to admit, since Theresa has identification with that name. She's eighteen, a single mother, who recently showed up in Tucson with her infant son. Since coming here, she's gone to and received help from several independent organizations, which certainly isn't unusual. What's strange in this case is that she hasn't applied for public assistance, as well. In fact, it appears she's avoided contacting any government agency.''

Eve frowned thoughtfully. ''Why, I wonder?''

''Barbara has a theory, and it's strictly that—a theory.''

''Which is?''

"Theresa Conroy's running from something."

Running from something. Eve's frown deepened as those words repeated in her mind. "The police?"

Cloris shrugged. "Maybe. But Barbara doesn't think so, and I value her judgment. If she's right, something else is going on. What's clear, though, is that Theresa wants to keep her child. With Barbara's help, she's been offered a job at a thrift store operated by a local charity, and at a salary good enough to rent one of the small furnished apartments in the area."

"And she needs someone to take care of her baby during the day," Eve summed up.

"There's no question that she can't afford to pay for child care at the moment." Cloris sighed. "While I'd like to say I don't have reservations about this, I do. There are some unknowns involved here. But, of course, it's your decision."

Eve's first thought was, How could she refuse? Her second thought was that she couldn't. "If Theresa Conroy wants to bring her baby here, she's more than welcome."

Cloris's lips curved in a faint smile. "I had a hunch you'd say that." She raised her glass. "A horse may've gotten the better of you today, Eve, but you have gumption. Here's to the start of something great."

"We're the only ones around here who feel that way, you know," Eve said, lifting a hand.

"Those cowboys will come around," Cloris replied as they clinked their glasses in a toast. "Wait and see."

Well, whether they did or not, Eve reflected, she was the boss, the big boss, and she'd do what she felt she had to do—make her own way, as she always had.

But that path can be lonely, an inner voice whispered. And she couldn't deny it. Deep down she wanted what most women wanted: a family of her own; a man to share her life. A special man. Maybe even a big, strong, rugged—

Eve hauled in that thought. It wouldn't do, she told herself. No, it wouldn't do at all to even so much as fantasize about the head honcho being that man. As things stood, he was the last man she should be looking to share anything with, beyond a business relationship. The very last one.

Why the heck did he have to be so damned attractive?

Chapter Four

Theresa Conroy was a lovely young woman. And a nervous one, Eve couldn't help noting as they faced each other over a crib in the newly decorated nursery. One of Eve's fondest childhood memories involved her first visit to the circus: the sounds, the smells, the sheer, colorful magic of it. Now those images, brought to life with bright cartoon characters, adorned the walls here in tribute to that memory. No one could honestly say the room wasn't cheerful.

The person Eve viewed, however, seemed anything but. What had put those dark circles under honey-brown eyes? she wondered, studying a narrow face flatteringly framed by long, fawn-colored hair. Unless she was mistaken, it was more than lack of sleep, though not physical illness. According to Cloris's friend Barbara, Theresa had passed a routine preemployment doctor's examination without a problem.

"So, when do you start your job?" Eve asked, deliberately keeping her voice light, echoing the same tone maintained since welcoming Theresa, who had pulled up in a rattling tan pickup probably older than she was. The fact that the truck's battered surface shined despite its shortcomings said a lot about Theresa.

"They told me I could start tomorrow," the reed-slim young woman replied. "That is, if you can take Max that soon."

At the sound of his name, Theresa's three-month-old son gurgled a response from the depths of the crib he'd been testing. Eve dropped her gaze and met eyes the same shade as Theresa's. But where everything about the mother was slim, everything about the baby was round—saucer-shaped eyes, chubby-cheeked face, sturdy body. And when it came to hair, the baby had almost none. Somehow that fuzzy head made him all the more adorable.

"I fell in love with this guy on sight," Eve confessed, reaching a hand down and finding one of her fingers quickly grabbed by a remarkably strong little fist.

"He's a sweetheart," Anna Montez, a petite, dark-haired, dark-eyed woman, tossed in with a soft chuckle as she walked by, her steps light on the newly scrubbed and polished tile floor.

"And we'd be happy to take him starting tomorrow," Eve added as the retired nurse and now part-time helper moved away.

"It's going to be hard leaving him." Theresa hesitated. "I won't be able to do it unless I'm sure he'll be safe."

Safe. The word didn't surprise Eve. Not in itself. She'd already reassured a few other new mothers who had agreed to take advantage of the day care center. All were being separated from their babies for the first time. So, worrying about their welfare was natural, Eve felt.

But something in Theresa's tone, something more than understandable concern, caused Eve to frown as she lifted her gaze. "Is there a particular reason why you're anxious about your son's safety, Theresa?"

Again her companion hesitated, shoving slender hands into front pockets of the well-washed chinos she wore with a pink cotton T-shirt. "No," she replied at last. "Not anything in particular."

Yes, something in particular, Eve thought. And kept that thought to herself. The last thing she wanted was to scare Theresa off. *If you don't push,* she told herself, *you might be able to eventually win this woman's confidence.* "I promise you we'll take excellent care of Max," she said.

As before, the baby reacted to the sound of his name, tightening his fist and regaining Eve's attention. "You sure know who you are, don't you?" she murmured. "And I bet you like being talked about."

Gurgling his agreement, Max kicked legs covered by a stretchy blue playsuit, avidly watching Eve's every move, as if he had such a zest for life that he didn't want to miss a second of anything that happened. He was far from the most beautiful baby she'd ever seen, yet that didn't seem to matter a speck. This tiny person, she decided, had character. She'd take it over beauty anyday.

She smiled widely. "We have some very special babies who'll be staying with us here, Max, but you just might turn out to be the most special of all."

Max wiggled his button nose and blew a frothy bubble in response to that statement, then joined in when his mother laughed out loud.

Good, Eve thought. Theresa Conroy needed some laughter in her life. Every new mother she'd met over the past few days faced hurdles. But this one could well be facing some challenges above and beyond the usual.

Whatever the truth of the matter was, Eve reflected, all she could do at the moment was fulfill her promise and keep a darling baby boy safe. *But safe from what?*

HE COULDN'T PUT IT OFF any longer, Ryder knew. Doing business meant dealing with paperwork, and this afternoon was a perfect time. One of the spring storms surging in off the Pacific had turned out to be big enough and strong enough to push its way into Arizona. Judging by the solid cloud cover rolling in from the west, it would hit before much longer. Maybe they'd get rain, maybe not. But they could count on getting wind, and plenty of it. Anyone who'd never seen a Southwest duststorm in action was bound to have a hard time fully appreciating what wind could do with desert sand, how it could whip up a grainy blanket as thick and dense as heavy fog.

A smart animal found shelter and stayed there until the whole thing was over. So did a smart man.

Ryder stepped into the ranch office. A quick glance around told him he was in luck. His boss was nowhere in sight. The babies must be keeping her busy. They had quickly grown to a bunch, he'd heard, once the nursery located on the other side of the house had opened for business.

For the first time, he was grateful for Eve's off-the-wall idea. He still didn't think much of it, but at least it was working in his favor. Combined with the designing activities he'd also heard about, it had postponed any more riding lessons. And since they hadn't seen much of each other during the past several days, there'd been little to remind him of what had happened during the first lesson.

Out of sight, out of mind. That old saying was holding true. *Except in the middle of the night.*

In the middle of the night, he remembered all too well what had happened. He'd already sworn never to ride double with a woman again. But it wasn't any woman wreaking havoc with his sleep. It wasn't any woman making him toss and turn and wonder if two people could actually make love while sharing a saddle. It was Eve Terry.

Ryder walked over to a table, set against one wall. The long slab of pine held a computer, laser printer and fax machine, all of which he'd talked Amos Cutter into buying. It had been a hard sell to a man whose distrust of modern technology had equaled his distaste for the female half of the population. But technology could be used to good advantage, Ryder had learned on the way to earning a college diploma. When it came to keeping track of ranch business, it had proved to be a godsend.

He tossed down a pile of handwritten notes, pulled out a hardwood chair and sank into it. Then he booted up the computer and quickly became absorbed in updating a variety of records, from livestock births to the latest round of expenses involved in maintaining a working ranch. Finally satisfied that his entries were complete, he logged on to the Internet to check on his personal investments. Most of the stocks he'd recently chosen were doing well, he found, pleased but hardly amazed by that fact. Many years earlier he'd discovered a knack for dipping into the stock market and pulling out at the right time. Slowly and surely he had turned his monthly salary into a fairly large sum of money—almost large enough to win him the Creedence Creek. Almost...

Ryder shut down the computer, shrugging off the familiar frustration of coming so close only to lose out. Instead of rehashing the past, what he needed to do was to make a fast exit. Before his boss showed up.

"Your luck's holding, Quinn," he muttered to himself as he quietly stepped into an empty hallway.

That was when his luck ran out.

A far door opened to let out a chorus of high wails. Warm wind rushed down the hall as Eve and Cloris appeared. Both were dressed in casual slacks and shirts, Eve's displaying a Western flair. One of her hands gripped the older woman's arm as if to support her. Cloris herself had a hand pressed to her shoulder. Dead certain something was wrong, Ryder instantly responded.

"It's just bruised, I'm sure," Cloris said above the din as he made his way toward them.

Eve caught sight of him and wasted no time in explaining. "The wind blew up out of nowhere and knocked over a lamp. Cloris tried to catch it before it hit the floor—"

"And only managed to ram my shoulder into a table edge," Cloris finished. "I'll be right as rain, though. Just need to put some ice on it to keep the swelling down."

"The window's stuck open," Eve continued. "The lamp broke and scared the babies, but they're fine. Our part-time worker is gone for the day, and I have to help Cloris. If you can get the window closed and keep an eye on things, I'll be back as soon as I can." The women quickly disappeared through another doorway leading to one of two bedrooms on the other side of the hall.

Even if he'd been given time to protest being left to his own devices, Ryder wasn't sure what he would have said. "Just get on with it," he told himself under his breath as he hurried into the nursery. Long strides took him to a window across the large room, where the wind still gusted in, flapping the curtains. Passing pieces of broken lamp, he reached over a small square table and gave the lower sash a hard tug. The window crashed closed. The wails around him rose to new heights.

And what the hell was he supposed to do next? he wondered, raking a hand through his hair. Whatever it was, he decided he was damned if he'd do it alone. He retraced his steps and poked his head out the door. "Pete!" he all but roared in the direction of the kitchen. "I need some help. Quick."

Then he turned back and took in details he'd so far ignored. The white cribs were no surprise. Likewise, the clown-strewn wallpaper Pete had agonized over. The babies themselves were certainly expected, although a half dozen yelling at the top of their tiny lungs was a daunting sight, Ryder had to admit.

The strongest of the cries drew his notice to a crib near the center of the room. He took a few cautious steps forward and viewed its occupant. A boy, he thought. Probably. It was hard to tell.

Then, walking closer, he noted the small, hand-painted sign that hung over the head of the crib, dangling from a shiny ribbon. Max, it said in bright, bold letters. A quick glance at other cribs found more signs, each displaying a different name. Eve's work, he decided. "And," he said, once again dropping his gaze, "I suppose that makes you Max."

It caught the child's attention. Tears still trickled down chubby cheeks, but he stopped crying and studied Ryder. They took each other's measure as Pete stomped in.

"What in blazes is going on?" he bellowed over the nonstop cries of the other babies.

Ryder shot him a look. "You and I are baby-sitting."

Pete's dark eyes went wide. "Jeez, Ry, I'd rather face down an ornery, two-headed bull than this setup."

In no mood to extend any sympathy, Ryder said flatly, "Well, we don't have much choice at the moment. So stop griping and do something."

"What?"

"How should I know? Sing to them, maybe."

"Sing…" Pete threw up his hands. "All right, if you say so. My singing can't be any worse than this caterwauling." He cleared his throat a few times and began a halting rendition of "Oh, Bury Me on the Lone Prairie." It was off-key enough to make music lovers weep.

Ryder winced as he looked down at Max. "I guess I can take it if you can, little guy. Are you okay, now?"

As though responding to that question, the baby frowned and pushed out his lower lip.

"Not quite okay, huh?" Ryder rested a hand on the railing. "I hate to tell you this, but if it's chow time, you'll have to wait. There's a bottle around here for you somewhere, I'm sure, but you'll be a lot better off being fed by someone who knows what they're doing."

Now that tiny lip began to tremble.

"No, don't start up again," Ryder said hastily. At a

loss as to what to do to ward off further tears, he reached down and gently patted a well-rounded tummy, felt the bulky padding under thin blue terry cloth dotted with dancing teddy bears. And it suddenly occurred to him that something other than food might be the problem.

"Oh, no," he muttered, looking into the baby's brown eyes, "don't tell me you need a diaper changed. *Please* don't tell me that."

But that's exactly what the baby seemed to imply as he squirmed and started to whimper.

"Sh— Shucks." Ryder stopped in the nick of time before issuing a word better left unspoken. It might have been his imagination, but those mournful eyes actually seemed to plead with him. "You're gonna make me do this, aren't you?" He sighed, long and hard, as he gave in to his fate. A smart man knew when he was licked. "Okay, I suppose I'll get the job done somehow. Just hang on for a minute."

He picked up the baby, discovered that compact body was heavier and more solid than he would have suspected. "You're not as fragile as I figured," he said, settling the boy into the crook of his arm. His seeking glance soon landed on a fluffy white pile stacked on a high, padded table just beyond a doorway leading to a smaller side room. Has to be the changing station, he told himself. And if anyone had predicted that morning that he'd be headed for it before the day was over, he would have called them flat-out crazy.

Pete broke off in midlyric. "Where're you going?" he asked into dead silence.

Only then was Ryder aware that the crying had stopped. "I have a date with a diaper change," he replied dryly.

Pete actually blanched. "I'd rather face a *three-*headed bull with murder on his mind."

Ryder made a quick sweep of the room and found several tiny eyes glued to Pete. "Just keep on singing," he advised. "This bunch probably got tired of trying to compete with you in the caterwauling department. I'd make sure it stays that way."

As he walked into the other room, the beginning strains of "Home on the Range" attacked his eardrums. He carefully laid his bundle down and considered his next move, grateful to see a row of metal snaps crossing a strategic area. At least he wouldn't have to get the kid out of that teddy-bear outfit.

"All right," he said. "Let's go for it." He popped the snaps open and soon viewed what he had to concede was a damn practical invention. He peeled back the twin tapes holding it in place, braced himself for the worst, was undeniably relieved to find the disposable diaper only wet as he pulled it away. "Thanks for that much, guy," he murmured as he bent over the child and reached toward the stack of clean diapers.

It was then he learned the hazards of changing a baby boy. In a heartbeat, the diaper he'd removed wasn't the only thing wet. The front of his denim shirt was soaked, as well. It took him a moment to realize what had happened. He looked down at his companion.

"Max, you little devil, you just peed on me."

For the first time, the baby smiled widely, then made a sound that could only be described as a chuckle.

EVE LEFT THE BEDROOM next to her own and pulled the door shut. She had helped Cloris undress, then filled an ice bag to soothe the injured shoulder. A minor injury, she was finally letting herself believe. She released a thankful breath, and as her worry eased, the sound of someone singing nearby won her full attention. At least, she supposed it could be called singing.

It wasn't Ryder Quinn, she decided without hesitation, although the voice was definitely male. No man who looked so good could sound so bad. Still, even with that assumption firmly in mind, she was far from prepared for what she found after a few steps took her to the nursery door.

Good grief.

She halted in the doorway, unable to believe her eyes, and frankly gawked. Pete Rawlins, his silver-haired head thrown back, kept right on belting out a Western ballad about tumbling tumbleweeds while surrounded by a silent audience. And that audience, each and every tiny member of it, was fast asleep.

Shaking her head in wonder, she walked forward and stood next to Pete. "I think it's safe to quit now," she said softly when he stopped long enough to take a breath. "They're in dreamland."

He jerked around toward her, clearly unaware of her presence until that moment. His sudden scowl came as no surprise. "I'm sure as shootin' ready to quit. I'm a cook, not a nursemaid."

She smiled despite that dubious welcome. "What you are is an amazing man." Which was no lie, she mused. Anyone who could bring peace out of chaos with nothing more than rusty vocal chords had to be amazing.

The compliment had him blinking before he narrowed his eyes. "Is this some kind of female trick?" he asked, suspicion underlining each word.

"No, it's some kind of female thanks...for your help." Before she even thought about it, she leaned forward and planted a brief kiss, no more than a peck, on a weathered cheek. "That's for coming to my rescue. I really do appreciate it."

"Um...ah..." The man who'd bristled with hostility seconds earlier now seemed at a total loss for words. Ducking his head, he turned and swiftly made for the door to the hall. "I guess it could've been worse," he grumbled without real heat, tossing the comment over his shoulder as he stomped out.

"You're the amazing one, getting Pete to admit that," a low voice said.

Eve whirled in the direction it had come from. Instantly she was the one rendered speechless.

She didn't know what startled her more, the sight of her business manager holding a smiling baby in his arms, or the fact that those muscled arms were bare—as bare as his hair-darkened chest. Fully covered, that chest was impressive; uncovered, it was dynamite.

"Um...ah... I see you've met Max," she got out at last, raising her gaze to meet Ryder's.

He walked forward with slow steps, his booted feet scraping softly on the floor. "We introduced ourselves. Then he conned me into taking off his dirty diaper. And then, before I could replace it, he pulled a fast one and did his duty on the front of my shirt."

She had to bite back a grin, taking in his rueful expression and well aware of what had put it there. "I guess you haven't—" Suddenly she couldn't go on. If she so much as opened her mouth, a laugh was bound to spill out.

"Changed a diaper before?" he finished. "No, I haven't. I had no idea of the dangers involved, either."

Then he waited. For her to say something, she was sure. But she was still struggling to foil that laugh.

Finally he lifted an eyebrow. "Cat got your tongue, Miz Eve?"

She drew in a short breath, managed somehow to maintain a sober expression. "I'm sorry Max...did what he did."

Just then, the baby gurgled out a small, merry chuckle. Ryder dropped a glance down at his burden. "You, on the other hand, aren't a bit sorry—are you, little guy?"

Another gurgling laugh had Eve joining in, because now she absolutely had to. The baby was just too precious, the situation just too funny, the wryly resigned grimace crossing a rugged face just too priceless.

Ryder switched his gaze back to the woman who found his predicament so amusing. Almost against his will, he felt himself charmed. At that moment she looked so young and carefree, nearly too young to be the hardheaded businessperson he knew she was. He took another step forward, stopped when he was mere inches from her, when certain parts of him didn't want to stop at all, when one part wanted to find out how that softly curved mouth tasted, and another wanted to explore every inch of those generous curves below it.

"You didn't laugh at Pete," he groused, a joking statement that came out huskier than he'd intended. Which, he reflected without humor, was what happened to a man when certain parts took control.

Gray eyes sparkled up at him. "Pete didn't get the full treatment."

"No, but he did get a thank-you kiss." He hadn't meant to say it. At least his brain hadn't. Yet it was too late to take it back. Too late to stop something from flaring to sizzle between them, as it had for a memorable moment on the day they'd met.

Eve's eyes widened as every trace of amusement disappeared in a flash. "Are you, ah, asking for a kiss?"

He could have said no. Instead he said, "If you think I deserve one," figuring that left it up to her. *Hardly, Quinn. You're the one who started this ball rolling.* He ignored that inner reminder. His body was already at war with itself.

The baby he held made no sound, as if sensing the adult tension in the room. Both males, large and small, waited for the woman they faced to speak, the sheer silence broken only by raindrops beginning a random patter on the tile roof.

After seconds that seemed like minutes, she released a long breath. "I suppose you deserve something."

"A kiss?" *Sure, Quinn, push it and dig yourself in deeper.*

"A thank-you one," she clarified with a level look, making that clear before she closed the final gap between them.

"Okay." He dipped his head.

"Okay." She lifted her chin.

He offered no choice of cheek or mouth, aiming straight for full lips shaded a clear red. And knew it was a mistake the moment they met his own. He'd assumed those lips were smooth as satin, imagined they were made to welcome a man's firm mouth. And he'd been right on both counts.

But he'd never suspected scarcely sampling them could knock him for a loop. He should have known, he told himself. From the first minute he'd gotten a good, long look at this woman and felt the impact in his gut, he should have known that nothing between them would be simple.

She didn't even *kiss* simple.

With no more than a featherlight touch, she made him crave, made him hungrier than he'd ever been, and not for food. He should put an end to it while it could still be considered a casual gesture, the voice of reason said. He heard it, but his priorities had already shifted. A man who craved badly enough took everything he could willingly get and was damned grateful for it. So he took and forgot about what he should do.

Eve's breath caught in her throat as the kiss continued. Her eyes drifted closed. Because she suddenly had to hold on to something, she blindly reached up a hand, curved it over the top of a broad shoulder. And knew it was a mistake the instant her palm met warm, bare skin.

Somehow that touch seemed even more intimate than the melding of their lips, made her even more aware of the fact that he was half-naked. If she hadn't touched him, her heart might not be spinning behind her ribs. If she hadn't touched him, her insides might not be doing a slow melt. If she hadn't touched him, she might still have at least some of her wits about her.

But she had touched him. And she'd gone off the deep end.

Now it seemed like an excellent plan to expand that touch, so she drew her hand down to where his chest hair began, a vivid reminder of the differences between male and female. Then it seemed like a great idea to explore a bit lower, so she did, brushing her palm over crisp curls and the taut skin beneath them, feeling the leanness and the strength. Oh, yes. His chest was nothing like hers.

She enjoyed that lingering journey, couldn't deny that her hormones relished every inch of it. They were, in fact, urging her on toward new horizons, whispering

how good the next few inches might feel. Mumbling—
No, not mumbling. They were…babbling.

Eve's eyes popped open. No, the *baby* was babbling.

She pulled back, retreated a step just as Max
squealed out loud. A glance his way showed a wide,
toothless smile. He was obviously as happy as her hormones had been. They were, truth be told, still skipping
around inside her. Settle down, she ordered, taking a
deep breath to help the process along.

And what in the world did she say to the man she'd
been totally losing herself in? Thank *you?* Hardly.

As it turned out, she didn't have a chance to say
much. Before she knew it, Ryder was carefully handing
the baby over to her, then rapidly making for the door
to the hall. "Looks like you can do without me now."
With that statement, tossed over one shoulder, he
wasted no time in stalking out.

Eve watched his hasty departure, wondered if he
even realized he was minus his shirt and now wore the
red imprint of her mouth on his own. "That's the second time a certain cowboy's left me in the dust, Max,"
she told her small companion. "My ego might be
smarting if I didn't suspect the head honcho was as
caught up in that kiss as I was."

Forgetting that kiss wouldn't be easy, she knew. Neither would the sight of a mile-wide chest on full display.

But the image that could really turn her inside out,
if she'd let it, was the memory of a big man holding a
tiny baby, an adorable baby boy whose sunny smile
clearly proved he had no fear of the man who held him
with such gentle strength.

That strong yet surprisingly gentle man had the
power to do more than attract her. He was someone

she could care for far beyond physical attraction. He was, truth be told, someone she could love…if she'd let herself, if she wasn't well aware of how foolish it would be to fall in love with a man who was waiting for her to pack up and leave.

She'd never been a foolish woman—certainly not when it came to men. No man had ever truly broken her heart, not even the two men she'd come to care for most at very different points in her life. Both had become successful Dallas businessmen, yet in many respects they'd contrasted as keenly as night and day.

Jack and Trevor. She remembered them well.

Almost from the moment she'd met Jack Hardy in a college English class, they'd been able to laugh together. At first the blond man with the stocky build had seemed like the brother she'd never had. Even after their relationship deepened, they'd had little trouble appreciating a good joke, in bed as well as out.

But the man with the easy grin had never so much as cracked a smile whenever she'd mentioned her career plans. Eventually she'd accepted the fact that she wasn't the kind of woman he really wanted…not when it came to a wife.

Trevor Wright, it could be argued, was Jack's complete opposite. Tall, dark and as lean as a whip, with a sense of humor as dry as the Sahara, Trevor fully supported a woman's right to combine marriage with a satisfying career. By then hers was going great guns, and a shared future looked promising.

At least, that was the case until it had dawned on her, finally winning her notice in all the hubbub of their busy lives, that Trevor was on a subtle yet constant, almost relentless, quest to help her lose weight. Once aware of it, it hadn't taken her long to realize that what this particular man really sought was a slender woman to share his life. And she would never be slender, not even minus the extra pounds she could have done without—then and now. She'd never be anything approaching model slim, not without resorting to sheer starvation.

So, as it had turned out, she wasn't the type of woman Trevor truly wanted, either.

Still, when both those relationships ended, it had been with little hard feelings on either participant's part, and no lasting wounds on hers. Maybe, Eve reflected, because she hadn't cared enough, loved enough to be badly hurt.

Nevertheless, she knew deep down that she *could* love terribly, and perhaps be hurt terribly. And possibly be wildly happy. A cynic, she wasn't. She believed happily-ever-afters happened.

But she was no fool, either. And she had no doubt that she'd be doing herself a big favor if she remembered that, when it came to getting involved with Ryder Quinn.

A crash of thunder silenced Eve's thoughts at the same time it woke up the room's sleeping occupants. Wails started in the blink of several abruptly opened eyes, with no rusty-voiced crooner in sight to lull them closed again.

A singer was something else she wasn't. Still, Eve decided, she had nothing to lose by giving Pete's method a try. The baby she held, and the only one not crying, babbled along beside her as she launched into the first chorus of "Happy Trails to You."

By the third chorus, her unimpressed audience forced her to concede that she lacked the grouchy cook's gift. She halted in midnote and looked down at

Max. "Thanks for your help, but I guess I'm a flop. It's back to the basics for this gal. Good thing I took that child-care course. At least I have some talent when it comes to dealing with diapers and baby bottles."

Max stopped babbling and smacked tiny lips in what could only be described as eager anticipation of his next meal.

HE WAS OUT ON THE RANGE again, this time more from need than choice. Yesterday's storm—a "danged doozy," in Pete's words—had blustered its way through, and every available man was out checking for damage in its wake. So far, Ryder thought as he headed the stallion toward the last piece of land on his agenda, he hadn't found much to concern him—certainly nothing serious enough to keep his mind off that kiss.

A thank-you kiss. Sure.

He had a hunch he wasn't the only one thinking about it, either. Eve had patently avoided making real eye contact over the dinner table last night. Then again, he had to admit that he hadn't been all that eager to meet her gaze after the way he'd practically shot from the nursery and out the back door. Letting her even suspect she could rattle him that badly was hardly smart. Letting himself get churned up enough to leave his shirt behind and not even realize it until the first wave of light rain hit bare skin was downright dumb.

And then fate, or maybe the worst of luck, had picked that particular moment to send Zeb and a few of the other, older hands riding by. There he'd been, steps from the ranch house, shirtless, and not about to admit to changing a diaper and being bested by a baby, not to that seasoned crew, which left him trading stare for stare and deliberately ignoring their eagle-eyed curiosity—until Zeb just happened to mention, ever so casually, that a tough man could look good wearing lipstick, if he really put his mind to it.

"And what the hell was I supposed to say?" Ryder muttered darkly. "No, I wasn't kissing the woman everyone who can see past a hat brim knows is partial to that shade of red?" He grimaced. "I guess I have to be grateful for the clap of thunder and sudden downpour that had all of us scattering for cover."

Lucky blew out what his owner chose to take for a sympathetic breath as they started up a rise. The sun had broken through at noontime, and already mud had dried to dusty dirt.

"Not that I think any of that wily bunch, as tight-lipped as they were on the subject this morning, forgot about the whole thing, friend," Ryder added in a grumble. "Probably no more than I'll be able to do the same."

Yet he did forget, or at least shoved aside, thoughts of the prior day's events as they crested the hill and he caught sight of someone crossing the desert on foot several yards below him. Someone he didn't recognize.

"Seems as though we've got ourselves a visitor, Lucky. That could be good. Or bad. I suppose we'll just have to find out."

Even at a distance, the lanky male taking long strides looked scarcely past his teens. Still, Ryder approached with caution, reminding himself that this stretch of land bordered on the outskirts of the city and consequently was closer than the rest of the ranch to the more unsavory elements a city could harbor. Determined to remember it, he kept a sharp eye open as a dark, shaggy-haired head suddenly turned as the sound of horse's hooves made itself known.

Stopping dead in his tracks, the stranger assumed a wary stance and waited as the gap between them closed. At a guess, he was no more than twenty, and obviously no more at ease with their unexpected encounter than the man who rode to meet him. He could have used a haircut, and a shave, as well, though his faded jeans and frayed gray sweatshirt were clean. Rather than the leather boots so common to the area, he wore canvas running shoes that had clearly traveled many miles.

"Hello, there," Ryder said mildly as he brought the stallion to a halt.

Deep brown eyes, gleaming with what could have been intelligence—or possibly sheer cunning—met his. "Hi."

No sense beating around the bush, Ryder decided. "Do you know you're on private land?" *And trespassing,* his tone implied, although he didn't say so.

A hesitation, short as it was, put the truth of the not-quite-quick-enough reply in doubt. "Yeah, I know. I'm looking for a job."

Without that hesitation, Ryder might have accepted it as fact. The person he viewed had been headed in the general direction of the ranch house, even if the gravel road leading to it was the more conventional route. "I'm Ryder Quinn, manager of the Creedence Creek Ranch. And you're…?"

"Kenny."

Which could actually be true, Ryder figured, considering the way it had just popped out. But he didn't miss the fact that no last name followed, even though he took the time to raise a hand and tip back his hat before he spoke. "Well, Kenny, I have to admit you don't look much like a cowpuncher. Do you have any experience?''

Again that hesitation, then, ''No, but maybe I could do something else.''

''Not much else to be done at the moment, I'm afraid.'' Despite his doubts, real regret tinged Ryder's low voice. Once he had crossed this same stretch of land seeking a job, eighteen years old and hoping against hope, for reasons a long way past the need to make a living, that he'd be allowed to stay.

And Amos Cutter had let him stay. It had been one of the happiest days of his young life.

Which was why he hated to turn anyone away. A month earlier he'd have probably given the kid a chance, let him earn at least a paycheck or two doing honest work for an honest wage, no matter how inexperienced he turned out to be.

But that was before a flock of babies had arrived on the ranch's doorstep. Ryder knew he could no longer just take a chance on anyone. Too much was at risk. Like it or not, there were some weird people in the world, and children had to be protected. References would have to be checked and double-checked before any new employee was hired on. Still, that didn't rule out offering help in another form.

''Could you use a stake to get you by for a few days?'' He didn't have much cash on him at the moment, but he'd readily give what he had.

''No, thanks, anyway,'' the person who called himself Kenny replied, shoving his hands in his jeans pockets. ''I've got enough to keep me going.''

Probably not for too long, Ryder thought even as he decided to let it drop. He wouldn't push anyone into accepting a handout. He knew the value of pride.

"Well then, no sense in going any farther. You'd better head back the way you came."

"Yeah, I will."

Ryder watched as the stranger turned around and started taking brisk strides, his long legs putting distance between them at a fast clip. Ten feet quickly became a hundred, then much more. And still Ryder watched. Only when the other man was totally lost to view did he drop his gaze and signal his readiness to move on with a light flick of the reins.

"I wonder what our visitor was really after." Ryder heaved a sigh as the horse started forward. "Or maybe my imagination's working overtime. Maybe he was just a kid looking for a job."

Lucky snorted, shaking his head and sending a caramel-colored mane dancing in the breeze.

"Okay, friend, I won't disagree with you. As far as both of us are concerned, the matter's still in doubt."

Chapter Five

Eve gave the Jeep's steering wheel a sharp twist to the left and began a climb up a dirt road steep enough to have her thinking that at the height of last night's storm the four-wheel-drive capabilities at her command might well have been necessary to achieve her objective. There was no question in her mind, though, that she would have achieved it. After weeks in a new environment, confidence in her ability to drive on more than smooth asphalt had grown by leaps and bounds. In contrast, six-lane freeways were fast becoming a distant memory. So were the endless sounds of a big city in constant motion.

Other memories had taken their place. One memory in particular stubbornly remained in the forefront. But then, she hadn't for a minute thought she could easily forget that kiss.

A thank-you kiss. Right.

Certain parts of her had no wish to forget it. They would have enthusiastically welcomed a repeat performance, she couldn't deny. Not that they were likely to get one. The chances were slim to none now, with the two parties in question scarcely looking at each other, much less engaging in any meaningful conversation.

Then again, what could she have said over the dinner table last evening? *Please pass the potatoes, and oh, by the way, do you want your shirt back?*

"That would have raised a few eyebrows," she told herself, "and accomplished nothing. Keeping your mouth closed was the wiser choice, no doubt about it. Now you can just leave the thing on the man's doorstep while he's out on the range, and you won't even have to feel guilty about the indignity it suffered, since you washed and ironed it yourself."

Hardly something she was in the habit of doing for a man, she reflected, and an event she'd made sure neither Pete nor Cloris witnessed. Once the shirt was returned, the whole episode would be over. Certainly its owner hardly seemed inclined to dwell on the subject. He'd been equally closemouthed, about the shirt and everything else.

Yes, all in all, this was the best way to handle it.

That conclusion reached, Eve allowed herself to relax and enjoy the short drive. Her spirits lifted right along with her steady progress upward. Cloris's shoulder was well on the mend, things in the nursery were back to normal, the gray morning had gradually given way to a perfect spring afternoon, dazzling with sunshine, and the only thing remaining to be done was to drop off her bundle and get out of Dodge before a roving cowboy returned.

After a few jogs and a final turn, the narrow road Eve climbed ended near the base of a one-story, wood-frame structure standing at the very top of the hill. Minus the high electrical wires strung on tall posts in the background, it probably would have looked much the same countless years earlier. A covered porch ran along the entire front of the building, beyond which openings for a door and two square windows had been cut. The window glass sparkled, only one of several telling signs she noted that pointed to regular efforts to maintain the place.

Nevertheless, despite those efforts, nothing she viewed could be described as anywhere near imposing. Solid, yes. Grand, never. Yet something about the house drew her. Perhaps its sheer age and the fact that it still stood firm, refusing to bow to anything the elements sent its way.

Eve picked up the tissue-wrapped shirt, slid out of the Jeep and started for the porch. She gazed ahead as she walked forward, then stopped in midstride as a thought struck her hard enough to still her completely.

This house was hers now. But it didn't feel like hers, not at all. And that surprised her. The sense of ownership, so proud and strong when it came to every other aspect of the ranch—land, buildings, animals—was absent here. For the first time since arriving with high hopes and a carload of luggage, she felt like an intruder.

Because Ryder Quinn lived here? she wondered. Impossible to say. This place was different, though. She knew it...she just didn't know why.

Then her thoughts scattered at the rumbling sound of an engine. Eve switched around to face the road, not even bothering to consider that it might be a visitor. He was back earlier than she'd expected, yet she had little doubt about who rapidly approached. The roving cowboy was headed home—not in the saddle, but behind a steering wheel.

Moments later the sight of a familiar blue pickup proved her right. Its driver negotiated the last curve with practiced ease and pulled up next to the Jeep, then got out and shut the door with a quiet thud. He looked very much as he had the first time they'd met, wearing a battered tan hat and a light coating of desert dust. Only now she knew who he was, knew keen intelligence went with the muscled body, knew that knowledge made him even more attractive…to her. Most of all, she knew she should do what she'd come here to do and leave as quickly as common courtesy would allow.

"Anything wrong?" he asked after several long strides took him to her.

Only then did she realize she was frowning. "Everything's fine," she replied, striving for a casual tone and achieving it. "I just stopped by to drop off your shirt. It's been washed and ironed." Conveniently omitting who had done the job, she held out her bundle.

He dropped his gaze, made no move to accept what she offered. "Thanks for getting it back to me, but it'll probably wind up dirty all over again if I put my grubby hands on it, even wrapped in that fancy tissue." He hesitated, so briefly that she wasn't entirely positive he had. "Why don't you come in? It won't take me long to clean up."

"No, that's okay," she said hastily.

Green eyes locked with gray. "It's your property, Eve," he reminded her softly.

So why does it seem to belong to you more than me? Even as the silent question formed, the truth of it hit her. For some reason she couldn't fathom, in some way she couldn't understand yet felt compelled to acknowledge, this house on the hilltop belonged to this man. Legally, she owned it. But *she* was the visitor.

Still, she could hardly tell him that; she was having

a hard time making sense of it herself. So she said, "I can come back some other day. There's no hurry."

His gaze didn't falter. "Might as well take a look at the place now, as long as you're here."

She could have come up with a reasonable excuse, would have in a heartbeat if she'd detected any real sign of reluctance on his part. And his logic was sound, she had to admit. Why not do it now? "Okay, I guess this is as good a time as any."

Together they climbed two steps up to the porch and walked past a long, high-backed wooden bench standing near the front door. Ryder ushered Eve in, then took off his hat and tossed it toward a row of metal hooks jutting from a roughly plastered wall. The hat spun in midair and landed so neatly that she gathered it was a daily routine.

"The layout's pretty plain," he said. "Living room in front, kitchen on one side of the hallway leading to the back, bathroom on the other, and two bedrooms at the rear. There's plenty to drink in the refrigerator. Why don't you help yourself to something and take a look around? I'll duck in the shower and be right back."

"All right," she agreed. "Can I get you something to drink while I'm at it?"

"A can of cola's fine. Glasses are in the cabinet over the sink. Don't bother with one for me." With that he strode toward the rear of the house and left her to her own devices, which suited Eve to a T: an inspection could be more comfortably conducted on her own.

As a start, she aimed an appraising gaze around her. Other than a portable air conditioner, set in a side window, the front of the house seemed as tied to the past indoors as out. A tall stone fireplace, the room's most striking feature, had to date back to when the place was built. Grouped near the hearth were a tweed sofa, an overstuffed chair, two end tables holding small lamps, and a faded rug with a Southwestern theme covering a portion of the bare wood floor. Nothing matched anything, everything was probably older than she was, yet the combined effect was surprisingly cozy. She had no trouble imagining logs crackling in the fireplace, casting a flickering red glow.

Eve walked around the room, laid her bundle on an end table and waited for the muffled sound of rushing water before starting down the hall. Two doors stood open at the end. On her left, a peek through the doorway revealed nothing much beyond a double bed and dresser, both made of aged knotty pine. As clean as the room was, it had a sterile, unused look about it. Not Ryder Quinn's bedroom, she decided. Intending another brief survey, she crossed the hall, glanced into the opposite room.

And then she could only stare as her gaze landed on a massive bed with a headboard reaching halfway to the ceiling. Made of gleaming mahogany, with a plain bedspread covering its wide mattress in a sea of blue, it looked much newer than anything she'd seen so far. The big man who slept there must have bought it, she mused. And even with him in it, there'd be plenty of space for another person. But then, beds built as huge as Montana were meant to be shared.

Eve turned away as that reflection proved too pointed. Thinking about beds was the last thing she needed, she told herself as she started back down the hall. The very last thing.

A few steps took her to a square entrance that opened into the kitchen. An electric stove, enameled sink, tall refrigerator and small Formica table with four chairs took up most of the room. The white appliances appeared fairly modern. In contrast, the aqua-colored table and chairs were definite relics of the past. To the continued rush of water coming from behind a closed door directly opposite, Eve crossed a checkered linoleum floor and opened the refrigerator, discovered breakfast fare and sandwich makings, as well as milk, juice, soda and beer. She pulled out two cans of cola, and decided she didn't need a glass, either.

Seconds after the sound of water ceased, she was back in the living room and headed for the front-porch bench. She had no intention of being close by when the bathroom door opened. Or of even being in the house. Every woman alive knew that a freshly showered male could be an all-too-appealing sight—with or without clothes. Maybe by the time this particular male made his way outside, he'd look a little less desirable.

You're the one who's all wet, Eve, if you really believe that, her common sense promptly informed her.

She didn't believe it. Not really. But she kept on going.

RYDER BUTTONED a clean denim shirt and raked a hand through his damp hair. He glanced into a mirror fogged with steam, thought about shaving and decided against it. It would mean keeping his guest waiting even longer.

"The thing is," he told his reflection with a frown, "Eve Terry seems about as much of a guest as I am, and it's more than the fact that she owns the place."

It would be nice to be able to explain that statement, he thought. Too bad he couldn't, not even to himself.

All he knew was that the moment he'd come around

the final curve and caught sight of her waiting at the top of the hill, something had slammed into him out of nowhere, something that said she fitted exactly where she was, standing tall, with the house at her back. For all he didn't understand it, he had felt it as clear as day.

He'd never been given to fanciful notions. And that's what bothered him. He couldn't chalk up what he'd felt to sheer imagination and forget it…any more than he could forget that sight. Everything about it had seemed so *right*—which had to be totally *wrong*.

Ryder blew out a breath and opened the bathroom door. After a quick search of the house, he made for the porch and found Eve seated on the bench. Again, despite the urban cowgirl outfit, she looked so natural in that spot. *You're losing it, Quinn.*

Determined not to broadcast that fact, he sat beside her in one easy motion and accepted the cola can she offered. He popped the top, took several large swallows. "Nothing like anything cold after a day on the desert," he said when his thirst had been satisfied.

"How did it go?" Eve crossed one booted foot over the other. "Did you find much damage?"

He leaned back and stretched out long, jeans-clad legs. A gentle breeze drifted over his bare feet. "Nothing major in the area I covered. By tomorrow, after everyone's checked in, I'll have a better idea, but I wouldn't worry too much about it."

She sipped her drink. "I wasn't worried, at least not about the land. It's the animals, what can happen to them outside in a serious storm, that bothered me."

"They're tough, and smarter than you might think. Even the littlest calf seems to come through fine when mama's around to watch out for it."

Eve nodded. "I guess most mothers have a way of doing that. Mine only gave me up because she felt she had to. I understand that even better after seeing how anxious the new moms I've met are about their babies' welfare and safety, even when there's no real reason to be concerned." She paused, staring straight ahead. "Then again, there's always the possibility."

Ryder picked up on that last remark. "Are you saying there might be a good reason in a particular case?"

Eve let out a soft sigh. "I can't be positive, but I do know that Theresa Conroy, Max's mother, is more concerned than usual. I tried asking her about it, and got nowhere."

His brows drew together. "Can't say that thrills me."

"It's not pleasant to think of any child's safety being in question," she said, "even though I've told myself that Max is getting the best care possible while he's here. Certainly no one on the ranch would harm him."

"You're right," he agreed. "I'd personally vouch for every man on the place." Then it occurred to him that someone had been on the ranch that very day who couldn't be vouched for. He straightened in his seat, then reached behind him toward a narrow windowsill and set the cola can down with an audible clink. "Damn and blast."

Eve shifted, turning until she faced him. "What's wrong?"

"I ran into someone on the range today." He went on to describe that meeting. "It could be he was just a drifter looking for a job," Ryder summed up, "but I've got my doubts."

She set her drink next to his. "And the man said his name was Kenny?"

"Uh-huh, which I halfway believe is true. I might not have let him get away so easily if I'd known what you just told me about Max's mother." He brushed a stray lock of dark hair off his forehead. "Nothing's going to happen to that little guy if I can help it."

"If *we* can help it," Eve tacked on resolutely. Then her sober expression lightened as a small smile formed. "He wrapped you right around one of his tiny fingers, didn't he?"

Ryder slanted her a look. "What makes you say that?"

"Because he did the same to me. I never had a chance." Her smile grew. "Max is special."

He discovered he couldn't deny it. "He may well be, but that doesn't mean I'm changing any more diapers."

"I'd have given a lot to see you change that one," she admitted wryly.

A rueful grin formed at the memory. At least he'd got the job done. "All in a day's work," he said with a shrug.

She shook her head. "It was above and beyond the call of duty."

"Well, you thanked me for it."

The words were out before he could haul them back. He would have swallowed them whole if he could have, but it was too late. All he could do was watch as gray eyes went wide, wait as the kiss they'd shared took on a life of its own and filled the scant space separating them. No baby was between them this time. Only that kiss, drawing them together.

Although neither moved a muscle, Ryder felt the pull. And the kiss hadn't even been a real one, he reflected. Not mouth-to-mouth, tongue-to-tongue real.

But maybe that was the problem. Maybe taking that kiss to its natural conclusion with a genuine, bona fide version would put an end to the whole matter. It might be worth testing that theory, he had to concede.

"Perhaps we should try that kiss again," Eve said gravely, stunning him by repeating his thoughts. Looking a lot more resigned than happy, she added, "I suspect it's going to be there until we finish it."

It took him a moment to find his voice. "If you think so," he said at last, not about to admit he'd come to the same conclusion. "I suppose we should just, ah, get on with it."

"Right." She tilted her chin. "Then it'll be behind us."

"Right." He bent his head. "Then we can forget it."

This time when his lips met hers, he was prepared for the welcoming softness, braced for his body's reaction. Now that he knew, he could handle it, he told himself as he slanted his mouth to take the kiss deeper, delved in as those soft lips parted for him. One lightly probing taste was all it took to tell him he knew nothing.

Then his body took over.

His arms reached out to draw her closer. His hands met behind her back. His palms slid over the smooth yellow cotton of her shirt. His fingers grazed the narrow ridge and back clasp of her bra. Instantly his mind envisioned her front, minus her clothes and fully open to his gaze. As the kiss continued, he couldn't keep one hand from slipping forward. He had to feel her, just feel her there, in the place his wayward eyes had wandered to on far more than one occasion since they'd met. She would be softest there, he had no doubt, found it to be true when, barely making contact, his fingers brushed across a full breast. That touch, as fleeting as it was, proved to be his undoing. Restraint toppled as he tasted more and wanted more.

In a matter of seconds he wanted it all.

EVE SHIVERED in Ryder's embrace. She had fought, and conquered, the urge to moan in pleasure at the touch of a strong hand stroking her breast so gently. It hadn't been easy. How could she have thought, even for the blink of an eye, that kissing this man again would solve anything? she wondered. Granted, it had seemed worth trying at the time, but now she knew differently. At least one part of her did.

You should put a stop to this, that part firmly contended. Another, more quietly persuasive part said, *Don't stop, not yet. It feels too good, he feels too good.* And even the smallest portion of her couldn't deny it. No man had ever felt this good to her. Never.

Then any thought of bringing things to a halt was wiped out as powerful arms flattened her against a hard chest and robbed her of the will to stop. Reaching up, she slid her hands over broad shoulders, tangled her tongue with the clever one roaming her mouth, and gave herself totally to the kiss.

Just one kiss.

One kiss that went on and on while the tension she'd sought to ease built and built. One kiss she couldn't begin to imagine breaking, even when breathing became as urgent as the overwhelming desire to feel those strong hands not only on her breasts but everywhere.

By the time the kiss ended endless moments later, she wanted everything.

"Oh, boy," she murmured, thinking out loud as she

buried her face in the crook of Ryder's neck and took in a lungful of air along with a knockout mixture of pine soap and pure male. "Boy, this is going to complicate things."

Suddenly Ryder went stock-still, then pulled back and released her so quickly that she had to catch herself to keep from falling forward. In a flash he was on his feet.

"You're right," he said as he carefully backed away. "We don't need any complications. It would be a helluva lot smarter to keep things on a business basis." With that he turned and started moving in earnest. "I have to put on my boots and, ah, see about some things. I'll catch you later." The last word was barely out when he beat a swift path into the house and closed the door.

Just like that he left her staring after him. Again. He had everything female inside her running around in circles, and he was gone. Again!

Fuming, Eve shot up. Her boots pounded on weathered wood as she stalked across the porch. "So even after all that, he wants it to be strictly business, does he?" she muttered to herself. "Well, the man has no idea how dedicated to business I can be...but he will. In fact, I think it's time the big boss made several things crystal clear. And I know exactly where to start."

She hopped in the Jeep, slammed the door and pulled away with a squeal. Headed downhill, she slowed only because she had to in order to remain on what road there was. Minutes later, back on flat land and up to full speed, she headed for the stable closest to the ranch house. She arrived there in record time, parked next to the corral and jumped out. She didn't stop until she stood beside a stall at the back of the building.

"Hello, Sable," she said calmly, staring straight into gleaming black eyes. "Remember me?"

The mare cocked her head, as if considering that question, then bobbed it in response.

"Of course you do." Eve lifted a wry brow. "Who could forget the memorable time we spent together? You got the better of me that day, my girl. But the fun's over, so listen up." She slid her hands up her sides and placed them on her hips. "First, in case you don't know it, I'm the one who happens to be providing you with food and shelter. Second, you can bet your gorgeous mane I expect something in return."

She paused, took a firm step forward. "So this is the way it's going to be. Tomorrow morning and every morning for however long it takes, you and I have a date in the corral. I'm going to ride you, and keep on riding you, maybe until your bony butt is as sore as mine. Before this whole thing is over, we'll take a tour of the ranch—miles and miles of it—and you will be a perfect angel for the entire trip, *no matter what.* Am I making myself plain?"

Judging by the wary look that seemed to form in Sable's ebony gaze, Eve figured the mare understood quite well.

"Good. And before you start feeling sorry for yourself," she added, "I'll tell you that you're not the only one I plan on explaining a few things to."

Oh, no, indeed, she thought as she spun around on one heel and left the stable. Setting a grouchy cook straight was next on her list, and with that objective in mind it didn't take her long to reach the ranch house. She arrived in the kitchen doorway just as the man she

sought pulled a large chunk of raw beef out of a sparkling new refrigerator. Great timing, she told herself as
she walked forward.

"I'd appreciate it, Pete, if you'd put that back and
save it for another meal." She deliberately tried for a
mild tone. Ever since they'd come face-to-face in the
nursery, Pete Rawlins hadn't been quite so hostile toward her. If possible, she hoped to keep it that way.

His sudden fierce frown told her how fragile that
hope was. "I always make a beef roast for supper on
Wednesday."

She leaned against the counter, assuming a casual
pose. "I'm in the mood for chicken."

"We just had chicken," he pointed out gruffly. "I
fried up some night before last."

And last night they'd had steak…again. "I'm not
thinking of fried. Roasting it whole is what I have in
mind, with a side of fresh vegetables and plain baked—
not mashed and drowning in butter—potatoes."

Pete's eyes narrowed to slits. "I don't take orders
about how to fix my food, never have and never will."

Eve let out a breath, forced herself to silently count
to ten. If they continued to lock horns, all-out war was
bound to be declared sooner or later. It could even have
him quitting, once he'd finally got it into his thick head
that she wasn't going anywhere. Hiring another cook
didn't worry her. She could find a replacement if she
had to.

But where would this man go? And at what cost?
After all, he'd spent a major part of his life on the
Creedence Creek. Leaving the ranch had to mean leaving behind many things, perhaps everything, he held
dear, although he was sure to be too ornery to admit
it.

She knew it, though, knew he'd be giving up far more than a job, and her conscience wouldn't allow her to let that happen without trying to prevent it. Not that she was backing down. She'd just have to try another tack.

"I'm not asking for a few healthy menu changes just for myself," she said, maintaining a mild tone. "I'm thinking about all of us—especially you."

If she'd just confessed to having eyeballs in the back of her head, he couldn't have looked more startled.

"Me?"

She folded her arms under her breasts. "Yes, you." *You're over sixty, and a possible heart attack waiting to happen if you don't watch out.* Rather than bluntly voice that thought, true as it might be, she tried for diplomacy. "You're in the prime of your life, Pete, but as a man grows more mature, he owes it to himself to keep his body as fit as possible, inside as well as out. You're a strong, vigorous person, and everyone who cares about you wants to see you stay that way."

Since he seemed speechless, she continued, "I think someone once said that the body is a temple, and food is its firm foundation." Or maybe no one had ever said it, she mused, but it sounded pretty good. "With that in mind, why don't you save the beef and make what I suggested for supper tonight? Please. For me...and for yourself."

Above the old, yet clearly well-maintained stove, a brass kitchen clock ticked away several seconds before he spoke. "I suppose it won't hurt to roast a chicken or two."

At the moment that grudging reply sounded like music to her ears. She had to hold back a smile. "And maybe you could make some fish on the grill once in a while?''

He hesitated, then managed a slight nod. "Lake trout's not bad if it's fresh caught. Neither is bass, come to think of it." Abruptly his frown returned, just as fierce as before. "But I'm telling you right now there's no way in holy Hades I am ever fixing any slimy shrimp."

"No shrimp," Eve quickly agreed. Then she leaned over the chunk of meat he still held out in front of him with both hands and planted another kiss on a rough cheek. "Thanks, Pete. Once again I'm in your debt."

Two down, she thought with satisfaction as she left the kitchen seconds later. One to go.

After her early-morning date in the corral, she would tackle the man who still had her temper on slow simmer and get a few more things straight.

Chapter Six

He was accustomed to giving orders, less familiar these days with being on the receiving end. Still, he had no trouble recognizing one when he heard it, Ryder reflected as he entered the ranch office and sat behind the desk. Young Cody Bodeen had passed it on with admirable tact, but the implication was plain.

"Miz Eve said to please meet her in the office at 10 a.m. sharp."

Ryder doubted that his boss had actually said *please*. Not after yesterday. He'd stood far enough back from a bare window to keep himself out of sight while he'd watched her make a roaring exit, putting the Jeep through its paces with a vengeance. As mad as a whole herd of howling heifers at branding time, that's what she'd been.

And every bit of it had been directed his way. Well aware of that, he'd invented an excuse and skipped dinner at the ranch house last night to give her temper time to settle. A smart man knew when to make himself scarce.

Heaving a sigh, Ryder leaned back in the swivel chair and crossed his arms over his chest. As far as he was concerned, her reaction was a long way from reasonable. They'd agreed to try something. The fact that it hadn't achieved what they'd intended was hardly his fault. Neither was what had happened during that all-too-real kiss. She'd responded to him every step of the way.

No, his fault, he supposed, was pulling back and putting some distance between them before things got completely out of hand. He didn't expect her to thank him for it, but he was damned if he'd apologize, either.

Women, he thought glumly, just as the woman in his thoughts walked in.

Despite having spent several hours on horseback, her totally unruffled appearance suggested she'd done nothing more strenuous that morning than pluck her eyebrows or polish her nails. But he knew exactly what she'd been up to, had even made dead sure Zeb was there in the corral to keep an expert eye on both her and the unpredictable mare.

Now Ryder watched as Eve approached, taking her time. After a pointed glance at the seat he occupied, she leaned one hip encased in formfitting denim against the side of the desk and gazed down at him. "Good morning."

Her voice was as calm, cool and collected as the rest of her. For some reason the whole package made him uneasy.

"Morning," he replied cautiously.

"Glad you could meet with me," she said, her tone briskly polite. "We need to discuss something." She tapped a red-tipped finger on the desk. "I think it's time I learned more about running the ranch."

That statement didn't surprise him. He'd figured she'd be looking to get more involved in a few things, sooner or later. It was only natural. "What exactly do you want to know?"

"Everything."

Now he was surprised, and knew it showed. *"Everything."*

Her gaze didn't waver. "Mmm-hmm. I'll leave it up to you where to begin, but ultimately I plan on being familiar with each and every aspect of managing the ranch."

A roundabout way of saying she wanted him to teach her his job, he told himself. Well, there were times when he preferred being flat-out blunt. "Thinking of tossing me out, Eve?"

"Not at all," she replied quickly and calmly, as though she'd been prepared for that question. "We have a six-month contract, remember?"

He nodded sharply in reply, remembering many things, including his firm conviction that his new boss wouldn't stay. He was still certain of that—or as near as made no difference. So far she'd adapted better than he'd expected, he had to admit. But that didn't mean boredom wouldn't set in before those six months were up.

And when it did, the Creedence Creek would be his. Finally.

In the meantime he'd follow orders, as much as it went against the grain. If she was determined to know more, he would show her. He knew just where to begin, too. Keeping detailed records that would satisfy the IRS at tax time could be the most tedious part of the job. To him, dealing with the meanest animal on the place was a picnic compared to that chore.

He straightened in his seat. "When do you want to start?"

Eve blinked at the easy agreement. Unless he missed his guess, she'd anticipated more of an argument, had probably geared up for it. She might have even been looking forward to locking horns, but he wasn't indulging her on that one.

"Getting started now suits me," she said after a moment of sheer silence.

"Okay. Let's go through some ranch records." He rose, walked over to the computer and pulled out a chair.

While he booted up, Eve pulled a chair next to his, sat down and leaned in for a closer view of the screen. Close enough, as it turned out, to rouse inner reminders of a real kiss best forgotten. More than close enough to spark a vivid memory of the feel of her breasts against him. Too damn close.

Ryder cleared his throat, and didn't miss the way his companion's quiet breathing stepped up just a little, just enough to make him more than suspect that he wasn't the only one finding it a challenge to be well within touching distance yet not quite touching. He took what comfort he could from that fact as he launched headlong into a lengthy explanation of a complicated spreadsheet.

Two hours later they were up to their ears in ranch bookkeeping. He was still explaining, and she was asking questions—about everything. After briefly breaking for a sandwich lunch, they headed back to the office for another session. By midafternoon, Ryder figured Eve's brain had to be on overload.

But the small pinched line between her eyes didn't stop her from summoning a smile as he shut down the computer. "Shall we say tomorrow at ten o'clock for another lesson?" she asked, just a little too brightly.

So she was game for more. Well, he would give it to her. "Sure," he said, his tone every bit as upbeat as hers even as he wondered just how far she intended to take this whole thing. It would, he decided, be interesting to find out.

AFTER ANOTHER LENGTHY SESSION at the computer the following day, Eve left the office and headed down the hall to her bedroom. Her head might feel full to bursting with all the information being crammed into it, but the rest of her was well pleased with the progress she was making.

She had Ryder to thank for much of that, she couldn't deny. As teachers went, he'd turned out to be an excellent one.

And she could also have him to thank for something else, Eve thought as she perched herself on the stool in front of her drafting table. An idea had been lurking in the back of her mind for weeks. One that just might have unconsciously begun to take form at her first sight of Ryder Quinn in a Western-cut suit. Memorable? Oh, yes. Maybe memorable enough to put her to wondering whether Western-style business wear for women—suits and accessories with a decidedly feminine flair—could have a viable market.

The concept would be a major shift from her past designing projects. Sassy Lady clothes had always been geared toward the casual, including next year's spring collection, to which she'd recently added some finishing touches. But maybe, just maybe, it was time to explore other possibilities. Coming up with a series of designs to send off to the manufacturer's corporate headquarters in New York was the first step.

Eve looked down at a wide slab of blank white paper. As always the challenge of filling that empty space, creating something where nothing existed, stirred her blood as well as her artistic instincts. She picked up a blunt-edged pen.

One practiced stroke gradually turned into hundreds, and time flew by until a quiet knock sounded on the open bedroom door. Eve had to haul herself back to her surroundings before she could focus on the person standing in the doorway. She put down her pen, flexing cramped fingers, and smiled at Theresa Conroy, who held her dozing son in the curve of her arms.

"Cloris said you wanted to see me before I left," Theresa said in her characteristically soft voice. Again, the jeans and T-shirt she wore were old yet spotlessly clean, her long, straight hair neatly brushed. And once again, those honey-brown eyes held a hint of sadness.

Eve resisted the urge to hop off the stool, walk over and give the young woman a companionable hug, telling herself not to push it. A hug wouldn't make Theresa's problems disappear, and offering too much in the way of friendship too soon might do more harm than good. Questions, a lot of them, remained. Today, Eve hoped to get the answer to one in particular.

"I wanted to ask how the job was coming along," she said mildly. Which was true. She was curious, though her real interest at the moment related to something else entirely.

"It's fine," Theresa replied, and seemed to mean it. "I keep busy, so the day is gone before I know it."

Eve remembered the old truck polished to a high gloss. This woman didn't fear hard work, that was plain. But other, less obvious signs said she feared something...or someone.

"I'm glad things are working out." Eve rolled

shoulders tight from maintaining the same position, the ache as familiar as an old friend. "I've been putting my nose to the grindstone, too. Would you like to see some designs in progress?"

Theresa nodded without hesitation and stepped forward. She carefully skirted around the growing stacks of discarded drawings littering the floor before reaching her objective.

"Forgive the mess. I'll shovel it out later." Eve's smile turned wry. "No one ever said the creative process had to be organized—or if they did, I missed it."

Theresa's mouth, bare of anything but lip gloss, rose at the corners as she gazed down at a zigzag string of sketches spread across the table.

"This is some early work for a new line I'm thinking of," Eve explained, going on to give more details. "When I'm satisfied that what I've come up with is worth passing along," she added, "I'll ship it off to New York and see what they have to say."

With a slight turn of her head, Theresa met Eve's gaze. "It must be wonderful, being so talented."

"I'm darned grateful for however much I have," Eve said simply, "but I'm hardly unique." She paused, recognizing an opportunity to insert something into the conversation. "Kendall Crane, one of my most demanding art professors, used to say that many people have talents locked inside themselves just waiting to break free. He was a great instructor, tough but fair. Now he's a friend, which means I'm allowed to call him…Kenny."

The jolt was slight, the eye blink quick. Nonetheless, a discerning gaze captured Theresa's response.

Eve took it all in with a bland expression while silently issuing an apology to her former teacher. Despite being far from stuffy, the sophisticated man with a thick thatch of silver-streaked hair and a penchant for wearing black turtlenecks would probably wince at the nickname. At least she'd quoted him correctly.

And she'd learned the answer to one particular question. Theresa Conroy knew someone named Kenny—someone Eve doubted was a casual acquaintance.

"I should be going now," the young woman said. "Thanks for showing me your work."

"You're welcome," Eve replied. And now she did reach out and place a hand on Theresa's arm, squeezing lightly before retreating. "Stop in and visit me again. I'm usually somewhere in the house around the time you pick up Max."

The baby stirred at the sound of his name, then blinked his eyes and opened them wide. "Well, hello, sweetheart," Eve said with a smile. "Your mom's taking you home, but we'll see you tomorrow."

Max raised a tiny hand and seemed to give her a wave. He couldn't know *bye-bye* yet, Eve thought. He was too young. Then again, she was beginning to believe this was one smart baby.

Theresa offered her own brief wave as she departed, leaving Eve to look after her and wonder about a chance visitor who'd called himself Kenny...if it had been chance.

She would tell Ryder about Theresa's reaction to that name, she decided. After all, there would be plenty of opportunity to discuss it. They'd be spending a lot of time together during the next few weeks. More than would please him, she was sure. A great deal more.

She was still fully determined to learn all she could about running the Creedence Creek, the whole business from top to bottom and not just the parts that staring at a computer could teach her. *Everything* was what she'd told Ryder. It would be interesting to see how he dealt with the realization that she meant it.

"THE WOMAN'S A SHE-DEVIL in disguise," Ryder declared from his seat on a sturdy sofa in the ranch house living room. His mood was dark, his temper as frayed around the edges as the scuffed chestnut-brown leather under him.

Pete picked up the remote control resting on an arm of the matching recliner he'd long ago staked out as his special spot and silenced a commercial on the big-screen television. "Now hold on, Ry. She's not that bad. Things could be worse."

Ryder knew his mouth was in danger of falling open as he speared his companion with a look. "*You're* saying she's not that bad?" His lips twisted. "I seem to remember your calling her a pure menace."

Pete looked down the legs stretched out in front of him, and made a production out of examining his boots. "That was before I, uh, got to know her." He lifted his gaze. "I'm not saying she's perfect, now. But she's better than that other female."

"Cloris?"

"Yep. Calling everybody sugar all the time." Pete leaned to one side, shortening the distance between them, and dropped his voice. "She's a dee-vor-say, you know."

"No, I didn't. Not that her being divorced has anything to do with anything. And as far as I can tell, you're the only one she calls sugar." Egged on by his troubles with another woman, Ryder added, "Maybe she's sweet on you."

Pete jerked back and made a face, looking as if he'd

just swallowed a sour lemon in two bites. "Jeez, Ry, don't even joke about a thing like that."

"Well, at least you can take comfort in the fact that you're not the one being hounded by a relentless female wanting to know everything about this and that and whatever." Ryder shook his head. "It started with ranch records, but it didn't end there, not by a long shot. Seems like nothing on the entire place is sacred. Now she wants to learn about *breeding techniques.*"

And the trouble was, he added to himself, certain parts of him were all but begging for the chance to give Eve a very private, very personal lesson on the subject. The more time he spent with her, the more he wanted to spend with her. Except, not doing anything remotely close to what they'd been doing.

Irritation fueled by frustration had long since set in, and today concern for her safety had been added to the mix when his headstrong boss had chosen this Saturday to take Sable on a daylong trip. Zeb and Cody had gone with her on that little jaunt. He, himself, had not been invited.

Since she'd been riding the mare regularly every morning for more than two weeks, odds were she could handle the horse. But that didn't stop him from worrying when he should be doing something constructive with the rest of his afternoon. He'd have to stew for at least another hour before they got back.

Or he could take a ride himself and get the edge off, he thought, and slapped his hands on his knees. "I'm going to saddle up Lucky and head out for a while. I'll be back in time for dinner. What's on the menu?"

"Grilled trout."

Ryder frowned at that news, more in puzzlement

than displeasure. "Didn't we already have fish once this week?"

Pete scrunched down in his seat. "We're having it again. And I don't need anybody giving me a hard time about it. If I want to keep my temple fit, I got to firm up the foundation."

Ryder could only stare. "What the hell does that mean?"

"It means we're having trout." Pete blew out a breath. "Why don't you take your ride? The wrestling championships come on in a minute, and I'm gonna miss the start if I keep flapping my jaws."

"Did you say wrestling, sugar?" a soft voice murmured.

Cloris Munroe looked nothing like a nurse today, Ryder decided as he rose, not in that gauzy floral-print top and flowing skirt. Then again, the woman leaning in the doorway wasn't in the nursing business at the moment. No babies were around to be cared for on the weekends.

Pete threw a disgruntled glance toward the door. "I said wrestling," he muttered, "a real sport for real men. And what in blazes do *you* know about it?"

"More than you'd expect," Cloris replied, ambling into the room. "When it comes to moves, I can tell a slam from a stunner, a pile-driver from a jackhammer, and then there's my own personal favorite—the figure-four leg lock."

"I'd say the lady knows her stuff," Ryder threw in just to stir things up, his mood improving.

"Humph" was Pete's comment as he stared straight ahead.

"You're a perceptive man, Ryder Quinn." Cloris aimed a sunny smile his way. "I've seen my share of wrestling matches, and I wouldn't mind watching the main bout today. It's bound to be a good one.''

"It'll be a danged doozy," Pete declared. "Grunt Brogan is one of the best." He shifted his gaze to the woman he plainly considered a pain in the posterior. "But you'd probably be cheering for Pretty Boy Mc-Coy."

Cloris sank down on the sofa in one graceful motion and stretched an arm across the back. "Actually Grunt is more my kind of guy."

Pete's salt-and-pepper brows climbed. "Are you telling me you're a Grunt Brogan fan?"

"I grunt right along with the rest of them when he steps into the ring, sugar."

"Sure, and I'm supposed to believe that. A fancy-dancy lady grunter."

Cloris didn't bother to reply. She just grunted a few times. Then she grinned. And then she grunted some more, really getting into it. High grunts, low grunts, loud grunts. There was nothing remotely ladylike about any of them.

"Well, I'll be a—" Pete gulped "—I don't know what."

Ryder left at that point and doubted anyone missed him. The television regained its voice as he strode down the hall. "Ladies and gentlemen, welcome to…" were the last blaring words he heard as he walked out the back door.

"SLAM HIM right into the canvas, Grunt. That's the way, you darling man!"

"Pretty Boy don't look so pretty now, does he? Hoo-eee!"

Eve came down the hall listening to those raised

voices. Wild cheers sounded in the background. She approached the living room and stopped dead in the doorway, not quite believing her eyes as she watched Cloris and Pete thrash around in their seats, apparently using body language to demonstrate instructions shouted at the two burly men dressed mainly in sweat who were grappling on the television screen.

Cody came to a halt beside Eve. "Seems like there's a wrestling match in progress," he drawled, pushing back his hat with two fingers. "It might go down nice with a frosty beer."

Eve had invited both her companions on the day's long ride over for a cold drink. Zeb had declined, saying he had to get home. Cody had wasted no time in accepting. "Why don't you go to the kitchen and help yourself?" she suggested. "There's beer in the refrigerator."

"Okay," Cody agreed, leaving Eve standing in the door and still recovering from the surprise of seeing a most unlikely couple in apparent total—if far from quiet—harmony. She had to smile at the sight, and then her mouth widened to a grin as she considered how her own day had gone.

Sable had behaved beautifully as they'd toured the ranch—miles and miles of it. It was a victory, Eve reflected, not only over a stubborn horse but a personal one, as well. She'd done something she hadn't been totally confident she could do.

And she'd done it without Ryder's help. Somehow that was important to her.

Not that he would have been thrilled to accompany her. He'd probably been all too happy to get rid of her for a day. But no matter how he felt, and despite a sore backside and various other aches, she felt terrific—a feeling she wanted to share.

"Hello, there," she said, walking into the room. She might have been invisible for all the attention she got.

"Don't let Pretty Boy flip you, Grunt," Pete ordered with a scowl.

"Get him in a leg lock!" Cloris added at the top of her lungs.

"I had a great day," Eve declared, raising her voice. Again she was completely ignored.

"I think you'd best wait until this is over, Miz Eve," Cody advised, entering with a long-necked bottle in one hand.

She sighed. "I suppose you're right, but I wanted to celebrate a little."

His eyes were bright with knowledge and perhaps a hint of sympathy as he met her gaze. "I guess I can understand that. Maybe…"

"Maybe what?" Eve prompted at the hesitation.

"A bunch of the hands spend Saturday nights at Bronco Billy's, more often than not. It's on the highway toward town. We down a couple of burgers, toss back a few drinks, dance—if the band's good and the women willing. Maybe you'd, uh, like to go with us tonight?"

Normally she would have politely declined. She'd already heard that Ryder often kept to himself, and she understood why. It was hard to maintain a supervisory role and socialize at the same time. But today wasn't a normal day. It was special, at least to her, and she couldn't resist the chance to celebrate in style, or at least as much style as a place called Bronco Billy's might have. "All right, I'd be happy to join you, but I'll need to shower and change first."

"Me, too." Cody grinned and raised his bottle. "Right after I finish this beer. How about if we pick you up at six?"

Eve looked at her wristwatch, found it was close to five o'clock. "Sounds good."

Cody dipped his head and walked around the back of the sofa to sit next to Cloris. "Who's winning?"

"Grunt Brogan, of course," she replied staunchly, not so much as glancing at the young man's way.

Eve took one more step forward. "I'm going to Bronco Billy's for dinner with Cody and a few of the other hands."

Finally she won Cloris's attention, for a second. "That's nice, dear. Have a good time."

"Don't order the pork ribs," Pete advised, throwing a look in her direction. "They make 'em too greasy." Then his scowl returned as his gaze shifted. "Come on, Grunt. Get him on the ropes and keep him there!"

Eve thought about sighing again, decided it would be a wasted effort. Instead, she turned and headed toward her bedroom. At least someone was willing to celebrate with her, she thought.

And if Cody Bodeen wasn't the rugged man who might have made the celebration really special by being truly pleased with her achievement, that was just too bad. She planned on having a good time without him.

RYDER TOOK HIS RIDE and felt better for the exercise. It had nothing to do with his getting a glimpse of Eve in the distance and seeing that she still safely occupied a saddle, he told himself, or with how he'd met up with Zeb later as the old wrangler was leaving the stable and learned for certain that she'd survived in one piece.

Nothing to do with it at all, he thought as he pushed

open the back door to the ranch house at six-thirty and started for the dining room. Finding Pete and Cloris seated there engaged in friendly conversation came as no surprise, given the afternoon's events. Likewise, the oval platter of just-grilled fish in the middle of the table. The only thing that gave him pause was something piled high in one of two round side dishes.

"Can that be rice, or am I dreaming?" The wry comment came as he pulled out a chair and sat down.

Pete slanted him a look. "What's wrong with rice?"

"Not a thing," he replied mildly, thinking that if rice had ever been served at this table before, he hadn't been around to see it.

"I think it's a delightful change," Cloris said, filling her plate.

"A body can't eat potatoes all the time," Pete added.

Never mind that the man had eaten a ton of them, Ryder reflected, taking the side dish that was passed his way. "You two look pretty pleased with yourselves. Grunt Brogan must have won."

"Slaughtered Pretty Boy," Cloris announced cheerfully.

Ryder spooned up some rice. "I guess we're not waiting for Eve." She was probably soaking sore muscles in a hot tub, he thought. Despite practicing every morning, an all-day ride wouldn't have been easy for her. Not that she hadn't brought it on herself. Still, he had to admire her for sticking with it, just as she'd stuck to taking in everything he'd shown her during the past few weeks. He supposed he had to admire that, as well, though he'd walk the entire ranch—in brand-new boots—before he'd admit it.

Cloris nudged the fish platter his way. "Eve won't be joining us tonight."

"Aha!" So she couldn't even make it to the table. Or maybe she just couldn't sit once she got there. He'd resist the urge to needle her about it the next time he saw her, Ryder decided, feeling generous as he slid some trout onto his plate.

Pete dished himself up some green beans. "She went to Bronco Billy's."

The platter Ryder had been holding met the table with a crash. "She did *what?*"

"It sounds like a fun place," Cloris tossed in.

"It's a rowdy place," Ryder informed her with a frown, "especially on a Saturday night, when all hell has been known to break loose." He switched his gaze back to Pete. "Why in blazes did she go there?"

"She wanted to celebrate her ride." Pete shook his head. "Don't know why anybody would want to celebrate sitting in a saddle all day with the sun beating down on them, but that's what she said before she and Cody left. She was all decked out, too, in a fancy outfit."

Ryder picked up his fork. "So she went with Cody?"

"And a bunch of the younger hands."

Now the fork hit the table with a clatter. "The bunch that generally drinks more than is good for them and gets into too many fights. And you let her go?"

Pete lifted one shoulder in a shrug. "What was I suppose to do, hog-tie the woman?"

Ryder blew out a disgusted breath. "It wouldn't have hurt to try."

Cloris wasted no time in laughing at that rueful remark. "I think Eve can handle herself, Ryder. Why don't you relax and eat your dinner?"

He picked up his fork again. "I'm eating my dinner. Then I'm going to Bronco Billy's. And then I'm going to see to a willful woman's well-being—whether she likes it or not."

"I'd say she's not gonna like it," Pete muttered, cutting into his fish.

Ryder stabbed a lone green bean clear through to his plate. "Too bad."

Chapter Seven

Bronco Billy's Sidewinder Saloon was like nothing Eve had ever experienced. She was no stranger to Western-style, bar-and-restaurant combinations with plenty of open space for dancing: the Dallas area had many. But this particular version was just old enough, brash enough and ragged enough around the edges to suggest it might actually have been doing business in the rough-and-ready days of the Wild West. Refined, it wasn't. Describing the place as even halfway civilized might be a stretch.

Eve loved it.

She smiled to herself as she sat at a large side table, thinking that Wyatt Earp and Doc Holliday would probably look totally at home if they shouldered their way through the oak double doors right now and sauntered over to the long bar, boot heels clicking on the scarred wood floor. Whisky might be more to their taste, but tonight beer was clearly the popular choice. Great quantities of it had been served during the past few hours, keeping the burly bartender busy.

Several waitresses, dressed much the same as many of their customers in jeans, checked shirts and wide-brim hats, stepped lively, delivering thick brown plates

heaped with food, mainly half-pound hamburgers with
all the fixings. Earlier Eve had indulged in one without
too much guilt. Now that fewer calories were being
consumed at home, thanks to Pete's cooperation, she
could afford to splurge a little on a night out.

"Enjoying yourself, Miz Eve?" Cody asked from
beside her.

She turned to him, allowed her inner smile to break
through. "You bet. This is a perfect place for a celebration." Not a sedate one, though, she added silently.
The noise level alone was equal to any New Year's
party she'd ever attended.

"A bunch of us had a bet going on how long it
would take you to tame that mulish mare," said a deep
voice coming from her other side.

Eve switched around to view Gabe Gentry, another
Creedence Creek ranch hand. He was Cody's age, or
perhaps slightly older. But where old-time gallantry
seemed to come naturally to Cody, Gabe was a black-
haired, blue-eyed version of a bad-boy cowboy. Many
of the younger women present had already thrown
meaningful looks his way. Given a few years to mature
to his full potential, he would be downright devastating
to the female of the species, Eve decided before calmly
asking, "Who won?"

Gabe grinned, showing a string of white teeth. "I
did."

"Beat me out by a couple of days," Cody grumbled.

"So I'm celebrating right along with you tonight,
boss," Gabe added. He pushed back a rickety chair,
got to his feet in one easy motion and gazed down.
"Would you like to dance?"

"I'm going to disappoint half the women in this

place if I take you up on that offer,'' Eve warned wryly.

Gabe's gleaming grin widened. ''I'll get around to them, don't worry.''

''In that case, okay,'' she said, rising.

He settled his gray hat more firmly on his head, then took her elbow and escorted her to a crowded dance floor backed by a six-man country band. ''Can you do the two-step?''

Eve laughed. ''I learned to do the Texas Two not long after I started walking.''

Gabe placed an arm lightly around her waist. ''Well, now, I'd say we're about to have a rip-roarin' good time.'' With a practiced flourish many men twice his age would have envied, he swung her into the middle of the crowd.

RYDER PUSHED a heavy door open with the flat of his hand and entered the saloon with a determined stride. He ignored the rowdy rendition of the ''Boot-Scootin' Boogie'' that hit his eardrums and glanced around the huge room, aiming his gaze from beneath the rim of his black Stetson. Being taller than most, he had little trouble looking over a sea of heads and spotting Cody and another hand seated at a side table close to the bar. He made his way through the crowd with little effort: people tended to leave a path open for someone of his size. A few acquaintances called out to him as he passed, the gist of most of their remarks being that they hadn't seen him here for some time, which was the bald truth. At one point in his life he'd frequented this place and others like it more than enough to earn a hell-raiser reputation. But those days were long over.

Not that B.B.'s, as many of its steady customers

called it, had changed. From all appearances it was as wild and woolly as ever. And that was exactly what he'd been afraid of.

Ryder reached his destination, pulled out a chair and sat down with his back to the center of the room. The startled looks displayed by the two younger men he faced told him how unexpected his visit was. But then, he'd expected nothing less.

"Evening, gentlemen." Ryder deliberately kept his tone mild, wondering exactly where a particular woman was, the one who'd brought him back to what could be argued as the roughest and toughest of his old haunts. He took in the small white purse with a long strap, hanging from the back of an empty chair next to Cody, and a short water glass half-filled with what had to be red wine, resting on the table. Assuming both belonged to Eve, he figured she probably wasn't far away.

Ryder's companions mumbled greetings too low to be made out above the din. In contrast the slinky brunette who approached with quick steps had no difficulty making herself heard.

"What'll you have?" she all but shouted.

"Bottle of Lone Star," Ryder replied.

The waitress looked him over, offered a saucy smile as she slapped a cocktail napkin featuring a picture of a bucking bronco on the table. "Good choice, darlin'. Be right back."

"She never calls me darlin'," Cody griped good-naturedly, his voice now loud enough to reach across the table.

Ryder leaned forward in his seat and tightened his jaw. "She may be calling you the cowboy who flew out a window headfirst, hat still on, if you can't come up with a damn good reason for bringing a greenhorn woman to a place like this.''

Cody swallowed. "Well, uh—" He stopped to clear his throat. "I was only trying to be friendly," he finally managed.

"Mmm-hmm. And how many fights have already broken out?"

"Just a little scuffle by the back door a while ago. I doubt Miz Eve even noticed. Only problem we've had so far was getting her a glass of wine. The bartender had a time finding some, but he came through. Luckily she wasn't particular about the color. And she's enjoying herself," Cody added hastily. "She flat-out told me so.''

The waitress slapped a frosty bottle down on the table. "Here you go."

"Thanks." Ryder dug in a jeans pocket and pulled out a bill more than big enough to cover the drink. "Keep the change."

"Thank *you,* darlin'.''

"So the greenhorn is enjoying herself, is she?" he asked as the waitress departed.

Cody aimed a glance over Ryder's shoulder and nodded. "If you'll turn around and take a look, you'll see for yourself."

Ryder turned. And looked. And stared.

His boss was having a good time, all right. A devil of a good one, judging by the way she was grinning from diamond-studded ear to ear, her face flushed below her short, shiny cap of golden hair. Gabe Gentry seemed equally pleased with the situation as the two scooted in tandem across the dance floor. Other dancers must have blocked his view earlier, Ryder decided. He'd never have missed them otherwise. Now space had been cleared all around them, obviously to give the star performers a chance to strut their stuff.

And as unexpected as that sight was, Ryder told himself he could have handled it with ease—or at least without any danger of his mouth going bone-dry—if the outfit Eve had picked out for this particular evening was anything like what she usually wore.

Too bad it wasn't. Tonight, the urban-cowgirl image had taken on a whole new dimension, starting with a snowy-white blouse that had small cutouts in the fabric across the shoulders and down the arms, allowing a clear view of the creamy skin beneath. Without those cutouts the high-necked blouse would have been almost prim. With them it was a totally different story.

Ryder slowly dropped his gaze, took in the stretchy red belt gripping a nipped-in waist as he made his way down to a stone-washed blue-denim skirt that ended at midthigh, well above the white boots moving in perfect time to the lively tune.

He'd never seen her legs. Which was probably why he couldn't look away. True, the fancy jeans she usually wore left little to the imagination when it came to their shape. But other than a memorable glimpse on the day they'd met the bogus snake, he'd never seen them in the flesh.

Now he was seeing them, Ryder thought. All nine smooth-and-silky yards of them. And so was every other man in the place.

That shouldn't bother him. It shouldn't…but it did.

Just then the song came to a rousing end. A loud chorus of cheers rose from the crowd as the couple in the spotlight left the floor. Ryder reached around for his beer and took a long swallow, because his mouth *had* gone bone-dry, then got up and waited as they approached. He knew the minute Eve spotted him. She came to a dead halt for a second, then continued walking toward him, her wide grin fading to an unreadable expression.

"Good evening," she said calmly when she was inches away.

"Evening," he replied, just as calmly.

"You're a mighty fine dancer, Miz Eve," Cody tossed in.

Now a small smile appeared. "Thanks." She glanced at Gabe. "I had a terrific partner."

Gabe tipped his hat, eyes twinkling. "I'm grateful for those kind words, ma'am." The band started up another tune, this one a bluesy ballad. "Care to do it again?"

"I think this is my dance," Ryder said, cutting in.

Eve blinked, finally showing some of the surprise she'd done her best not to show at her first sight of Ryder Quinn in this place of all places. He didn't socialize much with the rest of the crew, but here he was, looking devastating in denim, as usual. And now the man who kept taking off every time things got up close and personal wanted to dance with her?

"All right," she replied, because she had no idea what else to say. Except *no,* which would have been just plain rude. So she let him take her arm and silently lead her back toward a crowd of swaying couples, some locked in embraces steamy enough to turn up the heat in a room that was already overly warm despite its size.

Ryder put one arm around her waist, caught her right hand in his left and eased her into the group, deftly avoiding any collisions. He danced as well as Gabe Gentry, Eve soon decided. Not as showy, but with absolute confidence in his movements. And apparently he didn't feel the need to keep a conversation going, as the younger man had.

He waited so long before speaking that she almost jolted when he murmured in her ear. "You shouldn't be here, you know."

She pulled back slightly to gaze up at him, frowning in puzzlement. "Why not? The food's reasonably good, although the less said about the wine, the better. And country-western music suits me fine. Don't forget that where I come from, George Strait is right up there with Sam Houston in the hero department. Anyone worth his or her salt knows the lyrics to 'All My Exes Live in Texas.' And you can thank your lucky stars," she added candidly, "that I'm not about to sing them to you."

"Bronco Billy's still isn't your kind of place," Ryder replied, his tone quiet yet firm.

Her frown deepened. "I'll admit I've never been anywhere quite like it, but I thought I was fitting in fine."

"You won't when the fists start flying." As if to underscore that statement, a commotion broke out in a far corner of the room.

Ryder stopped in midstep. Eve turned her head and strained to see what was happening, only to find her view blocked by several clearly unconcerned couples who kept dancing while the band played on. "We're getting out of here," her partner told her flatly in the next breath.

Eve looked up at him. "It may be nothing, and I'm not ready to leave. I'm having a good time." *At least I was until you showed up,* she silently tacked on, far from pleased that he obviously assumed she'd meekly go along with whatever he said.

"I'm leaving." His expression turned grim. "And so are you—even if I have to toss you over my shoulder and cart you out."

Her mouth opened, shut, opened again. "You can't do that!"

"I can. And it won't even be remarkable enough to cause a scene. It's almost impossible to make a scene in this place." The sound of glass shattering seconded those words. "I think it's safe to say that no one will turn a hair if I carry you out of here right now."

The nerve of the man, she thought. Pulling away, she jammed her hands on her hips. "Lay one finger on me and you're fired."

He folded his arms across his chest. "Oh, no. We have a contract, remember? And I don't recall a clause in it to cover this sort of situation. Besides, it's not about the ranch tonight. It's just you and me, lady, and I'm not putting you at risk. You can press charges against me later, if you care to, but we're leaving, whether you walk or I haul you out."

She gritted her teeth, realizing he meant every word, and turned to stalk past the other couples. Cody was the only one still seated at the table when she got there.

"I think we'd best be going, Miz Eve," he said, casting a wary glance at the other side of the room. Glass crashed again as the band turned up the volume with another fast-paced tune.

"She's going," Ryder said from behind her. "With me."

Eve didn't bother to dignify that blunt statement with a response. She grabbed her purse and looked at Cody, forcing an unconcerned smile. "Thanks for inviting me tonight. I had a wonderful time." *Until now.*

Seconds later she slammed out the door and into the balmy, black-velvet night, well aware that her self-appointed keeper followed hard on her heels. Chin lifted and determined to end the evening as quickly as possible, she strode over to a familiar pickup parked on the outskirts of the wide gravel lot. She tried the passenger's door, found it unlocked and hopped in. Then she concentrated on fastening her seat belt and paying as little attention as possible to the man who slid in on the other side.

He gunned the engine to a start, shifted gears almost savagely as they made for the highway. Clearly he was in no better temper than she was. And she couldn't have cared less, she told herself. Let him be upset; he deserved it.

But he may actually have had your safety in mind, a niggling inner voice contended. "Bull crap," she muttered under her breath.

"What did you say?" he asked, biting out the words.

"Nothing."

"If you were cursing me," he added gruffly as he aimed the truck at a fast clip down a straight, dark road, "you can save yourself the trouble. You don't know that place and how a good time can turn into something else entirely. I do. And I'm not about to apologize for anything."

"I don't want an apology." What she wanted was his head on a platter. "Believe me, 'I'm sorry' wouldn't begin to make up for your high-handed attitude."

He slid a brief look her way, his hands clenched on

the steering wheel. "I was only trying to protect you, dammit."

"Well, next time, don't try so hard," she replied dryly, then was startled into gripping the door handle for balance an instant later as he abruptly pulled off on her side of the road. They jolted to a bumpy stop before he cut the engine with a flick of his wrist.

His eyes blazed in the silvery glow reflected by headlights set at full beam as he turned toward her. "I'll do whatever I feel I need to do, lady." He stopped, pinned her with an unwavering look intense enough to jangle every taut nerve in her body before he spoke again. "And, heaven help me, right now I need to—"

His lips came down on hers, wordlessly finishing the sentence with a swiftness that would have made her gasp if she'd been able to. But he gave her no chance to make a sound.

She wasn't sure how she came to be kissing him back, shaping her mouth to his, meeting his tongue with her own. All she knew was that it felt even better than the last time, made her want even more than she had before, had her heart hammering in her throat. A tide of physical longing swept away the last traces of her anger, leaving less belligerent though no less heated emotions in its wake. With the seat belt still holding her firmly in place, she raised her arms and fisted her hands in the silky hair at the nape of his neck. In that moment nothing mattered but the man who slipped his hands around her waist and pressed closer and closer. Only him.

And the kiss went on and on, sweet, sharp flavors blending, until Ryder finally lifted his head long moments later. Again his eyes pinned her in the darkness.

Willing her gaze not to waver, she met his stare with her own. "If you plan to take off and leave me again—"

"I'm not going anyplace," he said, breaking in, his voice deep and husky. "Even if my better judgment flat-out ordered me to get out and start walking, I couldn't do it. Not tonight." He hauled in a ragged breath. "If I were young and foolish enough, I'd try to make love to you right here. I have protection—that wouldn't be a problem. But I don't want it to be on the front seat of a truck, even if we could manage it. I want you in my bed. Badly." It was a stark admission.

He cupped her chin. "Tonight it's just you and me. No ranch, no contract, nothing but the two of us. Agreed?"

Only them. Only for tonight. Simple? Eve knew it wasn't, had little doubt Ryder was equally aware of that fact. Actions had consequences. Whatever happened tonight, tomorrow would follow, and the future would be forever changed, for the better or worse. But she could come to terms with tomorrow when the sun came up, she decided. Living for the moment—this moment—was too enticing to resist.

"Agreed," she said.

RYDER SWUNG onto the narrow road leading to the house at the top of the hill. One big hand gripped the wheel, the other held Eve's hand tightly. Not swallowed up by his, as a smaller woman's would surely have been, Eve's hand provided a solid press of flesh to flesh. Her palm was far softer than his own, granted, yet not quite as soft as he recalled from their first handshake. Regardless, the strength he'd once sensed beneath the silky skin remained.

And all he could think about was the prospect of that soft, strong hand touching him…everywhere.

It seemed as if they'd been driving for hours, although it had probably been no more than twenty minutes. Time ticked away with frustrating slowness as the wanting, the needing built inside him. Not much longer, he thought, aiming the truck at another turn in the familiar road. He let up on the gas, eased into the curve, despite certain portions of him urging breakneck speed. His sole intent when the evening started had been to keep Eve safe, he reminded himself. And he would do it, even if his entire body forcefully protested against driving cautiously on their upward, winding journey.

In the back of his mind a wary voice issued a very different protest. *Are you sure you're doing the smart thing, Quinn, making love to this woman?* He overrode its whispered message, as well. No doubts were allowed. Not tonight.

At last the final curve was negotiated with care and the place Ryder called home came into view. The porch light he'd left on welcomed their approach, a small, yellow beacon in the murky shadows beyond the truck's twin beams.

Ryder stared straight ahead. It always looked good to him, that old, sturdy, weatherworn house. He often saw it as a haven, but at the moment it looked like sheer heaven, because he would soon have the woman sitting beside him in his bed.

Too soon, if he didn't get a choke hold on his baser parts, he realized with a slight grimace. After all, he couldn't just rush her into the bedroom, could he? No, they'd have to at least talk a bit first. He had to hope she didn't have her mind set on a real conversation. A man could only do so much. Then again, Eve had shown no inclination to chat on the seemingly endless drive. After issuing a quiet agreement that had sent his pulse to pounding like a jackhammer, she'd barely made a sound.

Ryder stopped the truck steps from the foot of the porch. He killed the headlights, then the engine. A deep silence descended as he turned his head. Even in the darkness, the gray eyes that met his own gleamed with what could only be anticipation. Instantly wants and needs surged to the forefront.

"If we don't get out of here right now," he warned gruffly, "I *will* try to make love to you on the front seat."

She smiled a smile as old as the ages. "Then I suppose we'd better get going."

He shot out the door and came around to her side before she had time to do more than set both feet on the ground. Another smile, this one wry, appeared as he tugged her into an embrace. "I take it you're in a hurry."

"I'm about to explode," he said bluntly. Hardly a romantic declaration, he recognized, but he was too far gone to come up with flowery phrases. That was difficult enough to do even when his brain was fully functional.

Eve drew in a breath, imagining—vividly—the potential power of that threatened "explosion." The possibility was real, she knew, well aware of the coiled tension in the strong arms surrounding her.

"Let's go inside," she said, somehow managing to sound halfway calm while her heart raced.

Without another word, Ryder pulled her along with him to the front door. It closed behind them with a quiet click as he switched on an overhead light and turned toward her. "Can I, uh, get you anything?"

Beads of sweat dotting his brow below the rim of his black Stetson told her how much it had cost him to make that offer. Yet he had made it, trying to take things slow, it was clear. For some reason, that erased any need for hesitation on her part.

"Only you," she replied.

His eyes held hers. "You don't want to, ah, talk first?"

Her lips curved. "Let's talk during."

His sudden smile matched hers as he took her purse and hooked it on the doorknob. "I may be able to get a few words out. Barely."

With that, he picked her up, held her high against his chest and started for the rear of the house. Being swept off her feet and carried by a man was a far-from-common experience. Being so effortlessly carried by this one thrilled her, she couldn't deny. When they reached his sprawling bed, he lowered her to it before switching on a short brass lamp perched on a nearby nightstand. Then he straightened, reached up to remove his hat and launched it toward the top of the bed. It landed neatly on a rounded edge of the tall headboard.

She gazed up at him, arching one brow. "You'll have to teach me how to do that."

"Right now I plan on demonstrating how fast I can take boots off." He dealt with hers first, then his. In a matter of seconds he was stretched out full length beside her on top of the sea-of-blue bedspread. Then firm lips met hers, and a roving hand blazed a trail down her body. An avid mouth sparked inner cravings, quickly fired them to full-blown desire. Busy fingers fanned the flames.

Eve sucked in air when they broke for a breath, let it out in a sharp sigh when Ryder dipped his lips to her shoulder and pierced his tongue through one of the small cutouts in the fabric. It felt good. Unbelievably good.

"This is the damn sexiest blouse," he said, leaving that now-moist spot for another cutout farther down her arm, then another. "Hmm. It makes me want to lick you all over. And I plan on doing just that. Later." He lifted his head and touched one of the tiny pearl buttons that ran from her throat down to her waist. "You're going to have to help me with these. In the shape I'm in, I'll tear something."

She was in little better shape to do anything that required concentration. Luckily her fingers worked with a will of their own, unbuttoning the blouse without much trouble. She tackled the silver snaps on his shirt next, popping them open while he watched with a smoky gaze. Then their hands were on each other, seeking, finding, learning.

There was no restraint this time. She was free to touch him as she chose and did so eagerly, brushing her fingers over skin that was smooth in some places, rough in others and warm everywhere. He more than matched her enthusiasm, unhooking the clasp of her strapless bra and baring her to the waist before dipping his head and pressing his lips to her breasts. Rather than slow caresses, he used speed and heat and flash.

And it felt wonderful. Incredibly wonderful.

Finally his gaze returned hers. "You're driving me crazy." His voice came out in a near croak. "I have to have you, Eve. Now."

"Now," she agreed without hesitation.

They stood and undressed each other with a haste

bordering on desperation. Eve pulled back the bed-spread and slipped between crisp white sheets while Ryder rummaged in a nightstand drawer and retrieved a handful of foil packets. Keeping one, he tossed the rest down beside the lamp, then turned to the woman in his bed.

He was so stunningly male wearing nothing but skin, so powerfully, perfectly formed he took her breath away. She could have looked at him—just looked at him—for hours, if he and the wanting he'd created would have tolerated it. Neither would, she recognized, so she opened her arms to him.

Leaning over, he pulled back the sheet covering her and stared down, his gaze intent. "Lady, you are one beautiful sight."

She was far from beautiful, and she knew it. But that didn't seem to matter. Not now. Nothing mattered beyond closing the gap between them as she reached up and tugged him to her. He dealt with the protection while she stroked broad shoulders, and then he turned her on her back and rose over her. Their eyes linked, locked, as he positioned himself and surged inside.

"Yes," she murmured.

"Oh, yeah," he muttered.

Then speech was beyond them, and they were moving as one, giving and taking, lifting and thrusting, meeting needs and building more, over and over.

It felt... Eve searched for a word to describe what was happening, what had never happened before. Not to her. Somewhere from the depths of her an answer came. *Right.* That's how it felt. Amazingly, astoundingly right.

That was the last coherent thought she had.

Ryder watched as Eve's eyes drifted closed. He

clenched his teeth and held on to his control by a thread. Not yet, he told himself, making it as stern an order as he could muster. Never mind that his heart tripped, his breath hitched, his whole body verged on trembling like hard-packed ground during an all-out, wild-eyed stampede. Nothing mattered except the fact that he couldn't—wouldn't—let go until she did.

Sensing how close she was as she met him thrust for thrust, hoping that his instincts hadn't failed him, he put his upper weight on one arm and reached down between them to the place where they were joined. As he touched a special spot and flicked one long finger over it again and again, he could all but see her begin to fly.

The inner contractions launched him on his own soaring journey. Now he could join her, he thought, surging forward without restraint, breaking his self-imposed chains. Now he could lose himself in her. *Now.*

And now their cries came at the same moment, hers soft and low, his rough and deep. The sounds two people made when they were lost in each other.

Ryder gradually drifted back to reality, still breathing hard and half-dazed. Something had just happened, he realized. Something…important. At the moment, though, he wasn't inclined to mull over exactly what that meant. His brain was still fuzzy; his body still hummed. He was by no means sated. He planned to make love to the woman lying under him again. Soon.

Ah, she smelled good, he thought, taking in the scent of exotic flowers as he lifted his head from its resting place in the curve of a silky-skinned neck. She looked good, too, even with tousled hair and slightly smeared lipstick. He probably wore nearly as much of it as she did now, he reflected with a low chuckle.

Eve's eyes peeked open. "What are you laughing at?" she asked softly.

"I was wondering if your lipstick looks as good on me as it does on you."

A small smile formed as she studied his face. "It doesn't look bad."

Bending, he pressed a kiss to her cheek. "I think I prefer it on you." He shifted his upper body just enough to allow her more breathing room. "How do you feel?"

She sighed, a whoosh of sound. "Relaxed, as if I didn't have any bones at all."

"You have bones." He ran one hand over her shoulder and down her arm. "And they're very well put together."

Her smile grew. "Yours are put together even better."

He shook his head. "No way. I want you to spend the night with me," he added, and saw her smile fade.

"I'm not sure that's a good idea."

"I don't care whether it is or not," he informed her with blunt directness. "We can sort that out in the morning, but I want you here with me tonight. All night."

She caught her lower lip between her teeth. "I'd have to call Cloris. She might worry if I didn't come home."

"And you'd rather no one knew about any of this," he finished, wondering why that should irritate him. After all, he didn't want the whole thing broadcast, either. It was personal and private.

"I'm sure Cloris won't say anything if I ask her not to."

"And Pete sleeps like a stone on Sunday mornings, because he watches his favorite ancient Westerns on the late-late show Saturday nights. I'll have you home before he gets up." Sensing he was persuading her, Ryder let his mood lighten. "What have you done to Pete, anyway? He grilled fish again for dinner tonight, and fixed *rice* to go with it."

Her smile reappeared, just as he'd hoped it would. "You could say we had a heart-to-heart chat."

"Well, whatever you talked about, he's a changed man. He even thinks you're, and I quote, 'not so bad.'"

Her quiet laugh was plainly amused. "Praise indeed."

He brushed a stray lock of hair back from her forehead. "Will you stay?"

Eve hesitated, then slowly nodded. "I'll stay."

"Good." Ryder carefully eased himself away. "I have to take care of matters in the bathroom. The phone's on the dresser. Why don't you call Cloris, and I'll be right back." With that, he rose and made for the door to the hall.

Eve watched him depart. Despite her earlier hesitation, she didn't regret her decision. The truth was she wanted to spend the night exactly where she was. Maybe too much. But it wasn't tomorrow yet, she reminded herself. She still had time to live for the moment.

With some effort she pulled the top sheet around her and got up. A day in the saddle plus an evening on the town had her muscles protesting further movement. She did her best to ignore them. Two steps took her to a low dresser made of dark wood and topped by an elaborately carved mirror. She checked her reflection, found that she was positively glowing. Languid eyes and scarlet-smeared lips only added to the image of a woman who'd been fully pleasured.

And so she had been—to the hilt—and Ryder clearly knew it. He'd been looking a little smug around the edges when he'd left her. Something he had every right to be, she had to admit. On a scale of one to whatever number, the man was off the chart when it came to making love. One time was all it took to reach that conclusion. But it wouldn't be the only time. Oh, no. He hadn't asked her to stay just to sleep beside him.

He had plans.

Eve plucked a tissue from a box on the dresser top, wiped her mouth clean, and picked up the phone. Hopefully Cloris would answer rather than Pete.

"Creedence Creek Ranch," a lilting voice promptly greeted.

"Cloris, it's Eve."

"Well, hello." Surprise tinged that brief reply, along with unmistakable curiosity.

Which was only to be expected, Eve told herself. "I just wanted to let you know that I won't be home until tomorrow morning. Everything's fine," she added, "so don't worry."

After a silent second Cloris said mildly, "I take it Ryder found you. He stalked out of here a determined man, let me tell you."

Just then the man in question walked back into the bedroom without a stitch on. Eve struggled to hold on to her train of thought. "Yes, he, ah, found me."

A knowing chuckle came across the receiver. "I suspect that says it all." Cloris paused. "What goes without saying is that I'll keep this to myself, and Pete's

too tied up in a John Wayne fest on TV to spare a
thought for your whereabouts—or mine. I left after the
second movie. Not that The Duke isn't great, but a
woman can only take so much gunslinging in one
dose.''

Ryder stretched out on the wide mattress and linked
his hands behind his head. Eve swallowed, hard, as her
gaze slid over him, taking in a long length of skin
darkened almost to bronze by the soft lighting. ''I'll
see you tomorrow, Cloris,'' she managed to get out
before gently hanging up the phone. She found her
every move being calmly watched as she approached
the bed.

''I'd appreciate it if you'd drop that sheet and crawl
on top of me,'' Ryder drawled, his deep voice lazy.

But she'd didn't—because suddenly she couldn't.
Instead, she stilled completely as a mocking chorus of
other deep voices rose starkly from the shadows and
rang in her mind.

Yo, hefty hips.

Eve drew in a long breath, as much to steady herself
as to fill her lungs. Why had those words come back
to haunt her? she asked herself. Why now? She wanted,
or at least certain parts of her wanted, to do what Ryder
had so sexily suggested, but nagging doubts, brought
to full-blown life by a memory she couldn't quite forget, had her clinging to her covering.

A second passed before Ryder lifted a brow. ''Problem?''

*Yes, there's a problem. All at once I'm struggling
with the thought that, with the first headlong rush behind us, you won't be nearly as impressed with my
body as I am with yours.* But she wasn't about to say
any such thing. She had her pride, after all. Deciding

it would be easier if done quickly, she dropped the sheet in a heap and dove for him.

Ryder grunted at the impact when Eve landed. He'd been wondering at her uncertainty and could only be grateful that she'd decided to take him at his word. Still, he'd hadn't expected anything quite so forceful. "I have to admire your enthusiasm," he said with a low laugh, "but I had something more leisurely in mind." He dropped his arms, gripped her shoulders lightly and began to lift her upper body. "To begin with, I want to look my fill." And he did, until he became aware of how her whole body was stiffening, muscle by muscle, under his study.

He raised his gaze to lock with hers. "You're not comfortable with this—my looking at you—are you?"

"Not entirely," she conceded with a small sigh. "Anything I have is hardly special enough to rate a detailed study."

Ryder could only stare in response to that statement. "You have to be kidding," he said. But all at once he knew she was dead serious. Amazing, he told himself. "Have you any idea what I thought after getting a good look at you on the day we met?"

She shook her head.

"I thought you were a goddess."

Her mouth popped open. "A *goddess*. Now you're the one who has to be kidding."

"Truer words were never spoken," he assured her gravely. "I can't say I was totally happy coming to that conclusion at the time, but there's no question I did." He rolled her over until her back met the bed, then propped himself up on an elbow at her side. "And right now I can only say that my judgment was flat on target," he continued, stroking a hand over satiny curves, from full breasts to rounded hips to dimpled knees. "Your body is perfect to me, Eve, just as it is."

But doubts remained, and more than a few. He saw them flickering in her eyes and became determined to wipe them out. "I guess I'll have to show you," he murmured, replacing his hand with his lips, letting them roam at will. "Tasting every part of you seems like a terrific place to start." And he proceeded to do just that, sampling, relishing, savoring, inch by inch. When he finished, countless minutes later, he hoped he had erased everything except a hunger for physical release as great as his own.

Ryder rolled onto his back, quickly dealt with protection, then pulled Eve over him, so that she straddled his hips with her thighs. She looked down, face flushed, eyes gleaming. And not a doubt in sight, as least as far as he could make out, which made him a satisfied man.

Well, almost.

He lifted an arm, plucked his hat from the headboard and placed it on her head. Then he gave her what he fully intended to be a very wicked grin. "Why don't you ride me, lady?"

And so she did. Taking him up on that suggestion, and adding of few refinements of her own along the way, she rode him all the way to paradise.

THE LIGHT WOKE HER, just the sheer beginnings of dawn seeping through a bare bedroom window. Eve stretched, arching her back, and listened to the sure and steady breaths of the man beside her. He needed his sleep, she told herself. He had put in an adventuresome night, taxing his physical resources and demanding much from hers.

Not that she was complaining, Eve thought with the

softest of sighs. Even total exhaustion would be a small price to pay for what he and the night just past had given her—no, *inspired* in her, because it had to come from deep down inside.

She could only describe it as…respect. Not respect for herself as a person. Being raised by two wise and wonderful people, she'd had that from her earliest memories. But respect for her body, a woman's body that could give a man pleasure and receive it in kind.

Perfection didn't matter, she'd finally recognized. In the long run the world and all its varied notions of the ideal face and form didn't matter a speck. And neither did her own private notions on the subject—not when it came to herself. Like most people viewing a reflection in a mirror, she would probably never see anything close to perfection, not even if she lost every one of those stubborn extra pounds clinging to her.

Respect for one's own body was the important thing. And if another person, one special person, viewed it as perfect, that was all that truly mattered.

Ryder Quinn was special.

Over the course of the past several hours, he had become special to her. She could have tried to deny it, but she'd never been any good at fooling herself. *He was special.* Now she had to deal with that undeniable truth.

Eve quietly got out of bed and reached down toward a denim shirt lying among the clothes scattered over a well-worn rug patterned in blue. Taking in the tangy male scent of its owner, she pulled the shirt on and snapped it closed as she stood up, more to ward off the cool breeze slipping through a window opened several inches at the bottom than from any sense of modesty. She tiptoed out, visited the bathroom and came back minutes later to find Ryder still asleep, reclining on his back with the top sheet they'd retrieved sometime during the night bunched at his waist. He looked good enough to jump.

Instead, resisting that powerful temptation, Eve headed for the opened window, one of two at the rear of the room. The other held a unit air conditioner, bound to be needed at all times of the day and night once summer was in full swing. She looked out at the blooming, barely pink sky. After a moment she turned away, her gaze following the sun's path as it angled through clear glass. It landed, faintly shimmering, on something resting on the floor directly across the room, something she never expected to see, not here.

It was a cradle.

Slowly, feeling drawn for some reason, she stepped closer and crouched down. She brushed her fingers over wood darkened with age yet free of dust. Handmade. At least it appeared to be. "I wonder how old you are," she murmured.

"It could be older than both of us put together," came a quiet voice from behind her.

Ryder propped himself up on an elbow and watched as Eve quickly turned around to face him. Their eyes met and held as he slowly flicked the sheet aside, rose in one smooth motion and started toward her, feeling the first cool rush of morning air ripple its way down the long length of his bare body. Relishing it, he didn't even consider stopping to put anything on. Thankfully, he didn't feel he had to. Not after last night.

"The cradle might go back to when the house was built," he said, coming to a halt and crouching beside Eve. "Maybe it belonged to the first owners."

"A genuine antique." She looked back at the cradle and rocked it with a gentle motion.

One corner of Ryder's mouth kicked up. To him it meant something else entirely, but he figured it could be viewed that way. An antique. He supposed it was.

Reaching up, he wound his fingers in Eve's short hair. Golden silk, he decided, and as smoothly soft as the rest of her. All of her. He could testify to the fact, remembering every detail of what had passed between them.

He'd never be able to totally forget last night, he more than suspected. Because something had happened. Something important, as he'd already figured out. Something he still wasn't prepared to tackle. Not at the moment. One thing for dead sure, though, he was nowhere near ready to give it up after one short night.

He blew out a breath, thinking that things had gotten complicated in a hurry, and well aware that an inner wariness had predicted the probable outcome when he'd invited her to share his bed. A wariness he'd ignored, he reminded himself. But would he act differently if it were in his power to go back to that fateful moment in the truck?

No, he concluded without hesitation. What had followed had been just too good, too satisfying, too... extraordinary to change a blessed thing. Whatever the consequences, he couldn't regret it. Wise or not, he would do exactly what he had done and damn the consequences.

And, wise or not, he wanted to share more than a bed with this woman. He wanted—needed, he had to admit—to share a piece of the past he had always kept strictly private.

"How many mothers have rocked their babies in this cradle, do you suppose?" Eve asked, her voice as hushed as the silence all around them.

"I have no idea," he replied. "I only know that my mother rocked me there."

Her head whipped around. "In *this* cradle? I thought you said it could date back to…"

"When this house was built," he finished. "That's totally possible. I was born here," he went on, watching as gray eyes widened. "In this house, in this room. More than thirty years ago, I slept in that cradle."

Chapter Eight

Again Eve looked at the old, handmade cradle, and saw far more. Now she knew why this house was different, why, from her very first sight of it, a sense of ownership had eluded her. She owned it, yes. But the man at her side had a personal claim, one that went deeper than any legal title.

He had been born here.

And now his formidable determination to purchase the Creedence Creek made sense. *I believe Quinn wanted this property very badly,* Hank Swenson, the real estate broker, had said on the day they'd met. *Why, I couldn't tell you.*

Now Ryder, himself, had chosen to tell her. And only her, she reflected with confidence, suddenly sure no one else on the ranch knew what he had just revealed. The question was, how should she respond to that startling admission? As simply as possible might be best, she decided.

She faced him fully, found him studying her, and smiled. "You must have been a beautiful baby, cowboy."

It won her a small smile in return. "According to

my mother, I was a handful from the day I made up
my mind to get born in a hurry.''

''And you did it here,'' she summed up.

''That's right. My folks came to the Creedence
Creek one stormy afternoon, or so the story goes, when
my father heard that a new barn was being built and
thought he might get a job. He had several skills—
carpentry, in particular. My mother was pregnant at the
time with their first and, as it turned out, only child.
Without warning, she went into full-blown labor on the
way up the drive from the main highway. By the time
they arrived at the ranch house, I was champing at the
bit to get out. Amos Cutter gave my father some quick
directions to this place, which was vacant at the time,
and called the nearest hospital.''

''Hmm. Even in an emergency, he wasn't about to
have any female crossing his doorstep, was he?'' Eve
remarked dryly.

Ryder's laugh was low and amused. ''I guess not.
Things worked out fine, though. Apparently an ambu-
lance team arrived just in time to welcome me into the
world.''

''Sounds exciting.''

''My mother didn't think so.''

It was her turn to laugh. ''And how long did you
and your parents stay at the ranch?''

''Five years.'' Something in his tone left little doubt
that those early years were remembered fondly. ''My
father worked at various jobs around the place while
my mother studied. She took college courses through
the mail, more for the love of learning than to earn a
degree.'' He paused. ''We were happy here, for as long
as it lasted.''

But it didn't last, Eve thought, and knew he regretted that fact by the way his expression sobered.

"When I turned five, my folks wanted to take a tour of the West before I had to go to school the following year. We packed up and left, and spent the next several months almost constantly on the road. They enjoyed traveling, my father most of all. The need to keep moving seemed to grow as he got older, too, because we seldom spent more than a year in one place after that, just long enough for me to finish school in the spring. By fall we'd usually be somewhere else."

Sympathy was her gut reaction, and it must have showed, because he added, "It wasn't all bad, moving around. I got to see a lot of the country. And my folks did their best to make it fun. They were good people."

"Were?" she asked gently with the beginnings of a frown.

"They've both been gone for some time. When I graduated high school, I decided to try to get a job at the Creedence Creek or some other ranch in the area, if that failed. They dropped me off in Tucson, gave me all the money they had to spare and headed for the south of Mexico, somewhere they hadn't yet been. They were looking forward to a new adventure."

Ryder's voice turned stark, expressing little emotion, yet more serious for the lack of it. "Weeks later, I phoned an aunt who lived in northern Colorado. She was our point of contact, since my folks didn't know where I would be, and they'd made no firm plans to stay anywhere in particular. She broke the news that she'd received a call from the authorities in a small town on the Mexican coast. My folks had been killed in a car wreck a few days after I saw them last, and I never knew it."

"I'm sorry." What else could she say? "So you were left totally on your own at, what, eighteen?"

"Yes. And it was hard for a while, even though I had a job—thanks to Amos. By that time Pete had hired on as cook, and I formed some friendships. I made out okay."

More than okay, she thought. Far more. Ryder Quinn was a self-made man in the truest sense of the term. "Did Amos Cutter recognize you, or at least the name, after all those years?"

He shook his head. "Funny as it seems, I don't know. He never said anything, and neither did I. I was determined to get that job on my own, as if I were a complete stranger. I think he may have known, though. Sometimes I'd catch him studying me in a way that made me wonder. But I'll never know for sure."

Ryder stood up, pulling Eve along with him. "And that's enough about the past. I have something else on my mind that needs to be said." He lifted a hand, ran it through his sleep-mussed hair. "There's no way I can just chalk it up to a good time between the sheets and forget last night, Eve."

She hesitated, but only for a moment. "That makes two of us," she had to concede.

He gazed down at her, desire sparking to life in his eyes. "I want you again, right here and now, but here and now isn't going to be enough for me. We can be discreet about what happens next. I figure you'd prefer keeping this quiet, and I agree. But I want more than one night." The last was a soft yet blunt statement. "So I've laid my cards on the table, and you'll have to decide whether we continue this or not."

And what do you do now, Eve? she asked herself. She'd lived for the moment, gloried in it, but that would end when the sun came up to brilliantly light the day, as it would shortly.

Could she—or, more important, should she—continue this affair? Which is what it would be, she knew. An affair. And an open-ended one at that. The odds of anything permanent coming of it were doubtful at best.

When all was said and done, she still owned something this man wanted badly. After what he'd revealed, she was beginning to realize just how badly. Although he hadn't said as much, it wasn't difficult to conclude that Ryder Quinn wanted—needed—something that belonged to the past as well as the present. A spot uniquely his. One word might describe it best.

Roots.

And, for all that he wanted her, he wanted the Creedence Creek more. Of that she was certain. If she left, he would get what he wanted most.

If—*when*—she stayed, he might well decide to leave himself, once their six-month agreement was over and done with, and buy property of his own, something he could unquestionably afford to do. An affair, no matter how physically satisfying, wouldn't change the fact that he wasn't a man to work for someone else, not indefinitely.

Yet he did want her, and more than a little. Of that she was also certain.

And he had taken her into his confidence, made her feel special to him, whether she was or not. If the last few minutes hadn't happened, she might have been able to end it then and there—certainly the wisest choice, given the problems adding another aspect to their relationship could well create.

But they had happened, those brief, startling minutes, and she couldn't end it. Not now.

"I want you as much as you want me," she confessed. *Maybe more,* she admitted to herself as the spark in green eyes flared. "It's bound to complicate things, though, really complicate them, if we continue this," she felt compelled to tack on.

Ryder heaved a sigh. "Don't I damn well know it," he grumbled, and there was enough frustrated male in that statement to make Eve grin, despite everything.

"Are you up for the challenge?" she asked, reaching out to brush a hand across his chest.

He cocked an eyebrow, "I could make a crude comment on the subject."

She dropped a glance down his body. "Never mind, I get the picture." Her grin grew as he tugged her closer.

"Do we have a deal, lady?" His voice was husky, his meaning clear.

She lifted her arms and slipped them around his neck. "We have a deal, cowboy."

EVE STOOD on the back porch and watched as Ryder pulled away, his progress marked by a sun still low in the eastern sky. He had just dropped her off at the ranch house. No one else seemed to be around—not within seeing distance, at any rate—a fact the man disappearing at a fast clip had put to good use by kissing her witless, breathless and at length, until she somehow found the will to break away and get out of the truck.

Now she had to get herself together and face the day looking as though nothing remarkable had happened. No small task, she knew. It would have helped if her blouse and skirt hadn't spent the night on the floor, but that was just too bad. A few wrinkles wouldn't daunt her.

Eve took a deep breath, opened the back door and entered the house. With deliberate steps, she fixed her sights on a restoring dose of caffeine to ease the effects of too little sleep. By the time she walked through the kitchen doorway, she thought she'd achieved some measure of the calm-and-collected manner she'd been groping for. One glance at the person she encountered told her otherwise.

Smiling what had to be the slyest smile ever, Cloris stood near the stove and lifted a stoneware mug to her lips. Eyes as blue as the long, silky robe she wore sparkled as she aimed her gaze over the brown-edged rim.

"Good morning," Eve said, swallowing a sigh as she headed for the drip coffeemaker. She opened an overhead cabinet, retrieved a mug and filled it almost to the brim before reaching for a white carton set on the tiled countertop. Although the terra-cotta tiles were dull with age, the counter was scrupulously clean, like everything else in the kitchen. Pete, she thought, ran a tight ship.

"Morning," Cloris replied at last as Eve added milk to her coffee. The very lack of anything in the tone of that single word spoke volumes.

Eve took several grateful swallows, waited for the caffeine zing to hit her bloodstream before venturing another look at her companion. "I don't suppose there's any use in asking you to wipe your mind blank and forget the past twelve hours."

Cloris's smile returned. "No. I can pretend to forget, though, if you'd rather not talk about it."

As appealing as that notion was, Eve found there was something she had to know. "Were you surprised?"

"Not really," Cloris replied easily. "I suspected what's happened would happen, sooner or later."

Now Eve was surprised. "Why?"

"Because of the way I've caught Ryder looking at you on occasion, when he thought no one was watching, of course."

"Like how?"

"Like you were a seven-course gourmet meal with all the trimmings and he was a desperate man on the far side of starvation."

One corner of Eve's mouth rose. For some reason, that comment pleased her. "So you picked up on him."

"Mmm-hmm. But he wasn't the only one."

Eve frowned at that news. "I hope you're not about to tell me that I have ever looked like a man-hungry woman."

"Just a little around the edges, maybe. And just for one specific man." Cloris leaned against the counter. "Neither of you has been blatant about it."

"Well, thanks for that much," Eve muttered.

"It's hardly anything to fret about," Cloris pointed out. "If two single adults are attracted to each other and act on it, that's just nature taking its course."

Shaking her head, Eve said, "It's not anywhere near so simple, trust me."

Cloris mulled that over for a second. "You mean because you two have a business relationship?"

"Partly, yes. But mostly because of the ranch itself."

"Ah." Cloris nodded wisely. "Pete unbent enough after dinner last night to tell me that Ryder was ready to buy the property before you put in a bid."

"He's still ready to buy it," Eve said. *All he needs is me gone,* she added to herself, deciding not to disclose that particular piece of information. Their agreement was private, and she'd keep it that way.

"So you both want the place," Cloris summed up with a gracefully arched eyebrow. "Maybe something is escaping me, but I have to say that I fail to see an insurmountable problem here. If things between the two of you become really serious down the road, can't title to the ranch be shared? After all, married couples tend to do that."

Now Eve had to stare, finding herself speechless for a moment before she found her voice. "Married! Believe me, things are a long way from being anywhere near *that* serious."

"Well, of course," Cloris replied mildly. "First both parties involved have to fall in love."

And one party is already on her way, something inside Eve said. She hauled in a quick breath, all at once realizing the truth of that. *You'd better watch where you're going,* she warned her heart, *or you may wind up in pieces.*

She might be special to Ryder, yes. But love, real love, was something else entirely.

Eve's brows drew together. "No one's in love," she said stoutly, "and right now there's no getting around the fact that the ranch and who owns it stands foursquare between us. Maybe we can ignore it for a while, but it's not going to go away."

"And the future concerns you, I can see." Cloris's smile turned bittersweet as she pushed away from the counter. "If you want some advice, one woman to another, I'd say to take it a day at a time. No one can truly predict what will happen. I was once so sure my own marriage would last forever…and I was wrong.

My ex found someone younger. Almost young enough to be his daughter,'' she tacked on bluntly.

There wasn't a shred of self-pity in that Southern-tinged voice, and Eve could only admire Cloris for it. "He was a fool to let you go,'' she declared, and followed up that firm statement with another long swallow of coffee.

"I'd say you're right.'' Cloris squared her shoulders. "But that's all in the past. I'm concentrating on the present and enjoying every minute of it. I even have a date to go bowling this afternoon.''

"Good for you.'' Eve walked over to the sink to rinse out her empty mug. "Who's the lucky man, if you don't mind my asking?''

"I don't mind. It happens to be Pete.''

"*Pete.*'' Once again Eve found herself staring. "You're kidding.''

Cloris grinned.

"You're not kidding.''

"It's just a buddy thing. At least it is to him, I'm sure. We bonded over wrestling, and now he's curious to see if I can hold my own with a bowling ball.''

It was Eve's turn to grin a sly grin. "I more than suspect you can.''

"Oh, yes. The man doesn't know it, but if he plans to get the best of me, he has his work cut out for him.''

Eve was still grinning as she left the kitchen feeling far more cheerful than she had moments earlier. *Take it a day at a time,* Cloris had suggested, and Eve considered that statement as she entered her bedroom, decided it had its merits as she fell back on the bed with a grateful groan.

Following that advice would be easy today, she knew. On Sundays no one did much around the ranch, other than make sure the animals were fed. The first real challenge would come tomorrow. Oh, yes. Because tomorrow she and her business manager, who was now also her lover—as startling as it still seemed—would have to put aside their personal involvement and work together.

Eve suspected that would be a long way from easy.

"ARTIFICIAL INSEMINATION is used more and more for reproducing livestock," Ryder explained as he and Eve viewed one of the ranch's youngest additions on Monday afternoon. Dark eyes set in a small white face studied them in return. They were in the ranch's biggest barn—the very one his father had helped build—in an area set aside for the newest calves and the watchful cows tending them.

Predictably Eve had been eager to learn all there was to know about breeding methods, and Ryder had spent the past several hours doing his best to oblige her with a steady stream of information on everything ranging from age-old basics to the most modern techniques.

"Not so much doing things the, ah, old-fashioned way, hmm?" she murmured.

"In many cases, no." Not that he, himself, didn't prefer the tried-and-true method in that particular department, Ryder thought. In fact, he'd welcome the chance to personally demonstrate his preferences, if they'd been alone with no possibility of interruption. If this wasn't business.

Separating business from pleasure was proving to be a challenge, even more of one than he'd figured. He had to admit that he'd missed this woman last night. Missed holding her, touching her, being held and touched by her. Rationally he knew they couldn't spend every night together. Keeping anything quiet would be impossible under those conditions.

But he *had* missed her, dammit. Even now he wanted to reach out and tug her to him. Instead he jammed his hands in his jeans pockets and told himself to get a grip. He would have Eve back in his bed, or wherever else she would let him have her, soon.

"I take it the new methods apply to breeding horses as well as cattle." Nothing in Eve's matter-of-fact tone said she was having any trouble keeping her own mind on business.

"That's right," Ryder replied, vowing not to let himself get bent out of shape because she could handle the situation better than he could. "It gets the job done with less risk of injury to the animals."

One tawny eyebrow arched. "Injury?"

Ryder nodded. "It happens. The parties involved aren't always particular about the niceties when it comes to..."

"Getting the job done?" Eve supplied at his hesitation.

"Uh-huh."

"But, as you indicated, nature is still allowed to take its course sometimes." A small smile curved her lips. "I'd be willing to bet that huge horse you own is partial to the natural method. Has he sired many colts?"

"His fair share," Ryder replied.

Her smile grew. "The old-fashioned way?"

"Mostly," he admitted, well aware that his answer amused her, as if she knew he considered Lucky a friend and found it hard to deny the stallion the pleasure of mating with a willing mare. It was true, though. And if that was foolish sentimentality on his part, well, hell, then he was foolish.

"I think we're about done with this particular topic," he said, turning away from the stall. He was more than ready to be done with it. They might be discussing livestock, but it still involved sex—a subject he could do without right now.

"Okay," Eve agreed, and walked beside him toward a tall door leading to the outside. "What's next on the agenda?"

He aimed a sidelong glance her way. It was his chance to smile smugly, and he couldn't turn it down, although he didn't let it linger. "We've got branding scheduled first thing tomorrow. Not near as much as we do in the fall, but you'd have the chance to watch. Or help out, if you'd like," he added blandly as her brow knitted. For the first time that day, his companion looked a little off stride. He wouldn't be human, he told himself, if that sight didn't give him some satisfaction.

"We'll, uh, see," she said at last as they left the barn and met a bright blast of late-afternoon sunshine.

He tucked his tongue in his cheek. "If you're going to be busy with other things, I can postpone it for a day or two."

Eve blew out a breath. "No, I don't want you to do that."

"It's no trouble," he assured her gravely. Too gravely, he figured when she suddenly halted in mid-stride and pinned him with narrowed eyes.

"You don't think I can do it, do you?" She pointed a finger straight at his chest and rushed on before he could reply. "Well, you're wrong. I can do it."

He managed to maintain a straight face. "Never said you couldn't," he said mildly.

"I can do it," Eve repeated, and started for his truck

with brisk steps. She hopped in and shut the door with a firm thud that all but said, *You can bet your boots I'll do it.*

Not likely, Ryder concluded as he got behind the wheel. And if she did show up, she wouldn't stay long. Yet, being a smart man, he kept his conclusions to himself.

"I wonder what's in store for dinner," he said in the next breath as he headed for the ranch house. "If Pete makes rice again, I'll be forced to wonder whether it's really him or some alien life-form in disguise."

Eve gave in to a grin and let her irritation fade, deciding that it wouldn't accomplish anything. She'd deal with the far-from-appealing image of a red-hot branding iron tomorrow and prove to Ryder Quinn that she was no coward. She had absolutely no desire to deal with it at all, it was true. But she would. Somehow.

"Rice would be questionable," she replied, using her driest tone, "but if Pete makes stir-fry to go with it, I think we should call 911."

They shared a chuckle as Ryder pulled into the gravel driveway leading to the house. Eve waved at Cloris, who was toting a plump bag full of an infant's seemingly endless requirements as she walked one of the new mothers to her car. A towheaded baby rested in the young woman's arms.

Eve wanted to wrap her own arms around the man seated beside her. Wanted to press her nose in the crook of his neck and take a deep whiff of him. Wanted, yes, to lay her head on his shoulder, not because she was tired, but just to savor a brief rest against him.

None of which she could do. Not now. This was the professional part of their relationship, she reminded herself, as she had repeatedly throughout the day every time she'd had the urge to abandon professionalism and touch him. Not intimately, but with no boundaries, the way a woman felt free to touch a man when they'd been as physically close as two people could get.

As she'd suspected, working—and only working— with Ryder had not been easy. But she had made it through one whole day without revealing that fact. At least she hoped she had.

"How's Max doing?"

His question hauled her back to the present. "Fine, and babbling to beat the band when I popped into the nursery this morning. Theresa should be picking him up shortly. Since she works on the far side of the city, she's usually the last to arrive. Want to stop in and see him for a minute? He'd probably welcome the sight of a man after being coddled by women all day."

Ryder slid her a look. "Will this involve any diaper changing?"

She had to purse her lips to keep a laugh from spilling out. "No."

"All right, I'm game."

Ryder braked to a halt, cut the engine and removed his hat to lay it down on the gearshift. Moments later they entered the house at the back. Several steps down the hall took them past the ranch office to the doorway of the nursery. Going first, Eve started into the room— and immediately froze at the sight of a total stranger.

A stranger who had Max.

She drew in a sharp breath and stared at the young, dark-haired man who held the baby in the crook of one long arm. Surprisingly Max showed no fear. Eyes wide, he calmly viewed the person who held him. But Eve's response was another matter entirely. Her heart began to pound in a harsh beat.

"Well, hello, Kenny," Ryder said from behind her, placing a steadying hand on her shoulder. "Can't say I'm pleased to see you here." His deep voice was soft yet unmistakably edged with steel. "I suggest you put that baby back in his crib, very carefully, and move away from him."

"I'm not going to hurt him," the stranger assured them. Nevertheless, his eyes darted back and forth, as if seeking an escape route.

Ryder dropped his hand and stepped next to Eve. "Then put him down, nice and easy, and we'll talk about it."

The man called Kenny carefully returned Max to his crib and took a step back. Then he made his move. In a flash, he turned on one heel of his scuffed running shoes and headed for the doorway to the side room.

He didn't get far.

Reacting swiftly, Ryder launched himself forward and tackled the intruder to the floor. They rolled around and around, crashing into several of the empty cribs before Ryder wound up on top and kept the younger man pinned with the sheer force of his superior weight. Rising to his knees and still pressing forward with his arms, he stared daggers down at this captive.

"Now we'll talk," he bit out. "I want some answers. Fast."

But it was Theresa who spoke as she entered the room with Cloris a step behind. "Kenny!"

"What's all the ruckus?" Pete asked, following hard on their heels.

Ryder whipped his head around and fixed his gaze on Theresa. "Do you know this guy?"

"Yes, he's..." She hesitated, running her tongue over her lips. "Whatever happened, he didn't mean any harm. Let him go. Please."

Eve moved to put a bolstering arm around the younger woman's shoulders. "We can't do that, I'm afraid. I hate to say it, but this man may have been trying to kidnap Max."

Theresa's brown eyes went huge. "No, you don't understand."

Despite her still-racing heartbeat, Eve tried for a mild tone. "What don't I understand?"

Theresa hesitated again, then let out a quiet sigh. "Kenny Markham is my husband—and Max's father."

Eve couldn't help it. She had to stare. "He's Max's *father?*"

As if to make that perfectly plain, the baby issued a hearty squeal from his crib. He didn't sound a bit disturbed. He just sounded happy.

Chapter Nine

"So, let's start at the beginning," Eve said, viewing the group now seated in the dining room.

Theresa and Kenny, looking very much like a typical late-teen couple in their T-shirts and jeans, occupied chairs on one side of the table. Cloris and Pete faced them on the other. Eve and Ryder sat at opposite ends. As though worn-out from all the excitement, Max nodded sleepily in his mother's arms.

Kenny aimed a solemn, sidelong glance at Theresa. "I'm still not sure this is a good idea."

"We have to trust someone sometime," she replied, meeting his gaze. "And these are good people, I know they are."

"Plus I'm bigger than you," Ryder added, with a steely look at the younger man, "and you're not going anywhere until I hear the whole story."

Kenny released a resigned breath. "Okay, we'll do it your way, since between you and Theresa I don't seem to have much choice. The whole thing started when I came to Arizona from California a few years ago."

"That's not really the beginning," Theresa said gently. "Tell it all."

"Right." Kenny lifted a hand and raked it through shaggy hair that had clearly evaded a barber's scissors for some time. "There's no easy way to say this, so I'll cut to the quick. I was running from the law when I came here. That's the bald truth. And all because a couple of my friends—or I thought they were my friends—robbed a convenience store while I was waiting outside for them in my car. I didn't know what they'd planned to do, didn't know anything until later that night when they showed me the gun they'd used and a wad of bills. That was when I found out they'd pistol-whipped a clerk and emptied the cash register. A witness managed to get my license plate number, though, and that sent the cops looking for me."

"But they didn't find you," Ryder supplied, leaning forward to rest his denim-clad forearms on the table, "because you took off." His curt tone left no doubt as to how he felt on that score.

Kenny squared his shoulders. "Yeah, I did. And I had my reasons, although you might not think much of them. I'd been in trouble before, when I was a young jerk with more attitude than brains. Nothing serious enough to earn me a police record, but enough to make them question anything I had to say. They wouldn't have believed me."

"So you came to Arizona," Eve continued calmly, forestalling Ryder, who looked ready to offer another terse comment. "Where and when did you and Theresa meet?"

"At a rock concert in Tucson not long after I got here." For the first time the barest of smiles curved Kenny's mouth. "We wound up sitting next to each other, and even though she was with a group of her girlfriends, I never gave the rest a second glance after

I started talking to her. She was sixteen. I was eighteen.''

"And we fell in love," Theresa added, "although not right away. We became friends first, I suppose because we had a lot in common. Kenny came from a broken home and I never had much of a home life, myself. I was living in Indian Sands, a town about halfway between Tucson and the Mexican border, with my stepbrother, who's a lot older than I am.'' Her tone turned starkly sober. "He's the only relative I had left after my mother and stepfather had one drink too many at a summer party and decided to cool off with a swim across a usually dry creek flowing fast after a storm.'' She paused. "They never made it to the other side.''

"I'm sorry," Eve murmured.

Theresa shrugged. "I was sorry, too. It was a terrible thing. But, as I said, I never had much of a home life, even when they were around. My mother was usually too busy with other things to give me attention. My stepfather only gave me his last name. No one seemed to care much about me, until Kenny. He followed me to Indian Sands and got a job at one of the gas stations in town. My stepbrother didn't approve, to put it mildly, but we managed to see each other anyway. As time passed, we went from friends to something more. We wanted to get married, but I was underage.'' She paused. "Then I got pregnant, and everything fell apart.''

Pete slapped a hand on the table. "Jeez, boy, what in blazes were you thinking of to get a nice gal like this in trouble?''

"It wasn't all his fault," Theresa countered, instantly on the defense. "Kenny was willing to wait, but I wasn't. It seemed as though I'd been waiting my whole life to be really close to someone, and I couldn't wait any longer.''

Pete's stern gaze remained on Kenny. ''Didn't you ever hear of safe sex?''

Eve had to bite her lip to keep from smiling at that last, grumbled comment. Given Pete's well-displayed aversion to females, at least until recently, she'd had her doubts about his ever having been intimate with a woman. But apparently the man was up to speed in that department. ''I think we're wandering from the point here,'' she said, watching Theresa's young husband squirm and deciding to get him off the hook. Not that he didn't deserve to listen to a few hard words. Being the older of the two, he should also have been the wiser.

Eve looked at Theresa. ''What happened when you learned you were going to have a child?''

''My stepbrother, Lance, was absolutely furious when I told him.''

Eve blinked. ''Lance?''

Theresa's mouth turned down at the corners. ''It's short for Lancelot, if you can believe that. Lucifer, though, would be a better fit.''

''I take it he's not a nice man,'' Cloris tossed in, leaning back in her chair.

''He's as bad as they come,'' Kenny said flatly. ''The creep belongs behind bars.''

''Kenny's right. I suspect Lance has been involved in more than a few crooked deals.'' Theresa dropped her gaze to her now-sleeping son. ''And only someone truly corrupt could hit on the idea he came up with shortly after Max was born.''

Eve frowned. ''What idea?''

"Lance told me that there was a black market for babies…and he wanted to sell Max."

"Oh, my God." Eve was shocked down to her booted toes and knew it showed. "How in the world could anyone do something like that?"

"Greed," Ryder replied grimly. "If somebody is greedy enough, they'll do most anything for money. It really doesn't matter."

"I'm sorry to say I think you're right," Cloris said. "And babies, especially newborns, supposedly bring a high price. It seems that some desperate couples will pay almost anything rather than wait years for a legal adoption."

Ryder flexed his hands. "And the lowest of the low capitalize on it. I'd love to put a fist in that guy's face."

And I'd love to see you do it, Eve thought as she returned her gaze to Theresa. Normally she was opposed to violence, but in this case she'd be more than glad to make an exception. "What did you say to your stepbrother?"

"I wanted to yell at him, scream at him at the top of my lungs. But I didn't. Not after he went on to tell me he'd discovered what had happened in Kenny's past. I already knew about the robbery and believed Kenny was innocent. But Lance threatened to get him sent back to California, where he'd be locked up with hardened criminals. With no money for bail, he'd have to share a cell with them, be at their mercy while he waited for his trial. Lance would make sure that happened, he said, unless I went along with his plans for Max."

Kenny reached out and gently ran a hand down his wife's long, fawn-colored hair. "So, after Theresa told me about it," he said, continuing the story, "we took

Max and slipped out of town late one night. Theresa had just turned eighteen, and we were able to get married once we reached Tucson. But we were sure Lance would be looking for us, so we split up. I left the truck with Theresa and planned to hitchhike up to Phoenix, figuring I could find a way to let Lance know where I was and get him to thinking we had all headed north. He'd be looking for us for a long time in a city that big.''

Kenny gave his head a rueful shake. "That's what I meant to do, at any rate. Instead, I got mugged at a truck stop along the Interstate and wound up in a small-town hospital, flat on my back and mostly out of it for weeks. By the time I was able to make my way back to Tucson, Theresa had left the motel we'd been staying at, and she and Max were nowhere to be found. I did odd jobs to keep me going and finally came across someone at a local charity who remembered them. The woman had no idea where they were, but she mentioned the Creedence Creek and that a nursery had been opened to help single mothers. It seemed worth a try, so I came here—twice, as it turned out—and made it into the house the second time.''

"You're lucky I didn't break your neck," Ryder remarked with blunt directness, folding his arms across his chest.

"No, I'm the lucky one," Theresa corrected, aiming a sudden smile at the man beside her, "because I got my husband back in one piece. When time passed with no word, I was frantic with worry and running out of money. The only thing I knew was that I had to keep Max safe." She looked at Eve. "I'll never be able to thank you enough for allowing me to bring him here."

"I would have helped more if I'd had all the facts."

Eve sat forward and steepled her fingers. "I know you're still worried, but won't your stepbrother have given up searching for you after all this time?"

Once again Theresa's expression sobered. "No. I'm certain of that. Lance has never let anyone get too close to him during all the years I've known him. But I was the closest. I was family. To his way of thinking, I've betrayed him. He won't give up, believe me."

And it would be too risky not to believe, Eve decided. "Then we'll just have to deal with him."

"That won't be easy."

"No, it won't," Kenny said, immediately seconding Theresa and sounding equally convinced of that fact.

"But we can do it." It was as firm a statement as Eve could make.

Theresa's answering sigh was long and heartfelt. "You don't understand."

"What don't I understand?" Eve asked for the second time that day.

"Lance Conroy is a prominent, upstanding resident of Indian Sands. He may be bad to the core, greedy enough to do most anything for money and as crooked as they come—but he's also the local sheriff."

LATER THAT EVENING Eve and Ryder walked together toward the stable closest to the ranch house, their path marked by the silvery light of a nearly full moon. An owl hooted in the distance.

"I'm still having a hard time believing it," Eve said. "A crooked sheriff named Lancelot. It sounds like a cross between a play about King Arthur and a Roy Rogers movie."

"Unfortunately, it also appears to be real." Ryder grimaced. "At least we can make sure Max is safe while he's here. No one will get into the house again unless they're invited. I'll make dead certain of it.''

Eve let out a long breath. ''Thank goodness Theresa and Kenny agreed to stay at the ranch until we can come up with a way to straighten things out.'' A small smile broke through. ''I suspect they're having quite a reunion.''

''In your bedroom.''

''Well, they had to sleep somewhere, and that seemed like the best spot.''

''Even if it means you have to sleep in Cloris's room?''

She shrugged, a casual gesture. ''With two twin beds, we'll make out fine.''

It would be a helluva lot better if you stayed with me, Ryder thought, and didn't bother to say. Eve couldn't take up residence at his place without raising every eyebrow on the ranch. They both knew it.

But he didn't have to like it.

And while he had to admire her enthusiasm for seeing justice done, he was a long way from convinced that he liked the realities that came with it. Taking on a corrupt law-enforcement official could prove to be dangerous. He'd have preferred calling the local police and laying out the whole story, would have pushed for that plan if the probable outcome didn't involve their taking Kenny Markham away in handcuffs and shipping him back to California.

Ryder couldn't blame them, either. Kenny's earlier mistakes had stacked the deck against him, although he seemed to be walking the straight and narrow now. The past would still have to be faced, after this current mess was cleared up, but right now Max needed his father.

And, Ryder concluded with a brief frown as he opened the stable door and switched on the overhead lights, that meant he'd have to do his damnedest to keep the whole bunch of them safe. Including Eve.

Lucky greeted them, bobbing his caramel-colored head as they approached.

"Does he know there's a treat in store for him?" Eve asked.

"You bet. I don't dare come out here after dinner without one. My name would be mud." Ryder retrieved two carrots from a back pocket, handed one to Eve and gave Lucky the other. The horse downed it in three fast gulps.

"Glad to see your appetite hasn't failed you, friend," Ryder told the stallion, then watched as the corners of Eve's scarlet lips curved up.

"He's a cutie."

Ryder winced. "Horses, especially big ones, are never, ever *cute*."

"I'll try to remember that," Eve said with mock gravity. She turned and walked toward the back of the stable. Breaking off pieces of carrot along the way, she fed them to each horse they passed. By the time they reached a stall near the rear, one chunk remained.

Sable issued a whinny and sent her midnight-black mane dancing with a flick of her head as Eve stepped forward. "Glad to see me, are you?"

She offered the last of the carrot, chuckled as the mare delicately nibbled it around the edges before slowly munching and swallowing the whole. "I think my horse has better table manners than your horse."

Ryder recognized the pride in that statement—and the challenge. "But mine comes when I call him."

Turning to face him, Eve lifted her chin. "Sable

comes, too, now." She ran her tongue over her teeth. "Most of the time."

He took a half step forward, stopping when they were nearly chest to chest. "Speaking of time, are we off the clock now?"

"The clock?"

"As in, is the business part of this day over?" All it took was a nod to have him sweeping her up in his arms. He headed for a clean stall with brisk steps.

Eve pressed her lips to his ear. "Does this mean what I think it means?"

"If you think it means there's a roll in the hay in your future," he replied, his voice suddenly husky, "you're right on target."

An objection wouldn't have surprised him, but Eve merely laughed softly, apparently having few qualms about making love in a horse stall. And for that he could only be grateful. Still holding her tightly, he let himself fall backward into a short stack of hay.

"I guess I get to be on top," Eve murmured as she straddled him and tackled the snaps on his shirt.

"Hay isn't all that comfortable," he told her, making quick work of her own snaps "Fortunately, my jeans can stay mostly on." He grinned, wickedly. "Yours have to come off."

She gazed down at him, batted her lashes. "Oh, is that how it works?"

"Mmm-hmm. Guess I'll have to teach you."

"Could be quite an education. Making Love in the Hay 101?"

"What you really need is a demonstration," he said. And he didn't hesitate to proceed to give her one.

EVE GOT THROUGH the branding. Barely, she thought as she made her way to the kitchen afterward. She'd missed breakfast that morning, which was more than fine with her. At the moment she knew her stomach would be far from thrilled with the prospect of food to digest.

At least she'd done nothing to thoroughly disgrace herself during an endless hour in the corral—like putting a stop to the whole thing and launching a new trend in ranching: brandless cattle. The electric branding iron had helped, she couldn't deny. The livestock might not have fully appreciated the lack of anything plucked from a smoldering fire, but she'd breathed a little easier.

And she had done what she'd set out to do, had shown Ryder that she could deal with the harsher realities of ranch life. Somehow that was the most important thing.

"You all right?" Pete asked with a searching look as she walked through the doorway.

Eve let out a long breath. "I'm fine." She made for the refrigerator, deciding that a cold glass of orange juice sounded good and her stomach would probably go along with that judgment.

Pete returned to loading the dishwasher he'd finally started using regularly. "There's oatmeal left. I made up a big batch for those two skinny kids. Got to get some meat on their bones if they're gonna be a proper mom and pop to that baby."

Eve removed a gallon juice carton and filled a small glass full. "You know, Pete, I'm beginning to think you're a softie at heart."

Pete snorted his opinion of that statement. "I'm as tough as boot leather and hard as horseshoe nails." He shut the dishwasher door and turned to view her.

"And—have to admit it, because branding's not for sissies—you've got more grit than I figured you had."

His gruff tone held unmistakable respect, and Eve found she wouldn't have traded what she'd just heard for the most flattering of remarks. To her it was like getting a hard-won medal. "Thanks," she said, and fully meant it. "I'll take that as a compliment."

"Take what as a compliment?" Cloris asked lightly, entering the room with two empty baby bottles in hand.

"Nothing," Pete muttered, his voice suddenly dropping to a growl. "I got to go get groceries." With that terse comment, he stomped his way out.

Eve said, "And I thought we were getting along so well."

"You two are doing fine." Cloris turned on the water with a gush, adjusted it to a gentle flow and rinsed the bottles in the sink. "It's me he's upset with."

Eve set her glass on the counter, thinking that this was a new development. "I had the impression you and Pete were on your way to being buddies."

"So did Pete, until something he didn't expect happened last evening, after Theresa and Kenny turned in for the night, and you and Ryder, ah, disappeared for a while."

Eve ordered herself not to blush. To her relief her cheeks remained cool.

"Anyway," Cloris continued, "Pete suggested, ever so casually, that I go to a softball game with him. I declined."

"Not a fan?" Eve ventured.

"It's un-American not to like baseball." Cloris shut off the water. "I just wanted to make something plain."

Mystified, Eve asked, "And that would be?"

"He's a man. I'm a woman. If he wants us to socialize, he can ask me out on a real date, rather than
just suggesting I tag along with him."

Eve nodded slowly as understanding dawned.
"That's plain enough, all right. Pete's hardly the type,
though, to wine and dine a woman."

"He could be, will be, if he wants to go out with
me again," Cloris said, seemingly unconcerned with
the outcome. Then her expression sobered. "I'd like to
discuss something else, Eve, if you have a minute. Can
you come back to the nursery? I don't want to leave
the babies alone for long."

"Sure," Eve replied easily. She hardly had to be
talked into visiting the nursery. Usually she found herself there at some point in the day, and that was turning
out to be one of her favorite points. She knew it would
be hard to do without those visits if she had to give
them up. Then again, she couldn't imagine that happening. Not now.

Fortunately, she thought, she'd never had any reason
to question the wisdom of her decision to open the day
care center. In fact, as the weeks passed she became
even more convinced how right it was. Some people
might believe she'd been generous, but she knew the
truth. In the end, she was the one who'd reaped the
rewards, and they went far beyond money. Whatever
she gave she got back tenfold every time she watched
one of the young mothers holding her child and saw
the bond forming between them.

The thought had hit her more than once that she and
the woman who had given her life might have shared
many of those same moments if someone had been
there to offer help when help was needed most. Which

was probably a good part of why she had no doubt now that doing what she could to help was right.

What she did doubt, though—and more than a little—was that she'd changed Ryder's mind about setting up the nursery on the ranch. During all the time they'd spent together, he'd never so much as hinted that he might be coming around to her way of thinking, which meant he could well still be of the opinion that she'd made a mistake in turning the ranch into a *Bonanza* for babies, as he'd once put it. But as far as she was concerned, even though she could have done it somewhere else and accomplished the same purpose, she was glad she'd done it here.

"I'm shorthanded today," Cloris explained as she and Eve started for the doorway to the hall. "Anna came down with a cold and didn't want to pass it on. Theresa and Kenny volunteered to help out earlier, but I convinced them to take Max for a walk, since it's such a nice morning. Hopefully it will get their minds off their problems for a while. Which brings me to why I wanted to talk to you. Eve, I'm worried about them. And Max."

"I've been worried, too, I'll admit." Eve entered the nursery a short step behind Cloris. "After I got to bed last night, I stared at the ceiling and racked by brain, trying to come up with something that might help." She paused for a beat. "And I just may have."

Cloris whipped her head around and launched a probing look. "I have to say you don't seem all that happy about it."

"It's more like I've got a distinct hunch that a certain cowboy won't be happy. In fact, my idea may go over like a lead balloon." *Just like my plan to mix babies with ranch business,* she thought as she bent over one of the cribs and found a blue-eyed charmer with blond curls staring up at her. As little girls went, this one was gorgeous.

"Why don't you tell me about your idea?" Cloris suggested, bending over another crib, clean diaper in hand. "Maybe we can join forces and convince that certain cowboy."

It was, Eve decided, worth a try.

UNFORTUNATELY, Ryder reacted exactly as Eve had suspected he would. "You want to do *what?*" he all but roared, locking his gaze with hers as they stood and faced each other across opposite sides of a bright braid rug.

Eve had requested a meeting of all concerned after a casual lunch of soup and sandwiches. Now everyone was gathered in the ranch house living room. For once the large-screen television remained dark and silent, a stark contrast to Ryder's outburst.

"As I said," Eve replied calmly, "I want to go down to Indian Sands, nose around for a day or two and see what I can pick up."

He shook his head in clear disbelief. "And exactly what would you be looking for?"

She lifted one shoulder in a slight shrug. "Anything that strikes me the wrong way. Theresa said her step-brother could well be involved in some shady dealings. Maybe I can come up with something we could use to our advantage."

"Eve—"

She rushed on, determined to finish what she'd started. "If anyone gets curious as to why I'm there, I'll be a fashion designer seeking some local Western color, which wouldn't be much of a stretch."

"But it could turn into a risky situation in a flash," Ryder shot back, "if the wrong person gets wise to you."

"Oh, I hardly think that will happen," Cloris added, leaning in the doorway to the hall to keep one ear out for noises in the nursery. "Who would connect Eve with Theresa?"

Ryder flung up a hand. "Kenny made the connection."

"True," the younger man agreed from his seat on the long sofa next to his wife. Max lay in his arms, rapidly depleting the contents of a bottle. "But that was with the Creedence Creek itself, not the owner."

"Still, the chance for trouble is there," Ryder maintained, his jaw as rigid as his tone, "and small-town law enforcement can wield a lot of power in its own backyard. Anyone who's been stopped for a minor traffic violation in the middle of nowhere and wound up a lot poorer can tell you that."

"I got to agree with Ry," Pete said from his spot in his favorite chair. "Trouble could blow up real fast."

"Then, maybe," Cloris said in her Southern-belle drawl, "Eve should take a big, strong man with her."

Ryder aimed a knowing look at Eve. "So that's where this conversation is headed. And who am I supposed to be on this little jaunt you've dreamed up?"

Eve braced herself, well aware she was on shaky ground. "You could be a model."

For a moment his mouth worked but no sound followed. "A *model*," he got out at last. "A fashion model, you mean. A clothes horse."

"Heavens above," Pete whispered, sounding truly horrified.

Eve knew when to change gears. "All right, you

don't necessarily have to be a model." Although, he
was attractive enough to pull it off, she couldn't help
thinking. A glossy magazine shot featuring him would
have women readers drooling. Which brought up another thought. "You could be a photographer, instead.
That would work, as well, and we'd get some pictures
in the bargain."

Ryder set his teeth. "I am not going to be a model,"
he told her, spacing out the words. "Or a photographer.
Or anything else. Because I am not going. Period. And
neither, so help me, Eve, are you."

She'd intended to remain calm and collected during
this meeting, Eve reminded herself. So much for good
intentions. Shoulders straight, she took a firm step forward. "And how do you propose to stop me if I decide
to go without you?"

He jammed his fists on his hips. "I'll call the police
and give them the whole story."

"No, please, don't do that," Theresa said in a rush,
breaking in.

Ryder's gaze remained on the woman confronting
him. "It's up to Eve."

He wasn't bluffing. Eve was certain of that. "And
what do *you* suggest we do?" she countered.

"I suggest we think before we act. Then, when
we've latched on to a plan that looks like it'll give us
our best shot at getting this whole thing settled, we'll
put it in action—on our territory, where we hold the
upper hand, if we can make it happen that way. Why
tackle a lion in his den, after all, when your chances
are bound to be better almost anyplace else?" He
paused for a beat. "In the meantime, we wait. I know
that's hard, but it's also smart."

Eve tapped a toe on the carpet. It really galled her

to give in, yet what he'd just said made sense, she had to admit. He might be stubborn, he might be high-handed. But, blast it, he was also right.

"Okay," she agreed, just as a phone rang in another part of the house.

"I'll get it," Cloris offered, giving Eve a sympathetic look before she left.

Ryder plowed a hand through his hair, grimly aware that Eve was far from pleased with him. Which was just too bad, he thought, because this was too important to back down. She might be the boss when it came to ranch matters, but this had nothing to do with the ranch. Regardless of whether it pleased her or not, he wouldn't—couldn't—calmly go along with a scheme that had the potential for trouble written all over it. He'd put himself at risk, but not her, and he wasn't changing his mind about that.

Cloris reappeared in the doorway. "The call's for you, Eve."

"Right." Pivoting on one boot heel, Eve turned and walked out of the room, chin held high.

"I think she'd like my head on a fence pole," Ryder said with a rueful twist of his lips, speaking as much to himself as to the others in the room.

"Could be she wouldn't mind kicking another part of you," Pete muttered.

Max gurgled his agreement with that particular remark so heartily that all eyes turned his way. Then he slapped tiny hands together as if to emphasize the point.

Kenny gave the empty bottle to Theresa and looked down at his son. "Well, now that you got that out of your system, do you have anything more to say?"

Max promptly spit out a short stream of milk and followed it with a wide, toothless grin.

Even Ryder had to smile. "That little guy is something else," he said, shaking his head. "You know, the first day we met, he didn't waste any time in peeing on me. He really knows how to make an impression."

His comment produced a round of amused laughter, but it didn't last long. The room quickly grew quiet as Eve came back.

"That was a vice president of the clothing manufacturer I design for," she told them, her now mild tone and matching expression showing little emotion. "They want to meet as soon as possible to discuss a new line I'm proposing."

"The designs you showed me?" Theresa asked, her voice warming with enthusiasm.

"Yes."

"Oh, Eve, that's wonderful." Theresa turned to Kenny. "Eve's come up with an entire new line of clothes, something different from anything she's done before, and it's terrific."

Eve's gaze slowly moved to meet Ryder's. "I have to fly to New York. I won't be staying long, but I have to be at their offices in Manhattan the day after tomorrow."

Chapter Ten

It had happened, as he'd told himself it would, sooner or later. Eve Terry was headed back to the big time. It didn't, Ryder thought, get much bigger than New York.

This time she would be gone just long enough to complete her business. He had no doubt about that. And she'd stay at the ranch until Max and his parents were out of trouble. Even beyond caring about them, she would view their welfare as a personal commitment, and she would see it through. He knew her well enough to be convinced on that score.

But how long would Eve stay after everything settled down? That was the question. How long would ranch life continue to satisfy her after she'd been pulled back, even briefly, into the busy, bustling world she'd come from?

A world, Ryder had to admit, one stubborn part of him still told him she belonged in.

Once he would have been champing at the bit for her to leave for good. Now he was a long way from sure how he felt. All he knew for certain was that things had gotten about as complicated as they could get.

He was damn sure of that.

"How many bags do you figure she's packing?" Pete asked from his seat next to Ryder on the back porch stairs. Since there were only three steps, both men had their long legs bent and the flat of their boots firm on gravel. Earlier they'd shared a quiet dinner during which Eve had mostly pushed a plateful of food around before leaving to get ready for the flight she'd booked for the following day.

"One or two would be enough for a short trip, I suppose." Although that might be on the conservative side, Ryder reflected, considering all the baggage she'd lugged with her to Arizona.

"Told her I'd take her to the airport tomorrow," Pete tossed in. "I got an errand to do in town, anyway."

Ryder lifted a brow at that news, well aware that his companion normally avoided the city and its noise and traffic like the plague. "Looking to buy something you can't find in the local supermarket or hardware store?" It was the only reason he could think of for Pete to put himself through the ordeal.

Pete harrumphed. "Now that you mention it, I thought I'd scout around for a new jacket. That's not saying my old leather standby doesn't have some long years left," he added hastily. "Still, it might not be a bad idea to have something lighter that doesn't weigh a body down in the hot weather, don't you think?"

Ryder nodded, wondering what in blazes was going on. The man beside him had never shown any interest in clothes, other than to keep his own neat and clean. Most of Pete's Wranglers had been washed so often they were in danger of turning white.

"And that's not saying a man has to dress up," Pete added, "even if some highfalutin restaurants have snooty rules about it." He paused long enough to swat at a pesky fly buzzing by. "And talking about restaurants—"

"Were we talking about restaurants?" Ryder broke in, aiming a curious glance Pete's way.

"'Course we were. You got to pay better attention, Ry."

"Sorry, it's hard to keep up sometimes." Ryder did his best to look suitably chastened. "What about restaurants?"

"Well, I figure that some of them must have pretty decent chow—I mean the ones people pay good money to go to, not a diner by the side of the road."

"The food can be well worth the price," Ryder agreed. "But other things can be tricky. I've been in places where it's hard to even know what's listed on the menu, because it's written in French or Italian."

Pete's jaw dropped. "*Eye-talian.* How's a body supposed to order anything?"

"You point and pray you like what you get." Which was what he'd done, Ryder remembered, during his first visit to one of Tucson's finest. "And then there's the question of wine."

"Jumping Jehossaphat! You mean a man has to deal with *wine* if he wants to take a woman out?"

Ryder began to get a glimmer. "We're not talking about any particular man and woman, are we?"

All at once Pete seemed to find something fascinating to view in the distance. "'Course not. This is one of those, er, just-suppose situations."

"Uh-huh. Well, just supposing a man wound up in a fancy restaurant and was faced with a wine list, he could always ask the wine steward or the waiter to recommend something. Then all he'd have to do is nod gravely, as if he actually knew what they were talking about, and eventually agree with their suggestion."

"But does he have to drink the stuff?"

Ryder's lips twitched as he shook his head. "Not necessarily. He can order wine for the lady he's escorting, if that happens to be her preference, and maybe, ah, a good whisky for himself."

Pete released a long whoosh of sound and looked so relieved that Ryder had to grin, suddenly feeling better than he had for hours. Good enough, he decided, to let the devil take over for a minute.

"But the most important thing," he said slyly, "is not to tuck your napkin under your chin, Pete. I'm dead sure Cloris would take exception to that."

EVE PULLED UP to the house on the hill at just past ten o'clock. It was late by ranch standards, but she'd hoped to find a light still on at Ryder's place. To her disappointment only darkness met her gaze.

And what now? she wondered, thinking that the man who'd brought her here might not appreciate being hauled out of bed, especially after their earlier run-in. He'd said little at dinner, even less than she had, and she'd been quieter than usual herself. In her case she'd been mostly lost in thoughts of how much had changed in a brief space of time.

Only days ago she had no doubt that she would have been overjoyed at being invited to discuss what could be a tremendous opportunity to add a whole new dimension to the Sassy Lady line. More than the money she'd earn from her designs, it would be a labor of love, a chance to broaden the scope of her very own creation. Yes, less than a week earlier, she would have been thrilled by the possibilities and ready to face the challenge of making it happen.

But now, Eve had to admit, she found herself less than happy at the prospect of leaving, even for a short time. Rationally, she knew it made sense to go to New York, make her pitch, hopefully convince the manufacturer to proceed, and return as soon as possible. After all, as things stood, nothing earthshaking was likely to happen during the few days she'd be away.

And Max and his parents would be safe at the ranch while she was gone. She wouldn't have so much as considered going unless she believed that. Still, she would miss them, Eve knew, would miss the sight of Theresa's too-long-absent smile finally on display, and watching the way Kenny talked ''baby talk'' to his newfound son when he thought no one else was around. And she'd never be able to not miss Max and seeing how he viewed the world through those wide, curious eyes.

She'd miss hearing Cloris's lazy drawl, too, and even the sound of Pete's gruff grumbling. And she knew without a doubt she would miss the ranch.

But most of all she would miss Ryder. There was no denying the stark truth of that. And she couldn't leave without seeing him, she decided, still studying the dark house. If that meant getting him out of bed, she'd just have do it.

Eve shut down the engine, switched off the headlights and hopped from the Jeep. Seconds later she was crossing the porch when a small overhead light blinked on and the front door opened to reveal Ryder standing there. Although he looked fully alert, the quick glance she dropped down his body found him wearing no more than unsnapped jeans, as if he'd just pulled them on.

"I thought you might have been sleeping," she said as she walked toward him.

"No, I was awake." His gaze held a probing glint as it met hers. "I heard you coming up the road." He moved back from the door. "Come on in."

Accepting the invitation, Eve couldn't help but recall the last time she'd crossed this threshold and what had followed, that memorable night spent in a bed the size of Montana. But she couldn't start thinking along those lines—not now, she told herself. She had something to say, and there was no point in beating around the bush.

She turned to fully face the man standing beside her and linked her fingers behind her back. "I've come to eat crow. Not a lot," she added, "just my fair share, because I was wrong to let my temper take over this afternoon." She blew out a breath. "And you were right about how moving too quickly could be a mistake."

One dark eyebrow rose in response to that news. "But..." He let the word trail off, as if he knew she had more to say. And she did.

Her chin went up. "But I wasn't the only one at fault. You had every right to disagree with my idea, but you didn't have to get so, ah, *male* about it."

All at once his grin broke through. "Sorry. Every now and then my *maleness* tends to get the better of me."

"Humph. Must be all that testosterone." Despite her grumbling, Eve found herself relaxing for the first time in hours.

Ryder's grin widened as he folded his arms across his chest. "Sometimes I do put it to good use."

She couldn't argue with that, and also had no intention of giving him any satisfaction by agreeing. He wasn't off the hook yet, she thought. He just didn't know it.

"I have to say you could be a model," she told him, her tone perfectly sincere, more than suspecting that would wipe the grin off his face. When it did, she fought back a grin of her own and decided she was enjoying herself. "The agencies would fall all over themselves trying to sign you up, believe me. Man of the West. You'd be a sensation."

He winced, then scowled. "I'd rather be stripped naked and staked out over an anthill."

And now she had to laugh.

Instantly green eyes narrowed as he took a quick step forward, closing the gap between them. "You're putting me on."

She smiled a satisfied smile. "Maybe the next time we have a disagreement, you won't be so *male*."

His eyes took on a gleam as he reached for her. "Maybe. Then again, I could also put it to good use right now."

She slid her hands up his chest and wrapped her arms around his neck. "You certainly could."

Whatever she might have expected, it wasn't his suddenly solemn look. "What time does your flight take off tomorrow?"

Although her smile faded, her gaze didn't falter. "Midmorning. A little before ten."

"Will you stay with me tonight?"

"Yes," she replied without hesitation. It was exactly what she wanted. Her heart, as if it agreed completely, sped up in anticipation.

His grip tightened as he pressed her closer. Bending

his head, he brought his lips to her ear. "Tonight I won't rush things. I plan on taking my time with you." The warm brush of his breath only made her heart beat faster. "I'm going to pleasure you, and keep on pleasuring you. That's a promise."

Anticipation turned to sheer need as she went damp at his words and all they implied. "I'm not sure I can wait."

"I'm the one who has to wait," he told her. "You don't." He slid one large hand between them and cupped her. "You don't have to wait a minute." With that, his fingers pressed against her, the formfitting jeans she wore no barrier at all to the tempo he established with quick, clever strokes.

Eve's breath caught in her throat. "Don't you think we should, ah, go to bed?"

"Not yet."

"Oh." Now her breath came hard and fast and faster still. "Oh, goodness gracious."

"Let go, Eve," he urged, his own breath turning harsh as he redoubled his efforts. "Just let go."

And instants later she did, shuddering with the force of her release. He held her close through the aftershocks, held her up when she would have sagged as he pulled away.

"Now we'll try the bed."

Within seconds she was in his arms, and they were headed down the hall. She nuzzled her nose into the crook of his neck. "I probably shouldn't admit this, but I like it when you carry me."

Ryder's lips curved in response. He now knew the woman he held well enough to know that admission wouldn't have come easy. "Guess that's one thing we won't disagree on," he replied softly, "because I like carrying you."

He set her on her feet when they reached the bed. Then he switched on the bedside lamp and undressed her with care, touching as he chose to, looking his fill as silky skin was slowly revealed. She made no effort to hide anything from him as she had on their first night together, he couldn't help but notice, even as he took full advantage of her willingness to stand beside the bed while he tasted at his leisure and as he pleased.

And it pleased him to taste more than a little. A lot more. At last he let her slip between the sheets, then followed and stretched out beside her.

"You're wearing too many clothes," Eve murmured, running a hand down his body.

He caught her wrist, halting her progress as she reached his waist. "I'm keeping my pants on, for the moment." He raised her hand, pressed his lips to her palm. "And you have to keep your hands to yourself for a while."

One corner of her mouth kicked up. "Can't take it?"

He shook his head. "You'd have me ready to explode in no time," he admitted, "and I'm not going to let that happen, not until I've done exactly what I said I'd do."

With that he captured her mouth for a long, deep kiss that had them both gasping for air by the time it eventually ended. From there, inch by inch, his mouth blazed a trail down to her breasts and lingered at their pebbled tips, until her hips began to move against his in unmistakable invitation. Then his hands got busy and his fingers found her once again.

Ryder relished the soft moan signaling Eve's release

moments later. Satisfaction surged inside him at the sound. But it wasn't enough. Not nearly enough.

So he kept right on going.

Using his mouth this time, he gradually coaxed her to the peak again and nudged her over, knowing that for the past endless minutes the woman in his bed had thought of nothing and no one but him. And whatever happened in the future, she would not forget him, he vowed. Why he suddenly found that so important was beyond him. He only knew it was.

Moving in haste now, Ryder kicked off his jeans, applied protection as quickly as he could manage and covered Eve's body with his own. "Look at me," he said as he pressed forward. Gray eyes drifted open to meet his gaze.

"You won't forget the way we fit together, Eve. No matter what, you won't be able to forget it...or me."

And then he slipped inside, hauled in a breath at the sheer, gut-wrenching marvel of it. Finally giving in to his body's raging needs, he swiftly established the rhythm, let it build with each thrust, and then pushed it to new heights as Eve moaned again and gradually began to meet his increasingly rapid movements with her own.

"I don't think I can...do it again," she said on a ragged sigh.

"You can," he countered in a raspy whisper. "You will."

And, a few pounding heartbeats later, she did. He felt the inner tremors, felt himself start to shake as reality swiftly faded to a haze, until all that mattered was a man and woman locked in a vital search for fulfillment. Seconds later his low growl mingled with Eve's quiet cry as he let go completely and lost himself in what they had found together.

EVE WOKE UP in the middle of the night to the comforting feel of Ryder's arms wrapped tightly around her and the sound of his strong, steady breaths. Slowly she opened her eyes and met the murky darkness blanketing the room. Shimmering starlight slanting through the windows provided just enough light to make out the chiseled features of the sleeping man who held her. The sight quickly sparked a vivid memory of something he'd told her with almost fierce conviction.

You won't be able to forget.

And she couldn't deny it, not even to herself, well aware that she would never forget how he had so single-mindedly made love to her, as though she were the only woman in the world, how he'd brought her to the brink of what she'd thought was the limit of her capacity for pleasure and hurled her far beyond it. No, she would never forget the past few hours. And she would never, ever forget *him.* She was as sure of that as the sun's eventual rise in the east.

A woman didn't forget a man she'd fallen head over heels in love with.

Eve drew in a soft breath, staring straight ahead—straight into dark-lashed eyes concealed in sleep—as she confronted the truth of something that suddenly demanded to be acknowledged. She was in love with Ryder Quinn, deeply and completely. Anything she'd felt for any other man paled in comparison. And there was no going back. She was certain of that, as well.

Strangely enough, her heart wanted to rejoice, even though other parts of her knew it had just put itself at grave risk. Oh, foolish heart, she thought. It'll be your own fault if you wind up in pieces. Which it would be—because, to be fair, the man she studied had never given her any reason to expect more between them than what they had now.

And the last thing, the very last thing, she needed was to give him any hint of how her heart had just thrown caution to the wind. To do so would be light-years beyond foolish.

All at once those dark-lashed eyes slanted open. They blinked a few times before Ryder asked, "Why aren't you asleep?"

"I had things on my mind," she replied with total honesty.

He ran a hand down her spine, the rough flat of his palm on her far softer skin reminding her of the undeniable differences between them. "I'll be real disappointed," he said, "if you weren't thinking of me."

She arched her back. "I guess I shouldn't disappoint you."

"So you were thinking of me?"

"Mmm-hmm." *And that's all I intend to say on that subject.* "It occurs to me," she said instead, "that I got a lot of attention earlier." She tangled her legs with his. "I believe you deserve some, too."

"Does that mean you plan on having your way with me?" he asked, lifting a brow. "Please say yes," he added, fervently enough to make her smile.

Rather than responding, she wiggled a hand down between them and closed her fingers around a very basic part of him.

He sucked in a surge of air. "I guess that answers my question."

She began, then, to make love to him in earnest, and she did it gladly. Eagerly. Inventively. Over and over.

"How am I doing?" she asked much, much later, lifting her head from where it had been resting, far down his body.

"I think my eyes are permanently crossed."

"Mmm." She pressed a kiss to a muscled thigh. "Maybe if I start all over again, I can uncross them."

He groaned. "Either that or you'll kill me."

"Maybe we should just get to the grand finale," she murmured, inching her way up.

"I hate to say this," he remarked with a rueful sigh, "but the final act may be over." He raised a limp hand, let it drop. "Much as I'd liked to, I'm not sure I can...do it again."

"Trust me," Eve told him softly, feathering her lips over his, "you can."

And he did. But not alone. This time, he took her with him all the way.

HE WALKED HER to the Jeep at just past dawn, one long arm slung around her shoulders. Once again Ryder wore jeans and nothing else. Eve had no choice but to wear the shirt and jeans she'd come in, more of her clothing that had spent a night on the floor. Her reluctance to leave the ranch had only grown during the course of that night. Now, she thought, she'd be leaving behind the man she had tumbled into love with, however unwise the ways of her heart.

Then again, spending some time alone might actually be good, she had to admit. Maybe it would help her come to terms with the fact that Ryder might never feel what she felt now. And maybe she wouldn't miss him as much as she thought she would. Maybe.

Ryder slipped his arm from Eve's shoulders as they reached the Jeep. She turned and faced him, hoping no trace of her wayward heart lurked in her gaze. "I'll be back on Sunday afternoon," she said with all the casualness she could muster. "I've already booked a return flight." Since this was Wednesday, that would give her three full days, not counting travel time, to do what she was setting out to do.

"I'll pick you up at the airport," he told her, the even tone of his voice showing as little emotion as her own.

"That sounds good." She gave him details on the flight and time.

"I hope the trip goes well," he added. "There'll probably be plenty for you to do."

"It'll be busy," she agreed. "I have several meetings scheduled, starting with the marketing department. If I can get them onboard with what I'd like to do, I'll have a good shot at convincing the ultimate decision makers."

"You'll convince them," he said with assurance. "And you'll have a great time, being back in the thick of things."

Although his voice remained bland, something flickered in his gaze, something that told her his last statement held a wealth of meaning. "I don't especially want to be in the thick of things, as you put it. I'd rather be here at the ranch." *With you.*

He shrugged. "If you say so."

All at once it hit her right between the eyes and had them narrowing in sheer exasperation. Even after all the time she'd spent here, all she'd accomplished, all she'd learned, all she'd handled—including a crash course in cattle branding—Ryder still suspected a bit of life in the fast lane might have her leaving.

Not for a few days, but for good.

"I am coming back this weekend, no matter what."
She spaced out the words, emphasizing each in turn as
her gaze bored into his. "And I am *staying*."

But she had better make tracks right now, she told
herself, while she could still manage to keep from hiss-
ing at him. Despite everything, the last thing she
wanted was to leave with a quarrel hanging between
them.

Reaching up, Eve cupped the sides of Ryder's face,
prickly with a night's growth of dark beard, and kissed
him hard enough to rattle every one of their combined
teeth. "I'll see you on Sunday," she said as she
abruptly pulled away. Then she turned and hopped into
the Jeep. In a flash she was headed down the hill. At
the moment, as much as she cared about him, she was
more than ready to put some distance between them.

RYDER HEADED BACK to the house considering what
Eve had told him before she'd left in such a tearing
hurry. She'd meant what she'd said. He was sure of
that. She truly believed she was ready to stay at the
ranch for good. Looking into those gray eyes and seeing the formidable determination he'd witnessed there,
he was almost ready to believe it himself. Almost.

What he needed in order to truly believe, he recognized, was to hear her say it one more time, with the
same conviction, after she came back. Until then he
could only believe that anything could happen. Reasonable or not, that was how he felt.

*And how will you feel if she does wind up leaving,
Quinn? Or how about if she stays?*

The inner questions still rang in his mind as he entered the house. "I flat-out don't know," he finally

muttered in response. "It's all gotten too damn complicated."

He'd be better off trying to figure out how to solve a problem that had a chance of being solved, he decided. He made for the bathroom, intent on a shave and shower, thinking that once Eve's bring-a-man-to-his-knees-with-ease perfume no longer clung to his skin and clouded his brain, maybe he could come up with a way to help Theresa and Kenny permanently put their troubles behind them.

Maybe.

It dogged him throughout the day, and he was still searching for a stubbornly elusive solution to the young couple's problems when Pete joined him on the back porch of the ranch house that evening.

"I got shooed from the kitchen," Pete told him. "Those two youngsters insisted on tackling the supper dishes."

Ryder looked up from his seat on the top step and thumbed back his wide-brimmed black hat. "They need to feel they're doing their part."

"I know it. That's why I didn't make a fuss." Pete sank down beside him and launched a sidelong look. "Did I happen to mention that, even with all the blasted traffic, I got the boss to the airport in plenty of time for her flight?"

"You said that a short while ago, as I recall." And where was this headed? Ryder wondered. He hadn't missed the more than one speculative glance Pete had tossed his way during dinner.

"She didn't look happy when I dropped her off," Pete continued, disclosing that bit of information for the first time.

Most likely, she wasn't too happy with me, Ryder

reflected silently. Something else he recalled all too well was the edgy taste of frustration in Eve's last, bone-rattling kiss. "She probably perked up when she got to Manhattan," he said, deliberately keeping his tone light. "There's a lot to do and see. From her hotel room window alone, there's bound to be dozens of skyscrapers in sight." Not that he, himself, had actually seen them, not with his own eyes. Even his parents, as much as they'd traveled, had never made it to New York City.

Pete snorted. "Looking at buildings seems like a waste of time to me. If a body wants to see something tall, they can look at the mountains." He paused for a beat. "She likes the mountains, you know. Sometimes she'll sit at the supper table and just stare out the window at them."

Ryder nodded his agreement. He'd caught Eve doing that himself.

"Tell you what I think, Ry." Pete slapped a hand on his knee. "I think it wouldn't be so danged awful if she didn't get tired of this place."

That made Ryder's mouth curve, as brief and wry as the smile was. "She may not." And then again... No, he told himself. He wasn't getting into that now.

"Did you buy a new jacket?" he asked, abruptly switching subjects.

Pete slanted him another look. "Yep."

"Check out any restaurants while you were in town?"

"A few."

"Plan on making any dinner reservations?"

"Maybe."

Ryder was pursing his lips to foil another smile, this

one wholly amused, when the back door opened and Kenny stepped out.

"Am I interrupting anything?"

"Not much," Ryder replied easily. "Come on and join us." Both men scooted to one side to make room for a third person on the top step.

Kenny sat down next to Pete, folding his lanky body and stretching his long legs out in front of him. "Max is asleep, and Theresa and Cloris are talking about hairdos."

Pete made a face. "Well, you sure as shootin' did the right thing, coming out here. A man's got to have some male conversation."

"Wish I could be better company." Kenny's dark eyes revealed his worry. "I just hope that Theresa's stepbrother gets what's coming to him, and soon. Regardless of what happens here, though, I know I have to go back to California and straighten things out there."

"That, at least, might not be so hard," Ryder said. "It's occurred to me that your so-called friends could have gotten into more, and even deeper, trouble after you left. They were headed down that path, and may be behind bars now."

Kenny mulled that over as he brushed a lone mosquito from the pocket of the checked shirt Cody had lent him along with a pair of Wranglers. Only wellused canvas shoes belied his new ranch-hand image. "Yeah, they could be in jail," he agreed. "But how would that help me?"

"To my mind," Ryder explained, "the California authorities would be more likely to believe your story because you stayed out of trouble after the robbery, even held a steady job until recently. They could—I'm not saying they will, but they could—take all that into account and decide not to prosecute. But no matter what,'' he added firmly, ''I'll make sure you have a good lawyer to represent you.''

''Thanks.'' Kenny held out a hand, reaching around Pete. ''And I plan on paying you back for whatever the lawyer charges, down to the last penny.'' His tone was just as firm and edged with pride.

''We'll consider it a loan,'' Ryder said as their hand-shake was completed. ''The important thing is not to worry about what may happen down the road. It's the here and now that needs everything we can give it.''

''Ry's right,'' Pete tossed in. ''There's plenty for us to handle.''

Ryder's jaw tightened. ''And if I could find a way to do it, we'd get it all handled before Eve got back on Sunday.'' Because she wouldn't be content to stay on the sidelines, he knew. Eve would want to be fully involved, right up to her silky-skinned neck.

''She wouldn't like being left out,'' Pete declared with certainty.

''That doesn't concern me,'' Ryder said, and meant it. ''The bottom line is that she'd be safer away from here.''

''But before we can do anything, we have to figure out how to get the better of a big-shot, bad-guy sher-iff.'' Kenny heaved a sigh. ''I mean, who could take a man like that down?''

Pete lifted one shoulder in a shrug. ''Probably some-body as big and bad as he is.''

Something in those words captured Ryder's atten-tion. ''You just may have a point there,'' he said softly. *Big and bad.* The phrase repeated in his mind as he gazed into the distance. Then his thoughts began to race. Silent seconds passed before he surged to his feet, whipped around and looked down at the two still seated on the step.

''By God, Pete, I think you've done it.''

Chapter Eleven

Pete blinked. "What in blazes did I do?"

"Said something that finally got me headed in the right direction, I do believe." Ryder planted his fists on his hips. "*Big and bad.* Those were your words, and that's exactly what we have to deal with here. A crook with influence, not the common variety. It makes sense that to bring him down, we need someone with even more influence on our side. Someone whose word carries a lot of weight."

"I reckon our boss knows some big shots," Pete said.

"Only the state attorney general," Ryder replied dryly. "And Brad Pitt."

"Brad who?"

"Never mind, Pete. It doesn't matter who Eve knows. I want to keep her out of this completely, if I can manage it. So, the question is, who's the most influential person *we* know?"

They thought about that for a moment, and both came up with the identical answer at the same time. "Hank Swenson."

Kenny looked from one to the other. "Who's Hank Swenson?"

"Someone at the top of the heap when it comes to real estate brokers in this part of the country," Ryder said. "He handled the sale when Eve bought the ranch. He's as shrewd as they come, honest to the hilt and he has some friends in very high places."

Pete acknowledged that with a firm dip of his head. "Hank looks like a strong wind might blow him over, but deep down he's tough enough to tackle a tornado. And he's told me more than once about driving whatever model Cadillac he had at the time up to Phoenix to have lunch with the governor."

Kenny's mouth fell open. "Of Arizona?"

"You bet, youngster."

"So we'll call Hank, and if we can convince him to help us, he'll be our 'big guy,'" Ryder summed up. "But we need a bad guy, too, and I doubt anyone would believe Hank in that role." Ryder tapped a booted foot on gravel, stopped moments later as another thought hit him. "Then again, I may have come up with the perfect person for the part."

Pete tilted his head. "Who?"

Ryder flashed a grin. "Me."

"You!" His companions shot that back in unison.

"The *bad* guy?" Pete tacked on.

"Why not?" Ryder reached up and tugged his Stetson down low over his forehead. "After all, I've got the black hat."

ON SATURDAY AFTERNOON, Eve was pleased to be back in the Southwest and on her way to the ranch. No one had picked her up at the Tucson airport, but only because no one had answered when she'd phoned to report her arrival, a day earlier than planned. Calling that morning from New York, after her snap decision to catch the next flight out, would have been the smart thing, she supposed. Then again, the time difference would have meant hauling someone out of bed, and she'd actually never expected that with all the people staying at the ranch house at the moment, no one would be around. Even the phone at Ryder's place had just kept on ringing.

Not that it really mattered, because getting a taxi had proved to be no problem. In fact, the driver's bored eyes had taken on a sharp gleam at the knowledge that his passenger would be paying a healthy fare. Eve chuckled at the memory, glancing out a side window as they sped down the highway.

"Sounds like you're glad to be in sunny Arizona." The driver's gaze met Eve's in the rearview mirror.

"I am," Eve told the middle-aged man. "I live here."

He nodded wisely. "I figured you might from the outfit you're wearing."

Eve glanced down at the pale-pink embroidered shirt and khaki jeans she'd chosen for the trip back. As usual, they were her creations, more of the Sassy Lady line. A line that was about to be broadened in a big way, she thought, reflecting on the success of her mission. Western-style business wear for women would be sold in department stores across the country before too long, and the marketing people, bless them, had already come up with a gem of a tag dedicated to the new designs: The Lady Means Business.

To celebrate, Eve had treated the whole talented bunch to dinner the evening before, after concluding a series of meetings Friday afternoon. Her initial plan as of last night was to use an unexpectedly free Saturday to reacquaint herself with a city she'd visited several

times and had always found exciting. Instead, the realization had hit her, barely after waking at an early
hour, that what she really wanted was to get back to
the Creedence Creek as quickly as a high-flying jet
could get her there. New York was a great city, but
she had no wish to stay there, not even for one more
day.

She wanted to go home.

So here she was, headed to where she wanted to be,
and it wasn't long before a wide view of the ranch
summoned a smile. It looked, she thought, much the
same as it had at her very first sight of it. Old and
rooted to the past.

"Do you like living all the way out here?" the driver
asked as he pulled onto the road leading to the ranch.

Eve's smile grew to a grin. "I love living here."

"Guess that's what matters," he said with a to-each-
his-own lift of a shoulder. "I'm a city person, myself."

"So was I," Eve replied, "but things have
changed."

As they drove closer, she didn't miss the fact that
only her Jeep was parked in its usual spot. Everyone
must still be out, she concluded, and soon found that
to be the case as she walked through a quiet house with
her two pieces of luggage in hand, her footsteps echoing down the hall.

Eve poked her head into the nursery for a moment,
not because she really expected to discover anyone
there, but because it always cheered her to see the circus characters cavorting on the walls. What did the
babies think of it all? she wondered as her gaze stopped
to rest on the empty cribs and the hand-lettered signs
above them.

Maybe LeighAnn, the little charmer with the sunny

curls, would find the dancing bears a fascinating sight, while Stevie with the quickest grin of the whole bunch just might see himself perched on the back of a prancing purple elephant. Some of the other babies might prefer people—or as close as a riot of clowns chasing each other and managing a few handstands along the way fitted that description.

And Max... Well, maybe he'd be more interested in the pink puffs of cotton candy decorating the borders near the ceiling. Filling his tummy seemed high on Max's priority list, Eve had to admit, and she couldn't help wondering where he was right now.

Still, it didn't occur to her to worry as she left the nursery. No matter where everyone was, they were fine. Ryder would make sure of it, she knew without a doubt.

Eve sighed a heartfelt sigh. Lord, she had missed him. As frustratingly hardheaded as he could be on occasion, she had missed him, badly. And she missed him now, Eve acknowledged, entering the bedroom she and Cloris shared. Even as tired as she was, she missed him. Badly.

One glance at the bed she'd been using before she left was all Eve needed to decide to unpack later. She shut the bedroom door, tugged off short-heeled boots better suited to walking than riding, and stretched out with a soft groan. She'd concluded that traveling long distances at high speed could well be the world's most exhausting activity. She would take a dawn-to-dusk horse ride over jetting around any day. Which had her thoughts turning to her own horses, then centering on Sable, and that in turn had her thinking about something she wanted to buy.

Eve's last thought as she drifted into sleep was the

pleasing image of an elegant black mare all decked out in a shiny new saddle.

THE IMAGE filling Eve's mind as she slowly surfaced from her nap had nothing to do with horses. Rather, two humans were getting as close as two humans could get, and that was close, indeed. It was as steamy a dream as she had ever had, and the featured players were none other than a certain cowboy and her very own self.

Eve's pulse still raced, her blood still hummed, as her eyes blinked open. Good grief, she thought, blowing out a breath. Her body was certainly missing Ryder at the moment. What was that old saying? *There's never a man around when you truly need one.* Yes, that was it.

And this was definitely one of those times, Eve told herself as she sat up. Right now, she'd have to settle for a bracing shower to get herself back together. But first her thirst demanded something cold to drink.

Eve crossed the room in her stocking feet and opened the door. All was quiet as she began to silently make her way down the hall. Then the sound of someone speaking, loud enough to be heard, yet too distant to make out any more, drifted toward her. It seemed to come from the ranch office, so Eve made a quick detour and started that way.

She was steps from where the door stood open when a deep male voice she'd didn't recognize had her quickly stopping in her tracks.

"So I guess you're ready to do business, Quinn."

"I am." And that voice belonged to Ryder, Eve had no trouble recognizing.

"I had you checked—up, down and sideways—before I came here," the other man said.

Ryder's low chuckle held no hint of concern. "Somehow I figured you would, Conroy."

Conroy. Eve's breath caught in her throat. Could Ryder actually be talking to—

"Being sheriff has its advantages."

Eve swallowed, hard. As unbelievable as it seemed, Lancelot Conroy, Theresa's crooked-sheriff stepbrother, was just feet away.

"I expect you put the position to good use," Ryder remarked wryly.

"Let's just say I do my best," Lance Conroy didn't hesitate to reply.

The sly satisfaction in his tone made Eve's skin crawl. At that moment she would have liked nothing better than to walk into the office, lift an arm and smack the smug smirk she was sure she would find there off his face. But she couldn't, reason told her. All she could do was stand where she was, hands clenched at her sides.

"Okay," Ryder said. "Let's cut to the quick. You've seen your stepsister's belongings with your own eyes, so you know she's been staying at the ranch."

"Yeah, I don't doubt she's been hiding out here, along with her kid and the young punk she's so crazy about. Question is, where are they now?"

Again Ryder chuckled, low in his throat. "Before we get to that, there's the little matter of how much you'll pay for the information."

The figure tossed out so carelessly had Eve's eyes widening even as paper rustled. Not that she believed Ryder actually intended to take the money. She didn't believe that for a second. No, he was up to something else entirely, she was sure. She just didn't know exactly what.

"Sounds fair," Ryder replied mildly, "although I suspect you'll get a lot more for the baby."

"Maybe, but what I'm willing to pay—and that's in cold cash—will probably get you what you want." Lance Conroy's brief laugh held little humor. "I've got you pegged, Quinn."

"Do you?" Though he kept his tone bland, Eve caught the hint of challenge and could all but see Ryder cocking an eyebrow as he voiced that question.

"You can bet the fancy suit you're wearing that I do," Theresa's stepbrother replied. "Like I said, I checked you out. Seems as though, from all I've found out, you've been as honest as the day is long up till now. But even honest men have their price, and it's not always money. I know yours."

"And what would that be?"

"The Creedence Creek. That's your price," Lance Conroy said flatly. "You came from nothing, worked long and hard, and eventually made it to the top spot here. But you wanted more. Oh, yeah. From everything I've learned, you wanted to own this place, wanted it bad. And you almost had it. Almost. Until a pampered city broad bought it right out from under you."

Pampered city broad. Now Eve wanted to aim a hard kick at what she was certain would be a remarkably unattractive male backside.

"That's why you need the money, Quinn," the male in question continued. "You need to sweeten the pot so you can buy her out and send her packing."

"Well, well," Ryder said. "I guess you do have me figured out, Conroy,"

No, he doesn't, Eve told herself, positive of that, although she was far less sure of many things. Whatever was happening, though, and regardless of what happened next, she knew she had to stay as still as a statue and let Ryder play it out. She had to do that, no matter what.

But suddenly she couldn't. Not when a long, beefy arm came out of nowhere from behind her, caught her around the waist and picked her straight up in one rapid motion.

Before Eve could do more than blink, she was all but hurled through the doorway and into the ranch office. Luckily she landed on her feet, although she had to bend her knees and put one hand on the floor to keep her balance. Casting a swift look around her, the first thing she saw was a short stack of green treasury bills in large denominations fanned out over the new rust-colored rug she'd chosen for the room.

The next thing she saw as she raised her gaze was the business end of a long, shiny pistol trained squarely on her.

And then she took in the sight of the tall, blond-haired man who held it, discovered that she absolutely had to stare. Who would have believed it? she asked herself.

Rather than the villain she'd imagined, the person she viewed presented the perfect picture of a Western hero, from his snowy white hat, to his silver-studded belt and side holster, to nickel-toed boots. Or it would have been perfect, if there'd been any trace of warmth in icy-blue eyes that were shades lighter than his crisply pressed denim shirt and jeans.

"I found her just outside the door, Lance," a gruff

voice said from behind Eve, "standing there and listening for all she was worth."

Eve tossed a look over her shoulder and saw a big bear of a man whose sweat-stained beige hat and rough-hewed features did far better justice to a typical Western bad guy.

"I suppose this is your deputy," she said dryly, forcing a bravado she was a long way from feeling as she once again faced the man with the gun. "Or maybe it's the Incredible Hulk with a Wild West makeover."

"Merely a friend." Lance Conroy's dry tone equaled hers before he flicked a glance to his right that had Eve's gaze following. "Who is this, Quinn, and did you invite her to this little party?"

Although several steps away, Eve had no trouble noting the harsh lines creasing Ryder's brow and the rigid set of his jaw. He looked thoroughly displeased, disgruntled and disgusted—and in no mood to mince words.

"She's Eve Terry, the owner of the ranch, and I sure as hell didn't invite her," he replied grimly.

But Eve wasn't fooled. Despite his tone and an expression to match it, despite the charcoal-brown business suit he wore, despite everything he'd just said and all appearances to the contrary, she knew a true cowboy hero when she saw one.

"Then I suppose we have a problem," Lance Conroy muttered.

Ryder let out a breath and resisted the urge to clench his teeth. *You're damn right we have a problem,* he silently agreed. He widened his stance, giving as good an imitation as he could of someone who was totally in charge of his nerves when in fact everything inside him had just been thrown into full-blown chaos. One word from him—the prearranged word, shouted as a signal—would have the room filling with people. But he couldn't say it, not as long as that gun remained fixed on Eve.

God, he couldn't risk it.

Instead, he had to stand there, seemingly calm yet ready to move in an instant if given the chance. And all the while his heart thudded in his chest, and his blood ran swift and cold at the thought of anything happening to her.

He had to get the pistol aimed away from her, he knew. Somehow he had to do that. *He had to.*

Even if it meant getting it turned on him.

That's how much he cared about this woman, he suddenly realized. More than he'd ever known, until he'd seen a deadly weapon leveled straight at her. Something in the back of his mind told him he'd better think about that, long and hard.

And soon.

But right now he had to figure out how to get that gun pointed in a different direction. His direction. Maybe Lance Conroy's inflated ego, he decided after a second's consideration, was the way to accomplish it.

"You're not planning on doing anything really dumb, are you, Conroy?" Ryder asked, for the first time letting his tone display his contempt.

The sheriff flicked another glance his way. This time a scowl quickly darkened his features. "I wouldn't get too cocky, Quinn. I'm holding all the cards at the moment."

"That's right, you are." Ryder paused for a beat. "But I'd be willing to bet your palms start to sweat when the stakes get too high."

The gun wavered then, just enough to tell Ryder he was on the right track. The way to get to this scum was through his high-flown opinion of himself. "I'd put that thing away," he advised with blunt directness, "before your itchy finger gets the best of your brain."

"I never shoot unless I mean to," the other man countered, biting the words out.

Ryder's reply came swift and hard. "Then holster the damn thing and stop shooting off your mouth."

That clipped command finally produced results.

Ryder froze, stilling completely as the pistol barrel slowly slid in his direction. Eyes narrowed, he watched and waited without so much as a breath until he was positive that Eve was clear of the line of fire. Only then did he throw his arms out and launch himself forward in one driving motion, yelling a single word.

"Geronimo!"

Almost instantly he struck with the full force of his weight and yanked up the hand holding the gun. It went off with a deafening bang and sent a bullet hurtling toward the beamed ceiling as Pete and Hank Swenson rushed out of a small closet that had been turned into the office storeroom. Meanwhile, Cody Bodeen, Zeb Hollister and Gabe Gentry dashed in from the doorway to the hall.

Ryder quickly wrestled the gun away, leaned to one side and slid it under the heavy pine desk, out of reach. Swiftly taking advantage of that slight shift, Lance Conroy wrenched himself free and surged to his feet. When Hank moved to block his path to the door, he took the small man out with one blow that sent him flying off to the side.

Pete got into the action then, tackling someone far younger than himself to the floor, and managed to hold on until Ryder was able to fist both hands in the sheriff's shirt and haul him to his feet.

Ryder took time out for a sidelong glance and saw that the trio of ranch hands had the sheriff's companion surrounded. It looked as though the big man hadn't put up much of a fight, which, in Ryder's opinion, made him the smarter of the two crooks.

Hank and Pete got up and dusted themselves off.

"You both okay?" Ryder asked. At their nods he took one hand off his captive and pulled out a chair from the side table holding the computer, then glanced down at a long rip in the shoulder seam of his suit jacket.

"You have really ticked me off, Conroy. Do you have any idea how much I paid for this suit?" Ryder didn't bother waiting for an answer; he just shoved the other man in the chair, none too gently. "I suggest you stay put. Otherwise this whole crew is going to take you on and you'll probably wind up looking a lot worse than your hat." With that he reached down to retrieve a sadly dented white hat and tossed it in its owner's lap.

After a quiet second passed and it seemed as if the sheriff was taking that advice, Ryder pulled out another chair and fixed a steely stare on the burly man being guarded by the ranch hands. "Why don't you sit down, too?"

Silently the man lumbered across the room and sank into the chair. It groaned under his weight but held.

Ryder finally allowed himself a look Eve's way and found her standing off to one side with her hands clenched around a heavy brass paperweight shaped like a horseshoe. Usually it occupied a corner of the desk.

"Are you all right?" he asked, far from forgetting

as he started toward her that he'd been given a lot to mull over where this woman was concerned.

Just how important is she to you, Quinn? The words dogged his heels as he crossed the room, but there still was no time to consider what had happened in those gut-wrenching minutes when Eve could have shared more than a passing acquaintance with a bullet. He'd think about that question later, he told himself. Right now he had to admit that, reasonable or not, what he really wanted to do was grab her by the shoulders and shake her until her teeth rattled for putting herself in danger.

Eve drew in a steadying breath and watched Ryder approach. "I'm fine," she said at last as calmly as she could manage, remembering far too well how her heart had seemed to stop beating for endless seconds as he wrestled for control of the pistol. Now she wanted to rush into his arms, might actually have done it despite their audience, if his expression had been at all welcoming.

It wasn't.

"What the devil are you doing here?" he ground out in a low, rough murmur.

She gazed up at him and kept her own voice quiet. "I decided to come back a day early and caught a cab at the airport. The house was empty when I got here, so I lay down and took a nap in Cloris's room."

"A *nap*." He threw up his hands. "That's just terrific. Mind if I ask why you didn't call and let somebody know you were coming?"

Ignoring the fact that he was all but growling, she said, "I only decided this morning to catch an early flight. I tried to call when I got to Tucson, but no one answered the phone."

"Because no one was around," Ryder told her flatly. "Kenny took Theresa and Max over to Hank's place. Cloris went, too. And the rest of us have been busy working out last-minute details so we could try to catch a crook." He glanced down at the paperweight she still held. "What did you plan on doing with that?"

"I thought I'd hit someone over the head, if I had to." She aimed a disgusted glare at the two men seated under the watchful eyes of those standing around them. "And I'm really sorry I didn't have to."

All at once Ryder's expression turned as serious as she had ever seen it. "Do you know what could have happened to you, walking into something like that?"

"Yes," she replied without hesitation. "And I know what could have happened to you." Now she had to struggle even harder for a calm tone. "Good Lord, you threw yourself at a man holding a *gun*."

"It wasn't in my plans, believe me," Ryder countered with a hard frown. "I had no intention of letting him practice his fast draw. In fact, I was all set to take the money with one hand and put a quick fist in his gut with the other when you made your entrance. And I have to say the timing was lousy."

Eve's sudden frown matched his. "If you'd let me in on your plans," she grumbled, deciding it felt better to be irritated than to keep reliving that horrible, heart-stopping moment, "I wouldn't have made any entrance."

There was nothing pleased about Ryder's sharp nod of agreement before he brushed back several dark strands hanging over his forehead. "No, you wouldn't have shown up out of the blue—because you would have already been here, bound and determined to be in the middle of it."

She couldn't deny what he'd said, but she wasn't backing down, either. "You should have let me know."

Rather than respond to that staunch remark, he took the brass paperweight from her and set it back on the desk with a soft thud. "Come on," he said, letting the subject drop as he jerked his head toward the other people in the room, "we still have to deal with the bad guys."

Lance Conroy straightened in his seat as they approached. "You'll never make this stick, Quinn."

Ryder folded his arms across his chest and looked down at the other man. "Why don't you think so?"

"Because it's your word against mine."

"Not entirely." Ryder dipped his head toward Hank and Pete. "These two gentlemen heard everything you said."

Pete nodded. "You can hear real good in that closet when you got your ear pressed to the door."

The sheriff snorted. "And who's going to believe any of you over me?"

"Oh, I don't think that'll be much of be a problem," Hank said easily. "The senator who took time out from his busy schedule and accepted my invitation to play a round of golf yesterday will vouch for my character, I'm sure, even if I do manage to beat him once in a while."

An icy gaze widened a bit at that news before it narrowed. "I know a state senator or two myself."

Hank straightened his bola tie. "This one happens to be of the Uncle Sam variety. And while we were celebrating his winning putt at the clubhouse, I asked a few questions. He came up with the interesting information that the Federal boys have been curious about some things going on in your part of the world, Sheriff Conroy. Drug traffic and the like. Needless to say, I told him they should pay some special attention to you.''

"They're welcome to dig,'' Lance Conroy said smugly, "but they won't find anything. I'm clean.''

"Clean as dirty dishwater.'' Ryder's tone held nothing but disdain. "You may have covered your tracks, but you're not as smart as you think. Your first mistake was figuring that since you'd do anything to get what you want, so would I. The result is a stack of cash on the floor. How do you explain that?''

The sheriff shrugged. "I have no idea how the money got there. As far as I'm concerned, this is all an unfortunate misunderstanding. Like I said, Quinn, you'll never make it stick, even with witnesses—even big-shot witnesses,'' he tossed in with a glare at Hank. "Not even if you've got a tape going right now. Because nothing's really happened. If you try to get me in court on something I was supposedly planning to do, even if they'd allow hearsay or taped evidence, which I doubt, my record and the character witnesses I'll produce will win me a not-guilty verdict, assuming it goes to trial in the first place.''

"Well, I hate to say it,'' Hank remarked, "but you could be right. Getting you on something you intended to do wouldn't be easy, although you'd better believe we'd have tried it. Fortunately, we don't have to, since you've just given us a huge helping hand on getting you jailed for some past crimes.''

Blue eyes went to slits. "What the hell do you mean?''

The small man smiled like a fox. "Ryder was pretty sure when you told him you'd come alone today that you'd have a cohort with you, hiding like a snake in the grass, so we posted some men around the place—" he indicated the trio of ranch hands with a nod of his gray-rimmed head "—and asked them to keep out of sight and wait for unexpected company."

"When the big guy came sneaking around the side of the house and slipped in the front door, we were hard on his heels," Cody said. "In fact, we were close enough to get a peek at him grabbing Miz Eve, which gave me quite a jolt, I have to admit."

Ryder grimaced. "You're not the only one who got jolted." He took a deep breath. "But to get back to the matter at hand, deciding not to come alone was your second and biggest mistake, Conroy, because I'd be willing to bet that your partner in crime is a long way from clean. A fingerprint check would probably turn up some very interesting information."

The man seated beside the sheriff drew his bushy brows together. "So I did some time. So what?"

One corner of Ryder's mouth kicked up. "So are you on a wanted list now somewhere? For something that could put you behind bars again, for maybe a decade or two? Even if you're not, being charged as an accomplice in a baby-selling scheme could produce an entirely different verdict than the sheriff might get."

"Don't start spouting off," Lance Conroy advised his companion. "They have nothing on us."

"You mean they got nothing on *you*," the other man countered. He looked at Hank. "You're the big cheese here. Supposing I *was* wanted somewhere, could you help me get a deal?"

"Maybe." Hank toyed with a cuff of his green-checked shirt. "You murder anybody?"

Much to Eve's surprise, the Incredible Hulk actually

looked offended by that question. "Hell, no. I never got mixed up in anything that dicey. I don't even carry a gun."

Hank smiled his foxy smile. "Then I suppose I could try to get you less time than you might otherwise, if you help us by testifying to some things about the good lawman here."

Lance Conroy shot to his feet and stared down at his cohort. "You're a fool. They'll just use you to try to get me, and there's no guarantee they'll help you."

"No, you're the fool, Lance, if you think I'm gonna save your hide at the cost of mine."

"I guess it's time for a visit to the nearest police station," Ryder said.

"They'll never hold me," the sheriff declared. "One call to my lawyer and I'll be out before you can blink."

"No, I don't think so." Hank stroked the side of his jaw, where a bruise was already forming. "Right off I'm charging you with assault." The wily gleam in his eyes had Eve suspecting Hank had deliberately put himself in harm's way so he'd have reason to press charges.

"And I'm recommending you be held without bail," Hank added. "You may know a few judges in your part of the world, but you're on my turf now, and I know more than a few, myself."

The sheriff shoved his hat on his head. "I'm not saying another blasted thing until I see my lawyer."

Ryder's laugh held no amusement. "Finally, Conroy, you're acting smart." He retrieved the gun from under the desk, emptied it of ammunition and handed it to Hank. Then he looked at Eve. "I need to talk to you for a minute."

They moved steps away, out of hearing of the rest.

"I don't know when we'll be back," he told her. "Would you call Hank's place and let everybody there know what's going on?"

Eve nodded her agreement, though what she really longed to do was go with him. But she hadn't been invited, and this was his show, she reminded herself, however much she still thought he should have let her in on his plan.

"I'll see you later," he said.

"I'll be here," she replied, forcing a lightness she was far from feeling. "No matter what time you get back, I'll be up."

All at once his face settled into hard lines every bit as serious as his earlier expression. Silent seconds ticked by while he stared at her, just stared at her. Finally, his jaw still firmly clenched, he turned around and rejoined the group. Eve watched them file out through the office door, and then she was left alone in a suddenly quiet house.

Not that the quiet lasted for long, not after Kenny and Theresa arrived back from Hank's place with Max in tow and Cloris following behind them in her car. Eve met them at the door and took time out for hugs all around before Max blew her a bubble to welcome her back from her trip.

Despite the tense minutes that had rattled her nerves to the core and sent her pulse into overdrive only a short time earlier, she found herself smiling. "It's good to be home," she told the baby held securely in the curve of his father's arm. "I missed you, Max."

"Bub-bub," he replied, twitching a tiny nose.

Kenny puffed out his chest like a proud daddy. "I've been trying out 'dah-dah,' but it's probably too soon for him to pick that up."

"It might not be all that long," Eve said, looking down into wide eyes that sparkled with what she could only describe as intelligence. Once again she found herself thinking that this was one smart baby. Maybe someday he'd teach more than a few people a thing or two. But right now he was where he belonged—safe and sound at the Creedence Creek.

Yes, she thought, it was wonderful to be home, and she didn't change her mind one bit on that score during the hours that followed.

Dinner was a mix of leftovers from the refrigerator and lively conversation, especially when Pete and the three ranch hands returned in the middle of it with the welcome news that the cops were holding Lance Conroy and his cohort. Thanks to Hank Swenson, a judge had denied them bail.

Hank and Ryder had stayed behind, Pete explained, to meet with some higher-ups on the law-enforcement chain. "Ry said it looked as though things will work out fine and dandy. Odds are, once Conroy's so-called friend comes up with a heap of dirt and the Federal men get to digging, it'll be a long time before anybody has to worry about a crooked sheriff seeing a whole lot more than the view from a jail cell window."

"Amen to that," Eve said with a grateful sigh as she passed a platter of cold cuts.

"I suppose Ry'll stop back here after all the hoopla's over," Pete said, filling his plate. "Asked him as much on my way out the door, but all I got was a grunt—which was hardly amazing, seeing as how whenever he had a minute to spare from the Conroy deal, it seemed like Ry was mulling something over so hard that a body could almost hear the wheels spinning in his brain."

And what did that mean? Eve couldn't help but wonder. Unfortunately no answer came to mind. Maybe she'd find out more when Ryder got back, she told herself, and let the thought go.

After dinner, Cody hauled an old guitar out of his truck and sang some country-western songs. Luckily his voice was better than Pete's—and Eve's. The impromptu celebration gradually wound down when people began to yawn. It had been a long day for all of them. And especially for Eve, since her morning had started in New York.

She was one who remained awake, though, long after the house fell silent again. *I'll see you later,* Ryder had said, and remembering those words and the sober look he'd given her, she sat on the living room sofa, nursed a cup of coffee and waited.

But Ryder didn't come.

Chapter Twelve

"Maybe I should just mind my own business, but I can't help wondering what's wrong with Ryder." Cloris's soft voice drifted through the darkness as she and Eve lay across from each other in the bedroom they shared. Above them, an old ceiling fan spun a gentle breeze.

"He's brooding," Eve replied as she punched a pillow and turned over on her side. Having given it a great deal of thought, she was sure on that score. "Exactly what he's brooding about is another matter," she added. She had a good idea, though. One she wasn't sharing.

"Seems odd, since things have been going so well."

Eve couldn't argue with that. Three days had passed since Lance Conroy's arrest, and Hank had phoned that afternoon with the welcome news that a full-blown investigation was about to begin in the Indian Sands area. It looked as though the crooked sheriff's goose might well be truly cooked, and Eve couldn't have been happier about it.

Then, too, Kenny and Theresa were flying to California tomorrow, leaving Max at the ranch with Cloris and Eve, and a well-respected attorney would meet their flight. From all indications, Kenny would soon put his past behind him, and Eve could only be happy about the probable outcome.

On a strictly personal and private basis, though, she was a long way from happy.

"How are you and Pete doing?" she asked, both because she was curious and because it felt good to talk.

"I'm doing fine, but I think Pete's having a much delayed midlife crisis."

Eve blinked. "What?"

Cloris chuckled. "I'm joking, though he has been acting strange lately. More often than not, he's been two steps behind me, like a rock-solid shadow. And, maybe a half-dozen times a day, he opens his mouth to say something and snaps it shut in the next breath."

"Hmm. Well, at least he's not stomping out whenever you come into a room."

"I suppose we could call that progress." Cloris sighed. "Aren't men wonderful? Especially those who either avoid a woman altogether or lose their tongues when it comes to real communication if they are around."

"Some of them can be trying from time to time," Eve had to agree.

"Or maybe most of the time," Cloris added dryly. "Still, I'm not ready to give up on the male half of the population. All in all, they're just too useful in certain areas to do without them." She paused for a small yawn. "And don't you give up, either. Even if Ryder is brooding about something, he'll come out of it sooner or later."

At a loss as to how to respond to that, Eve remained silent.

"Guess it's time for me to shut my eyes," Cloris said on another yawn. "Good night, Eve."

"Good night." Eve closed her own eyes and stretched out on her back, knowing sleep would elude her, as it had for the last two nights. She'd been doing a lot of thinking, and it all centered on one man's recent behavior.

It wasn't that Ryder avoided her. Rather, he seemed to be somewhere else even when they were together, although they hadn't been totally alone for any length of time since her return from New York. He'd been busy helping Kenny find a lawyer—maybe busier than he'd needed to be, she had to admit. Whatever the case, there was no denying that he'd made no effort to be alone with her, no getting around the fact that he was brooding.

And she was very much afraid she knew why.

Ryder had finally—*finally*—come to the conclusion that she was staying at the Creedence Creek, which meant he wouldn't get an opportunity to buy the ranch. And the ranch was what he truly wanted, needed.

She'd known that all along, Eve told herself. Throughout every step of their relationship, she'd been fully aware of it. And she had no regrets about where those steps had taken her, no matter how difficult ending that relationship would be.

For her own sake, though, she knew it would be better to end it, and soon.

Even if she were special to Ryder on some level, being special was no longer enough for her. During the past few days, watching him while he seemed beyond her reach, her heart had learned a hard lesson: there was no substitute for love.

Still, there was no room for regret in what she felt.

And now she had a decision to make, one she'd already
mulled over for long hours, realizing that she and she
alone could offer Ryder the chance to have what he
truly wanted. Only weeks ago what she was considering would have been unthinkable. But weeks ago she
hadn't loved.

So, Eve, yes or no?

Yes. Yes, she would do it, she decided, letting out
a sudden, quiet breath. Even knowing full well the consequences involved, the final choice had been easier
than she'd imagined...because she loved. And because
she loved, Ryder Quinn would get the chance to have
what he truly wanted, needed and had spent a good
part of his life seeking.

Roots.

EVE FOUND RYDER in the ranch office late the following afternoon.

Kenny and Theresa had left to catch their flight to
California after lunch, and after Eve and Cloris had
assured and reassured them all the way out the door
that they were indeed doing the right thing in leaving
Max behind at the ranch. He would be well cared for
and, as Cloris put it, ''happy as a clam'' until they got
back.

Now Max was with Cloris and the rest of the babies
in the nursery, and Eve was ready to act on what she'd
chosen to do, having spent another wakeful night deciding exactly how she would handle it.

Knowing clothes and the subtle impact they could
make, selecting the perfect outfit for the occasion
hadn't been difficult. Her Western-cut shirt, made of
shiny gold cotton, was just a bit more sophisticated,

her formfitting bronze jeans just a bit flashier, than her usual mode of dress.

She had to play this right, she knew. The right image. The right words. The right tone.

"Hello," she said, forcing a light step as she entered the office.

Ryder sat behind the desk, wearing his usual denim. Pen in hand, he was filling out some forms. "Hi," he replied, looking up from his task. His expression was as even and unreadable as it had been for days.

"Do you have a minute? Now that things have settled down, I'd like to talk to you about something."

And now he did smile, just a little, as he put down his pen. "I guess I have to have a minute for the boss."

Eve propped a hip against a corner of the desk. "That's what I wanted to talk to you about, actually."

Ryder raised a questioning eyebrow and leaned back in the swivel chair.

"About being the boss, that is," she continued. "I'm not sure how to put this, except to say that I've discovered I don't want to be one anymore."

A puzzled frown formed while she watched. "And what exactly does that mean?"

This was it, she thought, and tried very hard to keep her voice as even as his earlier expression.

"It means I've decided to sell the ranch."

The old chair creaked a loud protest as Ryder sat straight up. For a startled moment he couldn't quite believe what his ears had heard. "You've decided to sell the ranch," he repeated slowly.

"That's right." Eve crossed her arms under her breasts. "Since you have the option to buy it, I wanted to tell you before anyone else."

And now he did believe, thinking that just when he'd

figured she was staying for good, she had apparently
chosen to give the whole thing up. Then again, he
hadn't been sure, Ryder reminded himself, remembering the doubts he still couldn't shake when she'd left
for New York.

"Was it the trip to the big city, Eve?"

"I suppose so," she agreed readily. "I didn't realize
how much I missed the hustle and bustle. The sidewalk
vendors, the shoppers scurrying back and forth, even
the crazy cab drivers. Not that I plan on moving to
Manhattan," she added. "That's too much hustle for
me on a regular basis. I think living in Tucson would
suit me fine, though. There's plenty to do, and being
closer to the airport would make traveling a lot easier."

She made it sound so reasonable. Unreasonably that
made him want to grit his teeth. "And what about the
nursery? Are you closing it down?"

"No, I don't plan on ever doing that. I'm just moving it. There are facilities all over Tucson I can rent.
Cloris would remain in charge, and the young mothers
we're helping now could take their babies there instead." She gazed down at him with a purse of her
lips. "As you once pointed out, operating a nursery
here probably isn't the most sensible setup."

"It was working out fine," Ryder found himself
countering. Once, he'd never have believed he would
admit that. But it was true, dammit. "You're really
going through with this, aren't you?"

She nodded. "And you'll have what you always
wanted, assuming you still want to buy the place."

He raised a hand and ran it through his hair. "Hell,
yes, I want to buy it if you're giving it up."

"It's for the best, Ryder," Eve said quietly. "It will
be best for both of us, in the long run."

"And about us?" he asked just as quietly, locking his gaze to hers.

Something flickered in her eyes, something he couldn't get a handle on. "I think it would be wise if we went our separate ways. You'll be busy with the ranch, and I'll have a lot on my hands, designing for the new line."

He could only continue to stare at her. "Is that what you really want?"

One second stretched to five before she spoke. "Yes."

Ryder blew out a breath. "I'm having a little trouble taking this all in." Which had to be the understatement of the year. He'd done his best to force a calm tone, when he actually wanted to pound on the desk with a clenched fist, take some of his fierce frustration out on bare wood. Days had passed since he'd asked himself just how important this woman was to him.

Now he knew. She was more important than anything. More important than something he'd worked toward for a major part of his life, more important than what he had always been fully determined to have.

More important than owning the Creedence Creek.

But he hadn't told her, because once he'd realized just how much Eve meant to him, things had gotten even more complicated as he'd found himself caught between a rock and a very hard place. It all boiled down to the fact that the woman he wanted more than anything owned what he'd been primed to get his hands on for years. How could he ever convince her that he really wanted her more than the ranch?

It was a hell of a question.

For days he'd been mulling it over and debating

whether he could even tell her how he felt…and now she was leaving. Not only the ranch. But him, too.

Eve pushed away from the desk. "It'll take a while to get the paperwork done and the sale completed. By the time it's all over, we both should be ready for some changes." She took a step back. "I have to tell Cloris. I'm not sure how she'll take it—" a small, wry smile formed "—but Pete will probably jump for joy at the news."

Ryder did his best to hang on to a calm tone. "I doubt it," he replied. "Not nearly as high as you might think, at any rate." As to how he himself felt, he was still reeling.

"I'll miss you, Eve." He had to say it.

"I'll miss you, too," she replied softly after a long moment. "But I'm not leaving yet, and I'll see you at dinner." With that, she turned away. Then, shoulders straight, she walked out while he watched.

And now he *did* bang a fist on the desk, hard enough to rattle the heavy horseshoe paperweight. It was the weapon she'd chosen to fight the bad guys, he remembered, staring down at it. He knew she would have used it, would have done what she had to do without cringing, if it had turned out to be necessary.

Eve Terry could be tough when it counted, he'd learned on several occasions. She'd faced a string of hurdles during the time she'd spent at the ranch, scaled them one by one with firm determination and pride in her achievements. From a stubborn mare to a stubborn cook to a stubborn cowboy, she'd won the respect of all—most especially him. Ryder's frown deepened at the memories. Despite his earlier and formidable conviction that she would give up the ranch someday, it made no sense now that she was actually willing to do it, just like that.

At least, it didn't make sense to him. Something was wrong. It was a gut feeling, but he had to go with it. Something was wrong, all right. And he damn sure wasn't about to waste any time finding out more.

Ryder slid back his chair, surged to his feet and made for the office door. A fast glance down the hall found Eve heading for the doorway to her bedroom. "Wait up, I want to talk to you," he said, grim intent underlining his words.

She came to a dead halt for a split second, then continued on her way. "Not now," she replied with a slight shake of her head, keeping her back to him.

"Yes, now."

Ryder stalked down the hall with quick strides and reached out an arm. Curving one hand around Eve's shoulder, he stopped her in midstep and turned her toward him.

That was when he saw the tears slowly sliding down her cheeks. Everything inside him clenched at the sight. This was a strong woman, one who wouldn't cry at the drop of a hat. Knowing that, her tears frankly terrified him.

"Good Lord, Eve. I don't know what's wrong, but I do know you don't want to leave the ranch. Nothing's going to make me believe different, so you might as well admit it."

Silent seconds passed before she spoke, her voice hoarse, her head bent. "All right. I don't want to leave."

He hauled in a breath. "Well, that's good, because I am not, by God, going to let you walk out on me. Not when I've finally figured out that I love you."

Misty gray eyes went wide in a flash as her head came up. "You love me?"

He lifted a hand and brushed her tears back with his thumb. "I've been driving myself crazy for days trying to decide if I should tell you or not."

She stared at him. "So that's why you've been brooding."

"I haven't been brooding." He shrugged. "Not exactly."

"Thinking hard, then." She sniffed what he hoped was a last sniff, because it tore him up. "Why did you have to think so hard about telling me?"

He figured the time for keeping things to himself was over. "Because of the ranch, and the fact that you own what I've been champing at the bit to own. If I proposed to you, it would only be natural for you to wonder about my motives."

Eve blinked her eyes dry as one word repeated in her mind. *Proposed.* "You want to get *married?*"

Ryder's mouth twisted in a rueful grimace. "Hell, I'm making a mess of this. Yes, I want to get married, and have kids, too. Even though you haven't told me how you feel, I'd ask you right this minute to take me on for life…if it weren't for the ranch."

Eve's lips curved softly as she turned to fully face him. "First, I suppose I should tell you that I love you."

Green eyes gleamed at that news before he tugged her into his arms. They closed around her, warm and strong. "I am mighty glad to hear you say that, even if it does put the final cap on complicating things."

"I'm also going to say that we could share the ranch," she added, "like most married couples would."

His expression sobered again as he shook his head. "No, Eve. I've thought this through, and the last thing I'll do is take half ownership from you." He paused for a beat. "Why did you give me that song and dance about deciding to leave here for the lure of city life?"

She had to be honest. "Because I thought you wanted the ranch more than me."

"And now?"

Eve looked deep into his eyes. "Do you want me, need me, more than the Creedence Creek?"

"Yes," he replied without hesitation. "No contest."

And her heart believed him.

"I know that now, Ryder. I truly do, and which one of us owns the ranch doesn't matter," she said, and meant it. "As far as I'm concerned, we can flip a coin to decide."

He gave his head another decisive shake. "I'm not about to do anything like that. It isn't as if the property is just sitting out there, ready to be bought, and we're flipping to see who gets the first chance to bid. You already own it."

"And my owning it is a problem," she summed up, finally understanding how serious he was about this.

"It is to me. I can't deny it. You may not have doubts now, but I flat-out couldn't stand it if you ever questioned down the road what I was really after."

And convincing him she would never doubt again would probably be impossible, she acknowledged with an inner sigh. She didn't want to say what she was about to say, and said it, anyway.

"Then I'll sell it to a third party, if that's the only solution. We can pool our resources and buy another place in the area, move the nursery there and take Pete and Cloris with us. We can start over together. That's the most important thing—that whatever happens in the future, we'll be together.''

Ryder's grip tightened as he rested his forehead on hers. "Lady, you are one in a million. Will you marry me?"

She wound her arms around his neck. "I thought you'd never ask." And then, letting her kiss answer for her, she kissed him with everything she had and everything she felt, kissed him long and hard, kissed him until they were both breathless and had to come up for air.

"Well, my word," a soft voice drawled when Ryder lifted his head at last.

He kept his gaze on Eve's. "I think we have company," he told her, his tone husky.

"You sure as shootin' do," another familiar voice replied.

Eve pulled back and turned to see Cloris standing steps away with Pete beside her and a wide-eyed Max propped up in her arms.

"Does this mean what I think it means?" Cloris asked arching an eyebrow.

Ryder settled an arm across Eve's shoulders. "It means we're getting married."

It also meant they might well be giving up the ranch, but Eve told herself she wouldn't dwell on that now. This was a time for celebration. A part of her heart might be heavy with the knowledge that a sale could be inevitable, but she wouldn't let that spoil the moment.

"Well, I'll be danged." Pete shook his head. "That rogue Gabe Gentry might've won another pool. They've been taking bets for days down at the bunkhouse on when you two would decide to get hitched."

"I guess we didn't keep things as quiet as we thought," Ryder muttered.

"I guess not," Eve agreed, matching his dry tone.

"Actually, I think I won," Cloris tossed in. "I had a hunch it wouldn't be too long."

Her sly statement got Pete's attention in a hurry. "You mean you've been visiting the bunkhouse?"

Cloris winked a playful wink. "There are some fine-looking men down there."

"That does it," Pete declared. "You and I have a date for supper Saturday night. And you'll have to dress up, woman, because the place I'm taking you doesn't only have fancy cloths on the tables, it's got *candles.*"

Cloris aimed a sparkling glance at the man beside her. "Whatever you say, sugar." Then she looked at Eve. "This means you may have to baby-sit on Saturday, if Theresa and Kenny can't make it back from California for a while."

"I'd be delighted," Eve replied, gazing down at Max, and she meant every word. "With your mom and dad fussing over you, sweetheart, you and I haven't had much of a chance to really talk lately."

Max smacked his tiny lips again and again, as though he were indeed trying to tell Eve something.

How precious, she told herself. Babies were one of the world's treasures as far as she was concerned, and a twinkle in the small, round eyes she viewed seemed to say that if the world had the ability to tap into their thoughts, the little people could solve a lot of problems.

A lot of problems.

The silent words echoed in Eve's ears. Or maybe just one very important problem, she reflected, struggling to capture the barest hint of something as it flitted through the corners of her mind. Gradually it began to take form, while those small eyes kept on twinkling. And then at last she had it.

Out of the mouths of babes...

Eve took a quick step forward. "Max, you *are* one smart baby. In fact, you're a genius!" Max squealed his agreement as she bent and kissed him squarely on his nearly bald head. "You've given me a great idea, bless your chubby little cheeks."

"Bah-bah," Max replied, looking thoroughly pleased.

"And now I have to try to do something with it," she added. Turning, she reached for Ryder's hand. "Excuse us a minute."

"I suppose they're gonna start kissing again," Pete said with resignation as Eve tugged Ryder into her bedroom.

Cloris laughed softly. "Sugar, I suspect they may wind up doing more than that."

Definitely more, Eve promised herself as she closed the door. But it would have to be later. "Now, about that idea—"

"The one Max gave you," Ryder finished warily, staring down at her with a creased brow. "I have to admit that's quite a trick since he can only babble at the moment."

She pursed her lips. "Let's just say he inspired me when he got me to thinking about babies."

"Babies," Ryder repeated, clearly at sea.

"Yes. I know you're in favor of having some. You wanted kids, you said."

"You bet I do. But we're getting married first," he said firmly.

"And then you can put all that 'maleness' to good

use and get me pregnant,'' she summed up with satisfaction. "But that's not my idea.''

The sudden curve of his mouth was just a bit wicked.
"Sounds like a good one, though.''

"It suits me, too,'' she conceded readily, "but the
idea Max sparked is about the ranch.'' Eve's expression quickly sobered. "I don't want to let it go to some
stranger, Ryder. I'm prepared to do that, and I will do
it. But, God, I don't want to.'' Her heart was in that
last statement. "And you don't want to let it go, either.
You couldn't, because it's a part of you. It always has
been.''

"Yes…'' He cleared his throat, all humor gone. "I
guess you could say that's true.''

Could there be the barest misty gleam in this rugged
man's eyes? Eve wondered. Maybe it was her imagination. Maybe not. But she knew Ryder's feelings went
deep, knew better than anyone else in the world that
he believed this was the only spot he could truly call
his own. Suddenly she found herself dangerously close
to losing her own composure completely.

"It's become a part of me, too,'' she told him, struggling to keep her voice steady. She paused, swallowed
hard. "Neither of us wants to lose it, and it suddenly
occurred to me, looking at Max, that there is a way we
could keep the ranch and leave which one of us actually owns it up to fate.''

Ryder raised an eyebrow at that. "Fate?''

"Yes. Not chance, as in the toss of a coin,'' she
added, referring to their earlier conversation, "but fate
in the form of someone who will be a part of both of
us.'' Eve drew in a breath, well aware that the ranch's
future hinged on what happened in the next few moments.

"My idea," she said, "is to let our firstborn child decide who owns the ranch. If the baby's a girl, the title will stay in my name and you'll put the money you would have used to buy the place into building it and making it even better than it is. If our first child is a boy, I'll sell the place to you and put the money I receive back into the ranch. Either way we'll be living in a place that's special to both of us...and so will our children."

She waited then for him to speak. And waited some more before the scant beginnings of a smile finally appeared. And when she thought she couldn't wait a single second longer, he cleared his throat again and spoke at last. "I'd say that's a pretty damn terrific idea."

With a loud whoop, Eve launched herself at Ryder. When he caught her in midair, she wound her arms around him and held on tight. "Then we're getting married, keeping the ranch and starting a family." She welcomed the stray tear that fell now, because it was one of pure joy. "Do we have a deal, cowboy?"

He leaned in and kissed that small tear from her cheek before his wide grin broke through. "We have a deal, lady."

Epilogue

Ryder tried hard not to groan in relief as he gazed down at his wife. She looked lovely, exhausted and undeniably pleased with her accomplishment. And so she should be, he told himself, his heart beating heavily with emotion. She had just given birth to two children in rapid succession, and both tawny-haired, green-eyed infants were the most beautiful babies ever. At least they were to him.

Only a little over an hour earlier, he'd been in sheer terror of something going wrong when Eve had gone into full-blown labor without warning. Their children had entered the world in the same room where he'd been born, in the house he and Eve had shared since their marriage a year before.

Over the course of the last several months, he thought he'd figured out why Eve had once looked so right to him standing at the top of the hill with the old house at her back. As far as he was concerned, it was because she'd been meant to live there someday. With him. And now with their children.

Thankfully, the paramedics had declared both new arrivals to be perfectly healthy, making their father a very grateful man. "I am one lucky son of a gun," he said.

Eve smiled up at her husband, then dropped a loving glance down at the twins, each wrapped in a blanket and carefully held in the crook of an arm. "These charmers are lucky, too," she told him. "On their mother's side alone, they have two sets of grandparents—I expect we'll have some visitors soon," she tossed in, "and Cloris and Pete to spoil them, as well. Ever since he and Cloris became a lot more than buddies, Pete's shown a surprising tendency to dote on the babies in the ranch nursery."

Not too long ago, Ryder reflected, he would never have expected to see Pete inching his way toward the altar, however slowly. "Plus there are a few ranch hands who I suspect will want their turn," he said, "not to mention Kenny and Theresa."

Kenny Markham had successfully put his past behind him, and he and Theresa now lived in Tucson. Kenny held a job in the booming building industry, while Theresa worked at a day care center for preschool children. Both attended college on a part-time basis, and as often as not, they stopped by the Creedence Creek on weekends, bringing their growing son with them.

"I think Max deserves to be an honorary big brother," Eve said, returning her gaze to Ryder's. "Somehow I still feel we have him to thank for the fact that we kept the ranch."

"You did your share there," Ryder reminded her.

Eve's smile turned wry. Yes, she'd done her share in that regard, she told herself. And more than her fair share when it came to her fast and furious struggle to bring new life into the world. But as it turned out, despite everything she'd accomplished, little had been solved.

"You realize this complicates things even more, cowboy. One boy and one girl on our first try." She let out a long breath. "Of course, Eli popped out a few minutes before Eliza, so technically—"

"No way, lady," Ryder said, breaking in with quiet firmness. "We're not letting anything be decided on a technicality, and that's that." He sat on the edge of the bed and leaned in for a closer view of his offspring. "We'll just have to try again."

"I suppose we could make the effort," Eve agreed with mock gravity, then gently hugged the twins to her, sure that no woman had ever been happier than she was at this moment.

"Da— darn right we'll make the effort," he told her, minding his language after the steady stream of frantic curses that had come before the babies appeared on the scene. He nodded with satisfaction, then dipped his head and lowered his mouth to hers. "I'm looking forward to it."

"Me, too," Eve said an instant before their lips met. She looked forward to many things, and they all included the rugged man who was now her husband and the father of her children. Her own personal cowboy.

Ryder Quinn had ridden into her life, and Eve firmly planned to never let him go.

* * * * *

Watch for Sharon Swan's next book,
coming in June from
Harlequin American Romance.

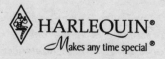

This Mother's Day
Give Your Mom
 A Royal Treat

Win a fabulous one-week vacation in
Puerto Rico for you and your mother at
the luxurious Inter-Continental San Juan
Resort & Casino. The prize includes round
trip airfare for two, breakfast daily and a
mother and daughter day of beauty
at the beachfront hotel's spa.

INTER·CONTINENTAL
San Juan
RESORT & CASINO

Here's all you have to do:

Tell us in 100 words or less how your
mother helped with the romance in your
life. It may be a story about your engagement,
wedding or those boyfriends when you were
a teenager or any other romantic advice
from your mother. The entry will be judged
based on its originality, emotionally
compelling nature and sincerity.
See official rules on following page.

Send your entry to:
Mother's Day Contest

In Canada	**In U.S.A.**
P.O. Box 637	P.O. Box 9076
Fort Erie, Ontario	3010 Walden Ave.
L2A 5X3	Buffalo, NY
	14269-9076

Or enter online at www.eHarlequin.com

PRROY

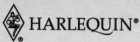

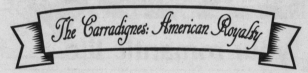